DREAMS
OF THE
LAST BORN

SCOTT PRUSSING

This is a work of fiction. All the characters or events portrayed in this novel are either fictitious or used fictitiously.

DREAMS OF THE LAST BORN

Scott Prussing Publishing
1027 Felspar St.
Suite 2
San Diego, CA 92109

ISBN: 061559977X
ISBN-13: 978-0615599779

This book is dedicated to some of my biggest fans and supporters. Without them, this print edition would not exist. Angie Brennan, Kristi Brolezi, Cindy Clark, Peggy Gatlin, Cheryl Gillespie, Lisa Hadley, Peggy Harrington, River Jordan, Michelle Olson, Dawn Rinks, Kathy Shader, Tina Taylor and Barbara Wilder.

PROLOGUE

Mandrar al-Eldra raced through the darkness, staggering and stumbling along a narrow dirt game trail that snaked through the old forest of Albion. His legs felt like they were encased in lead and his chest burned despite the briskness of the autumn air. Still, he plowed onward, scarcely feeling the unseen branches that tugged at the fabric of his dark cloak and whipped against his weathered cheeks above his thick red beard. He lumbered on, ignoring the protests of his over-taxed muscles even as he ignored the bleeding gashes that striped his arms and side, gashes far deeper than any branch could rip.

Flesh and sinew had their limits, though, no matter how indomitable the will that drove them. Mandrar sensed that loss of blood and long hours of flight were bringing his limit dangerously near. If it were only his life at stake, he would gladly have turned and faced his pursuers long ago, though such a course meant almost certain death. Sadly, that choice was not his to make, for he was the last of the Quirsi—if he died, the secrets of their magic would die with him. He could bear even that, if his sacrifice would assure that his enemies perished as well. But he knew better. His death would only make their ultimate victory more certain, with all of Perator falling under their cruel dominion. So instead he fled, buoyed by the faint hope that somehow in escape he might one day thwart their evil plans.

Finally, he could go no farther. Rest was no longer a luxury to be dreamed of—it was a mistress who could not be denied. He staggered off the path and collapsed into the leafy underbrush. Chest heaving, he lay where he fell, his cheek pressed against a pillow of damp moss. The dank, earthy scent filled his nostrils as he let his mind drift off into itself, free from any conscious thought, to seek whatever meager relaxation it could find.

How long he lay there, he knew not. It might have been minutes, it might have been an hour, but his breathing had quieted and his aching limbs had stopped quivering. Now he needed to replenish his depleted strength, for he knew his long flight had only just begun.

Gingerly, he pushed himself to his knees, and then up onto his tired feet. He listened carefully. The night was quiet; only the barest breeze rustled the browning leaves above him. Gathering his tattered cloak more tightly about his body, he threaded his way slowly among the gnarled trunks of a grove of ironwood trees, carefully searching the dark shadows between their snake-like roots for a talus plant. He allowed himself a small smile when he spotted a clump of telltale mottled yellow leaves. The tiny herb was barely six inches high, but it possessed powers and dangers far beyond its tiny size.

Dropping to one knee, he tore a piece of cloth from his cloak and used it to strip the small serrated leaves from the stem, carefully avoiding any contact with his skin. An oily irritant coated the leaves that would severely inflame unprotected flesh, but the talus root contained compounds that boosted energy and strength. When he had cleared the last leaf from the stem, he tossed the rag aside and pulled the stalk from the soft, yielding soil. He brushed the clinging dirt from the thick tap root, then snapped it off and put it into his mouth.

The fibrous root was tough to chew and carried a bitter taste, but Mandrar didn't care. His mouth began to tingle as he scanned the woods for a suitable place to complete his rejuvenation. He smiled when he spied the crimson leaves of a broad modoc tree. A moment later, he sat resting against its smooth gray trunk. He closed his eyes and slipped into a special Quirsi rejuvenation meditation. Chewing slowly upon the tart root, he let its juices strengthen his body while his spirit melded with the slow, even rhythms of the ancient modoc.

Thirty minutes later he opened his eyes, his strength and vitality much restored. With his renewed strength came renewed pain, for wounds such as his could not be cured by meditative rejuvenation alone. The deep gashes on his arms and side throbbed and burned. He gazed briefly at the crude, blood-soaked bandages he'd wrapped over his wounds. The soiled rags covered the worst of the injuries inflicted by the talons and jaws of the cursed Blood Hunters. Were it not for the sacrifice made by his aged mentor Phidias, these evil creatures—part man, part beast, part demon—would have destroyed him.

A single tear slid slowly down his leathery cheek. Wise and kindly old Phidias, among the most powerful and honored of all the Quirsi, had thrown himself upon the creatures, calling for Mandrar to flee even as he did so. Sensing the greater magic within Phidias, the Blood Hunters had swarmed the old man. Despite his powers, the struggle was no contest. The Blood Hunters had been bred to resist the magic of the Quirsi, and their razor sharp claws and wolf-like jaws had soon torn Phidias to pieces.

His sacrifice had allowed Mandrar to escape. The anguished cries of his brethren, mingled with the howls of the Blood Hunters, still rang in Mandrar's ears. The stench of blood and burning flesh was something he would not soon forget.

How ironic, he mused as he rested in the darkness, that he had been saved not by the magical powers he had labored so long to master, but rather by the simple strength and endurance of his youthful muscles. He had been among the youngest of the long-lived Quirsi, having passed his second century mark only a few years before. His mentor Phidias had seen seven centuries. Seven hundred years to develop his powers, to learn to control the forces in and around him. And now he was dead. All the others had perished as well. Mandrar's jaw tightened as he remembered one other who survived....

Nemidor! The cursed traitor behind their destruction. Mandrar's grief turned quickly to rage. The hated renegade had been among the highest of their order, but his ambitious soul could not be satisfied with even so exalted a place. Renouncing his ties to the Quirsi and their peaceful ways, Nemidor had journeyed to forbidden Malagorn, the land of darkness, and found a following among its denizens whose thirst for power and death matched his own.

Mandrar forced the memories from his mind; he could ill afford to allow hate and rage to sap his body of much needed strength. He breathed slowly and deeply, lifting his eyes to the dark sky. Through a mosaic of gaps in the branches above him he saw the pale circle of Primus beginning its slow descent into the last quarter of the western sky. The great moon should have been a shining jewel in the canopy of blackness above. Instead, the faded orb shone with less than half its customary brightness, its grandeur dimmed by the strange, deepening darkness that was inexorably creeping across the land.

In a few moments Ferus would rise in the east, beginning the *mocrah*, or false day, a two-hour period when the two moons shared the night sky, brightening the night into a pale twilight. In Malagorn, where the rays of the sun never reached, the *mocrah* was the only relief in the never-ending night. At least that's how it used to be, Mandrar thought. Recently, for reasons the Quirsi had been unable to discover, the *mocrah* had been growing steadily less bright. He guessed that unless something was done to stop the spreading darkness it would one day affect the sun itself.

He shook the troubling thoughts from his mind. His duty now was to escape and to survive, to insure that the powers and knowledge of the Quirsi would not be forever lost. If they were, the only chance to thwart Nemidor would vanish with them. Since the massacre, a plan had been germinating in Mandrar's mind. Though his scheme would take years to reach fruition, it offered the only hope he could see.

But first, he must somehow escape the Blood Hunters. He pushed himself up to his feet. His muscles still ached dully, but his exhaustion was gone, chased away by his special meditation and the invigorating juices of the talus root. He stood silently beneath the modoc, eyes closed, listening carefully. Though he heard no sounds of pursuit, he sensed a disruption, a rending of the natural spirit of the forest. The disturbance was still far away, but its source was unmistakable. The Blood Hunters remained on his trail. He had expected nothing less.

He started off into the darkness at a rhythmic trot his revitalized body could maintain for hours. As he ran, the night grew brighter as Ferus joined Primus in the night sky. Still, the *mocrah* was not nearly as bright as it should be. Mandrar scowled at this stark reminder of Nemidor's growing power.

More than speed and stamina would be needed to escape the Blood Hunters, he knew. The foul creatures, spawned by the black magic of Nemidor and the dark evil of Malagorn, had tasted his blood; they would pursue him relentlessly until they tasted it once again. Even his magic was useless, for it was now a beacon that would draw the demons to him. Cunning and woodcraft must suffice to hide his trail. Perator was a large world, and Mandrar had spent years studying its geography. There were many lands where a man could hide, even a Quirsi.

For six long months Mandrar continued his ceaseless journey, putting endless leagues behind him, changing direction at random, taking every advantage he could find to hide the signs of his passing. His way took him through thick forest and shady vale, across barren plains and over verdant hills. Rivers, canyons and two mighty mountain ranges fell behind him, but he would not trust distance alone to keep him safe. He scaled steep stone cliffs that would leave no marks of his passage and spent days floating down swiftly flowing rivers on crudely constructed rafts, never touching shore until he was ready to leave the water behind. He bypassed all towns and cities and avoided solitary travelers as well, so that none might speak even by accident of the passing of a red-haired man. Cold, wet and hunger were his constant companions, but he never once called forth his magic.

Finally, he decided he had journeyed far enough. The ruins of the Quirsi temple lay almost half a world behind him. His wounds had long since healed—only jagged white scars that striped his limbs and the ache in his heart remained. It was time at last to plant the seed he hoped would one day destroy his enemies. Some inner sense told him he had found just the place to do it.

The small, secluded village nestled in the valley below him was exactly what he'd been seeking. The spring sun warmed his back as he stretched out upon a granite outcropping, gazing down across leagues of rolling, unbroken forest stretching to the north, east and west. To the south he could see a wide swamp whose interior was hidden by a thinning curtain of morning mist. In the center of this isolation stood the village, little more than a collection of a few dozen crude wooden huts surrounded by a palisade of rough-hewn logs. A simple hamlet filled with simple, hard-working folk.

He had chanced upon the village almost a fortnight before. Despite the feeling inside him that this could be the place he sought, he had refused to make a hasty decision. Too much was at stake—he could not afford to be wrong. Since discovering the village, he had spent his days exploring the land around it, trekking leagues in every direction to make certain the town was as isolated as it appeared. And it was.

With no more reason to delay, he started down the hillside toward several small square fields cut into the forest at the north edge of the hamlet. As he descended the wooded slope, he felt a pounding in his chest far out of proportion to his physical efforts. For the first time in many long months, he was going to allow himself to be seen. He prayed he was not making a mistake.

As he emerged from the trees, a young blond woman pulling weeds at the edge of the nearest field spotted him. She looked up curiously as he drew nearer and a momentary shiver seemed to shake her slender frame. For an instant Mandrar thought he saw a look of startled recognition on her girlish face, but before he could be certain, the look was gone. She rose to her feet as he approached and met his gaze steadily, her pale blue eyes no longer betraying any astonishment.

"Forgive me if I startled you," Mandrar said gently. "I mean no harm."

"It was nothing," the woman replied, offering no further explanation. Her voice was soft, yet Mandrar saw strength in the eyes that studied him carefully. "Will you find what you seek here in Ishtor?" she asked enigmatically.

Mandrar hid his surprise behind a blank Quirsi mask. "Must I be seeking something? For in truth, I came to this valley but by chance."

"Chance is often the agent by which we find what we seek." She smiled and offered him her hand. "I am Aeta."

Mandrar took her hand. Her slender fingers were rough with calluses. He made a quick decision.

"I am Mandrar," he said, deciding to be honest with this woman and not worry about using his true name.

Aeta's crystal eyes remained fixed on his. Once again, he sensed recognition behind her look, but there was no time to question her because more villagers were approaching.

"I hope strangers are welcome here," he added.

Aeta cocked her head, as if amused by his words. "Would it really worry you if they were not?"

Mandrar smiled. "Perhaps not."

Aeta returned his smile. "They're just curious. We see few strangers here. And there is the color of your hair, red like a burning sunset."

Mandrar turned his gaze to the approaching villagers. All were dark-haired, with skin tanned a deep bronze. His eyes flashed back to Aeta. Her golden hair, which hung in a long thick braid over her shoulder, shone bright in the morning sunlight, and her fair skin was only lightly tanned. She looked as much out of place among these people as he did.

"What have you here, Aeta?" asked a burly man who was the first to reach them. There was little welcome in his tone, nor upon his gruff features.

Aeta edged closer to Mandrar. "Just a traveler who has chanced upon our village." There was none of the earlier warmth in her voice now. "He's called Mandrar. I have offered him our hospitality."

No such offer had yet been made, but Mandrar remained silent.

"This is Garith," Aeta told him.

Mandrar extended his hand, but Garith ignored it.

"He doesn't look like much of a threat," the big man said brusquely. "Since you have offered him hospitality, Aeta, *you* may feed him." Garith turned abruptly and strode back to his own section of the field. The other villagers waited a moment, unsure what to do, then followed Garith's example.

"I don't think your friend approves of me," Mandrar said.

"Garith approves of little besides himself," Aeta replied unconcernedly. "He's jealous. He thinks that someday I will be his woman."

"You have no mate?" Mandrar asked, finding himself pleased.

For a moment, Aeta studied him in silence, remembering. She had seen this handsome red-bearded face before, in her dreams. In the past, some of her visions had come to pass—here was yet another. She wondered what his arrival would mean, for her dreams had shown her nothing but his face.

"I've been waiting," she said at last.

Their eyes remained locked together for several moments. Mandrar knew her words revealed little of what she thought, but Aeta said no more on the subject.

"If I'm to feed you, I may as well get some work from you," she said, pointing down to a row of leafy green sprouts.

"Of course," laughed the last of the Quirsi as he dropped to his knees and began to weed.

CHAPTER 1

Aeta lay on her back atop a coarse grass sleeping mat, damp sweat plastering her soft white robe against her pale skin. The pain in her swollen belly rippled through her insides like jagged stones. She yearned to scream, to give in to the pain, yet no sound passed her lips. Even in her agony, Aeta sensed that to scream would be to admit defeat, to invite failure and bring the long sought event to a calamitous end, an end she was not certain she could bear. Instead, she clenched her fists in defiance, breathing deeply and digging her nails deep enough into her palms to draw blood as she forced herself to remain motionless upon the mat.

A momentary coolness swept across her forehead, brief seconds of blessed relief. For an instant she thought that *he* had returned, that he had come back to share her ordeal, bringing with him comfort and solace and strength. Then she heard the hoarse voice of Maigra.

"Soon, soon," the old woman whispered encouragingly as she gently wiped a wet cloth across Aeta's fevered brow. "It will all be ended soon."

It was not the pain that tortured Aeta. The pain she could bear. No, it was the cold despair that slowly engulfed her as she remembered the screams of other women during the past five years. One after another the labors of her friends and neighbors had failed, their agony proving fruitless. A curse had fallen upon their land; how or why, no one knew. With each passing year fewer and fewer women had become with child, and every pregnancy had ended with the delivery of a stillborn baby. She thought that somehow she would be different, but now she knew her doom would be the same. Hopelessness surged through her, draining her of the will to resist. A scream formed in her throat. This time, there would be no stopping it. She opened her mouth.

Just as the scream was about to burst from her throat, a familiar image began to materialize in her mind, rising from somewhere deep in her consciousness where her thoughts had not yet been twisted by the pain. Mandrar's red-bearded face, filled with strength and certainty, grew clearer with every moment. Once again, she heard the words he had spoken to her the night he left.

"You will give birth to a son," he had said, even after she told him there had been no children born in the valley for almost five years. "He will be strong, and he will be healthy. This I promise you."

The confidence and assurance in his voice still rang in her mind. His handsome face grew increasingly more real, until she thought she could reach out and touch him. She opened her eyes, fully expecting to see Mandrar bending over her. Instead she saw only Maigra, smiling down at her with a toothless grin.

Aeta managed a weak smile in return, and then closed her eyes and concentrated upon the image of her departed husband. He had told her from the beginning that he could not stay long, that every day he remained was a danger to the son he had said she would bear, and he had been true to his word. After just one brief month, a month filled with more laughter, happiness and love than she had ever known, he was gone. Yet somehow his thoughts had flown across the miles from wherever he had hidden himself, reaching her at precisely the moment of her sorest need. He was here, exactly as he had promised, sharing his strength with her.

A sharp spasm in her belly brought an end to the flight of Aeta's thoughts, but the clenching brought no pain. Instead, joy and fulfillment flooded through her as her child burst free from its protective haven into the world. A second later she heard its wailing cry—the most wonderful, miraculous sound she had ever heard.

"It's a boy," Maigra whispered joyously as she pressed the child into Aeta's arms.

Aeta hugged the mewling infant lovingly to her breast.

The news raced through the tiny village like wildfire. A child had been born, alive and healthy! The mysterious curse of barrenness was finally ended. Husbands and wives sang and danced in the dust of the street. The village came alive with a joy it had not known for far too long. Tonight, there would be love-making such as Ishtor had not seen in many, many moons, as five long years of fear and despair were washed away by the birth of Aeta's son.

She named him Thorogrin, child of hope. The people of Ishtor called him Feanor, meaning First Born, for they were certain his birth signaled a joyous new beginning for their land. But as time passed and no more children were born, Ishtor sank slowly back into sadness and despair. The villagers took to calling him Penderyn, the Last Born, leaving only Aeta and Maigra to call him by his rightful name. When the old nurse died when he was four, only his mother ever addressed him as Thorogrin.

Aeta leaned contentedly against the doorframe of her cabin, arms folded loosely across her chest, letting the spring sun bathe her skin as she watched Thorogrin skip happily toward her along the dusty street. She saw many traces of the long-departed Mandrar in her five-year-old son, and she felt a warm ache in her heart at the memory. His piercing gray eyes, set deep above high, strong cheekbones, matched his father's exactly. The fine, straight hair that hung almost to his shoulders was a light coppery color, for her own golden hue had softened the fiery red of his father's. His young face, seemingly stretched perpetually into a broad smile, mirrored his gay and loving nature. As the youngest child in a village almost bare of other children, he had been the happy recipient of the maternal love of every childless woman from the time he had been born.

She had done well, she thought, raising him alone these past five years. She wished it could have been different, that Mandrar could have stayed so they might have raised their son together, but she had learned to be happy with what she had. Closing her eyes, she let her mind drift back to that night almost six years before.

The mocrah *had just begun. Primus hung glowing in the western sky, while the pale disc of Ferus floated upon the treetops of the eastern ridge. Few stars were visible, for only the very brightest of them could penetrate the strange veil of darkness that seemed to be slowly, inexorably blotting out the sky. Aeta studied Mandrar's face as he gazed silently up into the heavens, lost in thought. The face of the man she loved could hold no secrets from her; she knew he was troubled and squeezed his hand in silent support.*

Finally, Mandrar turned to her. He clasped her shoulders gently in his strong hands and gazed deeply into her eyes. For a moment he said nothing. She locked her hands behind his waist and returned his gaze anxiously.

"It's time for me to leave," he said at last.

Aeta's heart sank. Though he had told her from the start that he could not stay long, she had buried his words in her happiness and her love.

"Must it be so soon?" Even as she spoke, she knew her plea was useless. But she had to try. "Can you not stay just a little longer?"

He shook his head. "I cannot, I must not," he replied gently, "though I wish with all my heart that I might. My enemies will not rest until they find me. Every day I remain, the danger grows. Our unborn son must not be risked."

"You said as much when you arrived," Aeta said, blinking hard to hold back her tears. *"Can you tell me nothing more?"*

"Tonight, I will tell you everything. You must listen well, for it shall fall to you to pass my words to our son when he is old enough to understand."

Aeta listened closely while Mandrar told his tale. He spoke of the Quirsi and of Phidias, of Nemidor and his treachery. When he told her of the Blood Hunters and how they had tasted his blood, she shuddered. She knew now that there truly was no chance he could stay.

"Will they never give up?" she asked sadly.

"Not until I am dead, or until Nemidor is defeated." Mandrar hugged her close. *"All this you must repeat to our son. He will be our hope against the powers of darkness. The blood of the Quirsi will flow in his veins, but he will be unknown to Nemidor and to the Blood Hunters. If the stars so decree it, he will be their doom."*

Aeta lifted her face from his chest. Something in his words, foreboding as they were, gave her hope. Her mind raced, seeking understanding. There was something he was leaving unsaid. In a moment, she had it.

"You will come back!" she said happily. *"You're the only one who can teach him, even as Phidias taught you."*

He nodded, smiling wistfully. *"When he is grown, I will return if I am able. Until then, my task lies elsewhere. The Blood Hunters must be drawn far from this place."*

"But what if something happens to you? What if you do not come back? What will become of him then?"

Mandrar smiled down at her. *"To see into the future is your gift, not mine, beloved."* His voice grew solemn. *"Our son's path has been chosen. To what future I have condemned him, only the years will tell."*

A warm hug from Thorogrin pulled Aeta from her reverie. She returned his embrace lovingly, playfully tousling his long copper hair as he buried his cheek against her stomach. That this delightful child, so full of love and joy, could be the son of whom Mandrar had spoken seemed impossible, but she knew it was true. He would grow up, and she would have to tell him the secret of his birth and of the dangerous destiny that lay before him. But that would be years from now, she promised herself. Let him enjoy the innocence of his childhood, for if Mandrar was right, there would be trials enough ahead for him. We have now, she told herself, and that's all that matters. For the moment she would push her worries about the future from her mind and simply enjoy the child her love for Mandrar had created.

The future arrived sooner than Aeta expected. And it arrived with no warning. Thorogrin was six when the first dream came.

He saw smoke—thick, billowing, black smoke that filled his vision. His whole world was engulfed by the dark, choking cloud. Behind the smoke he could only barely discern the red glow of fire.

He was moving. The curtain of smoke swirled around him as the glare of the fire grew steadily brighter. Now he could see flickering tongues of flame dancing within the smoke. And there was heat, too—blazing heat that seared his face as he drew closer to the raging inferno.

A dark figure materialized, surrounded by the flames. The image grew slowly clearer. It was a woman. The light of the fire reflected from her hair. Hair of gold. He saw her face. Mother! Her mouth stretched open, calling to him or screaming—he could not tell which. No sounds issued from her tortured mouth.

A terrified scream burst from his throat. "Motherrrr!!!"

Her son's scream yanked Aeta from her sleep. She bolted from her sleeping mat and rushed to his bed. His arms and legs thrashed inside his tangled blankets as he writhed in his sleep.

"Thorogrin," she said soothingly. "Wake up, my son." She caressed his face, trying to stroke the fear away. "I'm here. Everything is all right."

He opened his eyes. They were filled with pain and confusion.

"You had a dream, that's all," Aeta said softly. "It's over."

The image from his dream returned. "Mother!" he sobbed. He sat up and hugged her tightly, his cheek pressed against her welcoming breast. Aeta gently stroked his hair.

"It was so real," he said, his voice so low it was almost a whisper. "There was smoke, and fire. You were trapped. I couldn't reach you. You were screaming, but I couldn't hear you."

Aeta's arms tightened involuntarily around her son. She shuddered, glad that Thorogrin's head was still cradled against her breast, lest her face betray the chill fear that shot through her. She had seen the same nightmare, more than once, when she was a child scarcely older than Thorogrin. Even now she could see the smoke and feel the burning flames as they whipped around her. Not all her dreams came true, but many did. And now her son had seen the fire. Had he inherited her gift? Would this be one of the visions that someday came to be? She shook the thought from her mind.

How much should she tell her young son? How much did he need to know? She remembered how frightened she had been of her own first dream, so many years before. She made her decision. She would have to tell him about his dreams, for he would have others, and he must be prepared. But she would not allow him to worry. That she had shared this exact vision would remain her secret.

"It was only a dream," she said aloud.

Thorogrin pulled his head from her chest. His innocent gray eyes stared up into hers questioningly. "But it was so real, Mother. I breathed the smoke and felt the flames. It was not like other dreams."

Aeta cupped his copper head lovingly in her hands. He seemed so much older than his six years.

"Listen to me carefully, my son. You will have other dreams like this one, dreams that seem to be more than dreams. Some of these shall come to pass, but many will not." She kissed his forehead. "I know this is not easy for you to understand, but you must try. These dreams are a gift you and I share, yet they are also a curse, for we have no control over what we see and no way to know which might actually come to pass. Whether I would have given you this gift had I the choice, I do not know. But there was no choice. This power is within you, just as it is within me. I do not know from whence it arises, only that it is there."

She dropped her hands to his shoulders. "Heed my words, my son. Remember your dreams, but do not let them trouble you. Trust them not. Even the ones you see more than once may never be more than dreams. Use your visions to guide you only when there is no other way."

Thorogrin's unblinking eyes remained locked on hers the whole time she spoke. A frown creased his forehead, and for several moments he said nothing. Aeta knew he was struggling to comprehend the things she had said.

"I don't get it," he said at last. "But I will do as you say. I'll try not to let my dreams frighten me." He smiled warmly at her and then lay back sleepily upon his pillow. "Good night, Mother." His eyes slowly closed.

Aeta watched Thorogrin's face as he drifted back to sleep, glad that he seemed to have shaken his fears so easily. One day she would have to tell him other things, more frightening by far, but for now, the dreams were enough—more than enough. He was only a child. There was a limit to what he could bear. Mandrar's story would have to wait.

CHAPTER 2

"**P**enderyn! Are you home?"

"Penderyn! Come outside!"

Thorogrin was halfway through his breakfast when he heard Tal and Dal shouting his name from outside the hut. An impish grin brightened his youthful face as he looked expectantly across the table at his mother.

"Go ahead," Aeta laughed, unable to resist her son's beseeching look. "See what they want. It won't be the first time you didn't finish your breakfast."

Thorogrin's smile widened as he grabbed a thick piece of buttered bread from his plate and hurried outside, anxious to see what his friends wanted. As he stepped out of the cabin into the early morning sunlight, Tal and Dal charged toward him in a familiar game, their shoulder length black hair streaming behind them. The identical twins were twelve years old, five years older than Thorogrin and considerably larger and stronger, but he stood his ground, chewing his bread and waiting calmly with his arms folded across his chest as they bore down upon him. At the last moment each veered to the side, missing crashing into him by mere inches. He turned and faced them as they pulled themselves to a halt a few yards past him.

"You'd better be careful, Penderyn. One of these days, we're going to run right over you," Tal threatened.

"Stomp you right into the ground," Dal added.

"It takes more than the two of you to scare me," Thorogrin

said, laughing. "One of these days you'll quit trying."

The twins walked closer. "You probably wouldn't even run from a gryth, would you?" Dal asked teasingly.

"Not unless it was even uglier than you," Thorogrin replied, grinning. He ducked out of the way as Dal launched a playful punch at his head.

"Father's taking us into the swamp today," Tal said. "We're going to hunt ducks and look for troth eggs."

"He said you could come with us," Dal added, "if your mother says that it's okay."

Excitement shone from Thorogrin's eyes. So far, he had only been to the edge of the mist-enshrouded swamp. His mother had forbidden him to go any farther, citing the dangers of ever-shifting trails, sucking quicksand and fearsome beasts. Her words only enflamed his naturally adventuresome spirit, but he was an obedient child, so he had followed her wishes. Here was his chance to finally venture into the swamp's mysterious reaches.

"I'll ask her right now," he said eagerly. "Wait here."

He turned and scampered into the house. Aeta was cleaning the breakfast bowls from the table. Thorogrin's voice quivered with anticipation as he told his mother of the invitation and then begged for her permission. He held his breath while he awaited her decision.

Aeta hesitated, uncomfortable with the idea of her young son going into the swamp. He looked so small and frail standing there anxiously before her, but he had been associating with the older boys all his life and was growing up quickly. The swamp was dangerous, but there was danger aplenty in the world; he had to learn about it sooner or later. No matter how much she wished it, she could not shield him from everything. She searched her memory for any dreams about the swamp, any warnings of danger, but there were none. The twins' father Harren was a skilled woodsman and one of her closest friends. She knew he would look after her son.

"You may go," she said at last. "But be very careful, and mind exactly as Harren tells you."

"Thank you, Mama!" Thorogrin kissed her happily on the cheek and then raced out the door to tell his friends the good news.

Heart racing, Thorogrin gazed out into the mist-shrouded swamp. His mother had warned him countless times of its treacherous quicksand and the terrible beasts that dwelt in its murky waters, but he didn't know how many of her tales were true and how many she had made up just to frighten him from venturing into its dangerous confines. Soon he would know. He could taste the swamp's thick, musky air on his tongue as he stared out anxiously into the previously forbidden reaches. Most of the swamp was still hidden by the morning mist that lingered like tattered gray shrouds over much of the water, waiting to be lifted by the warming rays of the spring sun. Still, he could make out several small, humped islands in the distance, their soil held in place by the twisting, net-like roots of smooth-barked celeroth trees. The clumps of land seemed to Thorogrin like miniature planets, floating worlds of brown and green in a sky of gray.

Harren knelt on one knee in front of Penderyn and gave him his final instructions. The twins' father was tall and strong, with a tanned, clean-shaven face usually brightened by a warm smile.

"Stay close behind me, Penderyn," he said, his voice more serious than usual. He was not taking the responsibility of Penderyn's first journey into the swamp lightly. For added safety, he had enlisted the help of his cousin Vadar to join him and the three boys on this morning's trip.

"The paths of the swamp are constantly changing," Harren warned. "Always be cautious. What looks like solid ground may be just a thin covering of soil atop quicksand, so do not stray even a few steps from my path. And never, ever, enter the water. There are creatures in those hidden depths that would make a quick meal of you." He stood up and patted Penderyn on the head, reassuring him. "Watch closely and learn. Once you know the swamp there's no reason to fear it, but you must always respect it. Are you ready?"

Thorogrin nodded, not certain he wanted to trust his voice. Excitement mingled with nervous fear as he followed Harren into the gray, ghost-like world. Behind him came Tal and Dal in single file, with Vadar bringing up the rear.

The air was cool and moist, and filled with the thick, cloying odor of rotting vegetation. The haunting cries of unseen birds and the buzzing of insects filtered somberly through the grayness. Tiny droplets of mist dampened Thorogrin's clothing and clung to his cheeks like a layer of liquid down as they pushed farther into the swamp, but he took no notice. His attention remained focused on Harren and on the damp soil beneath his feet. The ground seemed solid enough, but he watched closely as Harren carefully tested the path with the butt of his spear before every step, and he tried to step exactly in Harren's footprints. For the first few minutes Thorogrin concentrated solely on his steps, oblivious to everything else around him, but gradually grew confident enough to risk a few, brief glimpses out to his left and right.

They followed a path less than four feet wide and often barely half a foot above the gently lapping waters on either side. The green, silt-laden water was too murky to see more than a few inches into its depths, but Thorogrin's imagination filled it with the terrifying creatures described so vividly in the many tales he had heard. As the sun climbed higher in the sky the mist steadily evaporated, and the increased brightness made the place seem less unfriendly and threatening.

Single file, the small party slowly traversed the twisting pathways for almost half an hour before they finally reached their destination, an egg-shaped island a hundred yards long with a rounded hump in the center. The entire island was held together by the largest clump of celeroth trees Thorogrin had yet seen. For scores of years, the trees' tangled webs of roots had collected silt and soil until all but the top of the roots had disappeared, slowly building the island upon which the group now stood. Dark green ferns and thick mosses grew in the moist soil near the isle's edges, while up on the higher and drier interior tall grasses and small shrubs had gained a foothold amongst the trees. Harren signaled for silence as they made their way toward the crest of the hump.

"Get your bows ready, boys," he whispered. "There should be game on the open water beyond this island. Don't forget to use string arrows."

As they crept through the trees to the far side of the narrow island, Thorogrin spotted a flock of speckled brown and white waterfowl winging toward them. In just a few moments, the birds would be within range. As he had practiced many times in the fields outside the village, he carefully coiled the thin twine attached to his arrow and laid it at his feet. He grasped his bow tightly. Until now, he had aimed only at trees and targets, which he missed far more often than he hit. How he would hit a flying bird he didn't know, but he was determined to give it his best. Licking his lips nervously, he concentrated on the rapidly approaching birds.

When the waterfowl were less than a hundred feet away, Harren gave the command to fire. Five arrows streaked through the sky, their thin lines of twine streaming behind them. Three barbed points buried into the breasts of birds as Harren, Vadar and Dal all hit their marks. Thorogrin watched in disappointment as his own arrow flew several feet wide of its target.

"I got mine!" Dal cried elatedly as his bird fell with a splash. "Right in the center!"

Harren and Vadar were busily pulling in their length of twine, dragging their birds quickly across the surface of the water.

22

"You'd better hurry," Harren warned Dal, whose excitement over his well-aimed shot caused him momentarily to forget about his string.

Suddenly, a loud splash erupted from the still water and a pair of dripping green jaws thrust upward through the surface. Sharp teeth snapped down upon Dal's bird, and the twine was yanked from his hand as the carcass disappeared.

Harren laughed gently at the distraught look that twisted his son's face. "That, boys, was a terriwarg. Now you see why it's important to retrieve your prey as quickly as possible—and why we don't attach the string to our belt." He rubbed the top of Dal's head. "Cheer up, son. You made a fine shot. Next time, you won't forget to pull your bird in quickly."

"It was a *great* shot, Dal," Tal encouraged as he dragged in his own empty arrow.

"I wish I could shoot like that," Thorogrin added enviously. Dal's sadness melted under their continued praise. In a moment, he was smiling again.

"Let's show Penderyn how to gather troth eggs," Harren suggested.

Thorogrin listened closely as Harren described the habits of the amphibious troth, a large, tortoise-like creature whose giant eggs were an important source of food for the village and were the main reason its people ventured into the swamp. While it might be some time before he was skilled enough with his bow to bring down a duck, Thorogrin saw no reason he shouldn't be able to find eggs if he paid attention.

Harren led them carefully out onto the moist, sandy dirt along the leeward shore. The morning had warmed nicely, melting away the mist, and the sun felt good on Thorogrin's face as he watched Harren force the butt of his spear into the soft, yielding soil.

"Troth eggs are never buried deeper than two feet," Harren explained as he pulled his spear from the soil. "The shells are thick—almost as hard as rock. So we use our spear or a stick to find them. Once we've located one, we dig."

Harren pushed his spear into the ground a second time, and then a third. This time, it sank barely a foot. He let go of the shaft and turned to Thorogrin. "Try to push it deeper."

Thorogrin grabbed the wooden shaft with both hands. He pushed down with all his strength, but the spear would sink no deeper.

"That tells you you've found an egg," Harren said.

The three boys dropped to their knees and began digging eagerly into the soil around Harren's spear. The moist dirt yielded easily to their efforts, and in only a few minutes they had scooped out a shallow hole several feet across. At the bottom of the hollow lay three large, light green eggs, each almost a hand's width in girth.

"That's a very good start," Harren said as each boy carefully lifted an egg and placed it into a cloth sack Vadar had taken from his pack. "Since you boys don't have spears, we'll find some sticks among the trees. Then all of us can hunt for the next batch."

Harren stayed close to Thorogrin as he searched for a suitable stick. By the time he found one, a slightly crooked length of celeroth branch two fingers thick, Vadar and the twins had already begun probing the soil of a rounded peninsula a few yards from where the first eggs had been uncovered. So far they had not begun digging, so Thorogrin knew they had not yet discovered any eggs.

"Let's try over here," Harren suggested, indicating a more narrow stretch of beach to their right. "Perhaps we'll have better luck."

Thorogrin followed Harren to within seven or eight feet of the water's edge and eagerly pushed his stick into the ground. It sank easily.

"Nothing here," he reported, his enthusiasm dimming not a bit as he pulled his stick from the sandy soil and plunged it back down a few feet to the right. When his second attempt came up empty as well, he moved immediately to a third try. This time his stick struck something solid.

"I've got one!" he cried happily.

He dropped to his knees and began scooping furiously at the moist sand, as if his treasure might disappear if he delayed too long in digging. In a moment his fingers struck something solid. He brushed away the remaining layer of soil and was rewarded by a small patch of green.

"Here it is!" he cried proudly. "I found one."

A glance toward the twins showed him they had yet to locate a place to dig and had moved farther out onto the sandy peninsula in search of better luck.

Proud that he had been the first to discover an egg, Thorogrin returned to his digging, eager to see how many eggs he had found. He carefully unearthed a second egg and was working on a third when a shrill scream from one of the twins pummeled his ears. He jerked his head around. His eyes widened in horror as he watched a giant terriwarg climb from the water near the base of the peninsula. Vadar and the twins were cut off, trapped farther out upon the small finger of land.

The fearsome reptile was longer than three full-grown men, with a long, tapering tail making up a third of its length. Thick, dark green scales, wet and glistening with slime from the swamp, covered the creature's body. It stood on four short, bent legs that kept its belly close to the ground, but its arched back and thick neck raised its elongated snout almost as high as a man's head. The monster's jaws looked longer than Thorogrin's arm, with a slithering red tongue that darted in and out between twin rows of yellow, dagger-like teeth. Terriwargs seldom left their home in the swamp's depths to hunt upon the land, but that was no matter now. This one had, and Vadar and the twins were trapped before it.

Vadar pushed Tal and Dal behind him and gallantly faced the

terriwarg with his spear. It seemed a puny weapon against such a beast, but he had no other choice. There was nowhere to run. To enter the water meant certain death, and there was no way past the terriwarg back to the higher ground of the island. He jabbed futilely at the monster's head, aiming for the lidless eyes, trying desperately to stem its advance while staying beyond the reach of the snapping jaws.

While Vadar thrust at the beast with his spear, Harren raced toward the terriwarg, shouting as he ran, hoping to distract the creature long enough for his sons and Vadar to scramble past it to the safety of the trees. The monster paid him no heed. Its attention was focused entirely on the meal in front of it. Slowly it plodded forward, forcing Vadar closer and closer to the end of the beach. Already Tal and Dal huddled at the water's edge.

Harren hoisted his spear high above his head and plunged it downward with both hands, using all the strength of his powerful shoulders. A sharp crack split the air as the spear snapped in two, its fire-hardened point unable to pierce the beast's scaly armor. At almost the same instant, the huge tail swung around with surprising swiftness, striking Harren with the force of battering ram. The blow sent him sprawling across the beach, where he lay senseless upon the dirt. The terriwarg paid him no more attention. Low, menacing growls rumbled from its throat as it advanced toward its helpless prey.

CHAPTER 3

Thorogrin watched helplessly as Harren's spear shattered against the terriwarg's thick scales. He tried to scream a warning as the huge tail swung toward Harren's back, but his call was too late. With Harren lying senseless on the ground, the reptile continued its relentless advance toward Vadar and the twins, as heedless of Vadar's thrusts as of the sting of an insect. Thorogrin knew his arrows would be even more useless than the men's spears, but he had to try something, so he fit an arrow to his bow and let fly. The terriwarg was a target even he could not miss, but the arrow glanced harmlessly off the monster's scaly side. Tears welled in Thorogrin's eyes, blurring his vision. His friends were doomed. He squeezed his bow tightly. He must not cry.

He wiped the tears from his eyes, but his vision remained blurred. Somehow, the world had turned gray and shadowy, as if some outside force had seized control of his sight. He tried to blink the grayness away, straining to assert his will, but whatever power assailed him was too strong. The mist continued to deepen, enveloping him.

Images began to take shape in the grayness. They were faint and indistinct, but somehow Thorogrin knew that what he was seeing was important. He surrendered himself to the fog, struggling instead to bring the dim forms into focus. The vision grew steadily clearer, slowly replacing the reality in front of him. And yet vision and reality were nearly the same. One of his dreams, he thought, though he did not remember it. Yet now the recollection of the vision seeped into his consciousness, triggered by the actual event.

Gray mist, thick and shadowy, surrounded him. Danger filled the air. He could smell it, he could taste it. Slowly, the mist began to lighten. A huge dark bulk took shape in the grayness. He saw long, terrible jaws, filled with jagged teeth. The menace engulfed him, yet the monster seemed unaware of his presence. Three smaller shapes appeared, just beyond the gaping jaws. The danger he sensed was to them, not him. He struggled to see more clearly, but was unable to pierce the shadowy mist.

A new figure appeared, this one behind the beast. He felt a closeness to it, a kinship. The cursed mist! Why would it not lift? What was he seeing? Suddenly, the figure leaped upon the monster's tail and raced up along its back. Atop the shoulders it halted, just behind the mighty head. What was it doing? The beast shuddered, and then blackness enveloped the scene.

Thorogrin blinked. The image was gone, replaced by the terrible reality. His friends had reached the end of the sand; they could retreat no farther. He hesitated, remembering the dream. If only the vision had been more clear. But there was no more time, and no other way. He scampered toward the terriwarg, grabbing Harren's splintered spear as he ran. Driven by instinct and heedless of anything but the danger to his friends, he leaped upon the terriwarg's back, at the base of its thick tail. The monster's fetid stench assailed his nostrils as he worked his way forward along its back, fighting to maintain his balance upon the wet, slimy scales. Atop the shoulders he stopped. The scales here were even thicker. How could he hope to penetrate them?

He looked more closely. Between the scales at the base of the creature's neck he spied a narrow gap, wide enough for his spear, provided he struck precisely. Still, the beast's skin looked tough and leathery. He would need all his strength to pierce even the unprotected hide. He raised the broken spear above his head, holding it with both hands. There was no room for error. He had to hit an impossibly tiny target with all his strength. The lives of his friends depended on him. It seemed a hopeless task. He held the spear poised above him. His arms began to tremble. He couldn't do it!

He felt his arms weaken. The spear began to slip from his grasp. It was hopeless. What madness had brought him here? Tears begin to fill his eyes.

Once again, some inner force seemed to seize control of his mind, guiding him. He closed his eyes and took two deep, slow breaths. His hands steadied as renewed strength flowed into his slender arms. When he opened his eyes, he stared down at his target, blotting all else from his mind. He saw only the narrow gap between the thick scales. There was nothing else—no terriwarg, no swamp, no friends in danger. Only the gap.

Suddenly, a series of shimmering streaks of multi-colored light filled the air in front of him. The red, blue, yellow and green beams all pointed down to the same tiny spot—the gap in the terriwarg's scales.

Calmness enveloped Thorogrin. He knew he was ready. With all his strength, he plunged the spear downward. The point slashed into the gap between the scales, slicing through the leathery skin straight into the terriwarg's spinal cord, severing it completely. The beast shuddered violently, hurling Thorogrin from its back, and then collapsed dead upon the beach.

He saw a figure cloaked in black, facing away from him. Man-like in form, its true shape was hidden beneath the folds of a dark, hooded cloak. Slowly it turned toward him, as if just now becoming aware of his presence.

No face was visible within the shadow of the hood,

only blackness. And two yellow eyes, glowing ever brighter, transfixing him with their stare. Evil washed over him. The hypnotic power of the shining eyes pulled at his soul.

A cloaked arm stretched toward him. A dark, clawed finger beckoned him closer. He tried to resist, but felt himself being drawn helplessly toward the demon.

Thorogrin awoke with a shudder. He was lying on his back. His companions huddled over him, their faces etched with concern. Relief flooded through him. The menacing hooded figure had been only a dream. His eyes fell on the lifeless carcass of the terriwarg stretched out upon the sand. Had he done that? He remembered standing atop the beast, the broken spear in his hands, but the rest was a blank. His friends were safe, though. That was all that mattered.

"Penderyn, are you all right?" Harren asked worriedly.

Thorogrin nodded. He rose shakily to his feet, helped by Tal and Dal.

"That was the bravest thing I ever saw!" Dal said excitedly, keeping hold of his friend's arm even after he was on his feet.

"Like something out of the old stories!" Tal added, his voice just as excited as his brother's.

While the twins fawned over Thorogrin, Harren edged over to the dead terriwarg. He studied the broken spear that protruded from the narrow gap between the bony scales, shaking his head in awe and disbelief. The tiny groove was the only place the monster could have been harmed. The strength and skill behind the killing blow was astonishing. He wondered how the boy had he even known what to do, let alone found the skill to accomplish it.

The others joined Harren alongside the giant carcass. A chill swept over Thorogrin as he reached out and gingerly laid his hand upon the beast's scaly side, trembling at what he had done. What magic had guided his thrust? Surely it could have been nothing else but magic. The memory of those moments was gone, though. He struggled to remember, to bring them back to his consciousness, but his mind remained blank.

Harren watched him closely. For a moment, the boy looked far older than his years. "What's wrong, Penderyn?"

Thorogrin shook his head and let the troublesome thoughts slip away. "Nothing," he said, smiling now, his boyish enthusiasm returning. "I guess I didn't expect quite so much excitement today."

Harren grinned. "Neither did we." He nudged the giant carcass with his foot. "I think we'd best get out of here now. This much meat will not lie unattended for long."

Even as he spoke a splash erupted from the swamp behind them. They turned and saw a giant head break the surface of the water and begin to glide slowly toward them, coming to feast on its cousin's body. The boys needed no further encouragement to leave.

Vadar took the lead as they threaded their way back through the swamp. Behind him, Tal and Dal pressed close to Thorogrin, praising his bravery and constantly repeating what they had seen, afraid they might forget some small detail if they spoke of anything else for even one moment. Thorogrin basked happily in his friends' admiration, the confused thoughts and feelings that had troubled him forgotten for now.

Though Thorogrin gave no more serious thought to his actions, Harren had been thinking of little else the entire journey back. By the time they came to the edge of the swamp, he had reached a decision.

"Let's rest a bit," he said as they emerged from the swamp. "Sit down, boys. There's something we need to talk about."

The three youths found a patch of soft grass just off the trail and sat down together, Tal and Dal flanking Thorogrin. Vadar knelt nearby on one knee, waiting expectantly. Harren squatted in front of the boys, so that his face was level with theirs.

"Boys, what I have to say is very important," he began, his somber tone emphasizing the seriousness of his words. "I want you to keep what happened today our secret. You cannot tell anyone."

"A secret?" Dal exclaimed in disbelief. "Why can't we tell? Penderyn is a hero. He should be in a song, or a story."

"I don't understand, Father," Tal said, puzzled. He looked from his father's face to Thorogrin's. "Why can't we talk about what Penderyn did?"

"I'll try to explain," Harren replied quietly. He waited a moment, gathering his thoughts so he could explain in a way the boys might understand. "What Penderyn did back there was indeed miraculous. There's no question he's a hero. We owe your lives to him, and I will be forever grateful. But what he did back there is not easily explained. In some mysterious way, he is different from the rest of us."

Thorogrin thought immediately of his dreams. He had never spoken of them to anyone besides his mother. Did others not have them? "I don't feel different," he protested, worried what all this might mean.

"That may be," Harren said, "but you are." He saw the crestfallen look on Thorgrin's face and affectionately rubbed his damp copper hair. "Don't worry," he said with a smile. "It doesn't matter to us. We love you more than ever. But to others, your difference might be perceived as a threat. Already there are those among us who seek to blame you for our difficulties, for the increasing harshness of our winters and our failing crops. I speak of Garith and his followers. They point to your birth, a full five years after Tal and Dal. They remember the strangeness of your father and would make a demon of him. They might use the miracle of your victory as a further sign that you are different, and then twist it to prove their earlier warnings."

"Is Penderyn really different?" Dal asked, looking at his friend in a new light.

Harren nodded. "In some mysterious way, yes, I believe he is. That difference saved your lives today. But Penderyn is no threat, despite what Garith would try to have people believe."

"Garith is a jealous fool," Vadar said angrily. "He has long wanted Aeta for his mate and sees Penderyn as an obstacle to his desires. But there are those who listen to him," he admitted.

"Do you boys understand why you must say nothing?" Harren asked.

The twins nodded in unison. Thorogrin looked worriedly from one to the other, wondering how they felt after their father's words. They were his closest friends; he hoped nothing would change that.

Tal draped his arm around Thorogrin's shoulder. "Don't worry, Penderyn. We don't care what anyone says. You're our friend."

"And a hero besides," Dal said adamantly. "Even if we can't tell anyone."

Time passed. Weeks turned into months and months faded into years. Though it was never forgotten, no word was ever mentioned of Penderyn's deed, except when the three boys were alone. Penderyn did not even tell his mother about the incident, to spare her the worry he knew the tale would bring. As the months slipped by, the three friends spoke of the slaying of the terriwarg less and less frequently, and when no new glimpses into Penderyn's mysterious "difference" came to pass, the whole thing slowly faded in their minds, until at last it was simply a fond memory, one that had never been explained. One other thing faded as well from Penderyn's memory, though even more slowly—the image of the dark, hooded figure, eyes glowing yellow in its unseen face.

CHAPTER 4

The still air of the woods had grown cool as the slanting rays of the autumn sun filtered through the half-bare trees at an increasingly sharp angle, and the crisp blue hue of the sky was beginning to fade into a powdery pastel as the day ebbed to a close. Crouched in the thin underbrush, Thorogrin gently pried an arrow from the carcass of a plump brown rabbit, applying a firm, yet gentle pressure as he worked the shaft slowly back and forth. With a wet, slurping sound, the arrowhead finally popped free. Smiling proudly, he shoved the arrow into his quiver and slung the rabbit over his shoulder. This was his third kill today—as many as Dal and only one less than Tal.

The twins waited for him back by the trail, perched comfortably on a smooth, waist high granite boulder that forced the path to twist around it. Each had a bulging leather pack leaning against the rock next to him. Thorogrin's slightly less full pack rested on the ground nearby. Tal noted the lengthening shadows and glanced up toward the sun.

"We'd better think about starting back," he said to his brother. "Night's not far off."

"And we've still a ways to go," Dal agreed. He called out to Thorogrin. "Penderyn, it's time to get going."

"On my way," Thorogrin replied, emerging onto the trail a few seconds later and nonchalantly dropping the rabbit carcass into his pack. He peeked at the twins from the corner of his eye, making sure they noted just how plump his latest kill was. At sixteen, the twins were young men now, yet they always treated him as an equal and asked him along whenever they went hunting. Still, he wanted to make sure they knew he was pulling his weight. Tal and Dal remained mirror images of each other, almost six feet tall with lean, wiry bodies, but as they had grown Tal's slightly bolder nature had come to the fore. His posture was just a fraction more erect than Dal's, and he was a bit more assertive in his bearing. Only eleven, Thorogrin was almost a full head shorter than both.

"We'll need to hurry a bit to make sure we beat the darkness," Tal said.

He slid down off the rock and hoisting his pack over his shoulder. Thorogrin and Dal did likewise. Dal took the lead as they headed northward through the thinning forest, their feet crunching loudly on the layer of dead leaves that coated much of the path. With their hunting done, there was no longer any need for stealth, so they moved quickly. Thorogrin followed closely behind Dal, half-walking, half-scrambling as he tried to match the stride of his taller friend. They had been hunting all day, and the leagues were beginning to take their toll on his young legs, but he voiced no complaint; he knew the dangers of the darkness as well as anyone. When they reached Ishtor, he would have plenty of time to rest.

Dal turned his head to say something to his companions behind him. Distracted, he failed to notice a thick root, half hidden by the fallen leaves, protruding across the trail. His toe caught in the crack between root and dirt, sending him sprawling face first toward the ground. He managed to get a hand out just in time to break the brunt of his fall.

Thorogrin dropped quickly to his knee at his friend's side.

"Are you all right?"

"I'll be fine," Dal replied. His mouth twisted into an embarrassed grin as he rolled into a sitting position and brushed away the dead leaves clinging to the front of his tunic. "How clumsy of me—you'd think I'd have learned how to walk through the woods by now."

He pushed himself gingerly to his feet. "Let's get go..." A gasp of pain cut off his words as he stepped forward. He clutched at Thorogrin's arm to keep from tumbling back to the ground.

"What is it?" Tal asked worriedly.

"My ankle," Dal said, holding the injured foot off the ground. "It's worse than I thought. I don't think I can walk on it."

"Sit down," Tal ordered. He and Thorogrin lowered Dal softly onto the path and then Tal gently probed the injured joint with his fingers. "I don't think anything's broken, but it may be a few days before you can walk on it. We'll have to carry you back."

"No way," Dal protested. "We'd never make it before dark."

Tal shrugged. "You have a better idea?"

Dal looked around, thinking. "Help me up into one of these trees," he said after a moment. "I'll be safe up there while you and Penderyn head home to tell them what happened. You can come back for me in the morning."

"Nothing doing," Tal replied adamantly. "I'm not leaving you alone out here all night."

"I could run back for help while you wait with Dal," Thorogrin offered.

Dal smiled warmly at his young friend. "Oh, no," he said. "I'd rather hop home on one foot than explain to your mother why we let you travel alone so close to nightfall."

"Then we're back where we started," Tal said ruefully. "We'd better think of something, and quickly."

"We passed a small cave on the way out this morning," Thorogrin said. "I don't think it's too far ahead. We could spend the night there."

Tal looked at his brother. "What do you say?"

Dal shrugged. "I can't think of anything better. Can you?"

Tal shook his head. He and Thorogrin hoisted Dal gently to

his feet. Dal draped his arm around Tal's shoulder for support.

"Lead on, Penderyn," Tal said.

Thorogrin started slowly down the trail. He kept one eye on the narrow path while he scanned the woods to their left, searching for the opening to the cave. Deepening shadows mottled the tree-covered hillsides, making difficult to see very far up into the trees. Several times he thought he'd spotted the cave, but after taking a couple of steps off the trail, he discovered he had been fooled by a trick of the uneven light. As the minutes passed, he grew anxious. Darkness was drawing nearer. Tal and Dal had accepted his certainty that the cave was close by. If he didn't find it soon, they would have to try something else. Precious time would have been wasted. He could not let his friends down.

Finally, he spotted it. About fifty paces up the hill, next to a rough gray outcrop, just as he remembered. This was no trick of the shadows.

"There it is!" he shouted, pointing up to the dark opening.

"Good work, Penderyn," Tal said. He lowered his brother gently to the ground. "Stay with Dal while I make sure the cave is unoccupied. We don't want to be the guests of honor at some beast's dinner."

He fit an arrow to his bowstring and crept silently up the ridge toward the cave, stopping when he reached the shadow of the rock that flanked the entrance. He listened carefully while his eyes adjusted to the darkness inside. Hearing no sounds, he moved cautiously into the dimness. The cave was not a big one, only about four feet high and no more than ten feet deep, but it was empty, which was all that really mattered.

"It's perfect," he called to his companions as he scrambled back down the hillside. "Big enough for all of us to squeeze into, and we should be able block up the entrance pretty easily."

"I'll start gathering some wood while you help Dal up to the cave," Thorogrin said. "We'll have a nice warm fire going in no time."

"What do you say to some tasty roasted rabbit for dinner, Dal?" Thorogrin suggested with a wry smile as he lit the kindling to a small fire just outside the entrance of the cave.

"Sounds like the perfect choice," Dal said with a laugh. "And since it's my fault we're stuck here, I'll do the messy work." Dragging his injured leg behind him, Dal crawled outside the cave and began skinning one of the rabbits.

Before long, the aroma of roasted rabbit filled the cavern. The trio ate ravenously, their appetites whetted by their long day of hunting. They talked little until they had finished.

"Our parents will be worried," Thorogrin remarked as they sat by the fire, enjoying its crackling warmth and watching the flickering shadows dance like crazed demons upon the uneven cavern walls. Outside, the night was dark and chill, but its cold fingers failed to breach the comfort of the fire-warmed cave. Despite his worries about his mother, Thorogrin felt wonderfully content.

"Father knows we can take care of ourselves," replied Tal. "I'm sure he'll be able to reassure your mother as well."

"I hope you're right," Thorogrin said. He yawned, the warmth of the fire beginning to make him drowsy.

"Why don't you two get some sleep," Dal suggested. "I'll take the first watch. My ankle's going to keep me awake for a while anyhow."

"Wake me when you get tired," Tal ordered. "I'll take the second turn."

"Don't forget me, Tal," Thorogrin said adamantly. "I want to do my share."

"Don't worry, you'll get your turn," Tal replied with a chuckle as he stretched out on the bed of dried leaves they had fashioned on the cavern floor.

Reassured that he would not be overlooked, Thorogrin rested his head upon his leather quiver and was soon fast asleep.

He saw a face, faint and far away. Nothing else—just a face, floating in blackness, growing larger, clearer. The face was hauntingly familiar, yet unknown. Long hair and a thick beard. The hair and beard grew brighter. They were red, almost like fire. Who was it? He struggled to see.

The outline began to blur, the color to darken. The hair and beard had transformed into a hood, the face now lost in dark shadow. Two yellow eyes shone from the blackness. Eyes whose hypnotic pull he had felt before. Terror filled him as he strained against their pull.

The eyes faded and the hood reverted to hair. For a moment, the original face stared back at him, until once again it began to change. The fiery red hair grew ever brighter, until it was hair no longer. Dancing tongues of flame reared in its place as the face disappeared. Nothing was left but the flames. He felt their heat as they surrounded him.

Suddenly, the scene became familiar. He saw a figure trapped within the flames. It was a woman—with hair of gold. Her arms reached out to him. He watched as her face grew clearer, but he already knew who it was. His mother's anguished expression bit deep into his heart. Her mouth stretched into a scream, a scream he had never heard in his previous dreams.

But this time, her voice rose above the roar of the fire, her cry filled with agony and despair. "Mandrar! Thorogrin!"

"Motherrr!"

Thorogrin's tortured scream echoed through the cavern, snapping Dal's head around and jerking Tal awake.

"Penderyn, what's wrong?" Dal asked.

Thorogrin paid Dal no attention. His mind was focused on only one thing as he sprang to his feet and leaped over the glowing fire that blocked the cave's entrance. He plunged into the darkness beyond, unarmed, unthinking. He knew only that he must reach his mother, before it was too late. This time, his dream had been different. This one had been all too real. He scrambled down the hillside and raced away toward Ishtor.

"Go after him, Tal!" Dal shouted. "Hurry!"

Tal grabbed his bow and arrows and darted from the cave without wasting time to reply. He crashed down the ridge to the trail. Dal would be safe enough, but Penderyn was running madly through the night, alone and unarmed. He must overtake his young friend, if not to stop him, then to protect him.

Thorogrin ran with a speed born of utter desperation, his slender body refusing to acknowledge fatigue as he sped through the darkness, his way along the narrow trail guided only by the dim light of Primus. He cared nothing for the branches that whipped against him, or of the fell creatures that hunted in the blackness. Every fiber of his being was centered on one goal: to somehow reach his mother and prevent the horrible doom foretold by his dream.

Tal raced after him, his longer stride slowly closing the distance between them, until at last he ran at Thorogrin's heels. Thorogrin glanced back in acknowledgment but said nothing, nor did he slacken his pace. Tal made no attempt to stop or slow him. Thorogrin's determination was clear; nothing Tal could say would make him stop. So Tal was content to run with Thorogrin, lending what protection he could as they dashed madly through the night.

The distance to Ishtor evaporated rapidly. In less than an hour they were running up the last hill before the village. A bright yellow glow illuminated the treetops along the crest of the ridge above them. Tal thought at first that it marked the rise of Ferus, but a glimpse behind him showed it was much too early for the *mocrah*; Primus was still too high in the sky. A feeling of dread foreboding stole over him.

Thorogrin took no notice at all of the brightening sky. His mind was filled only with the need to reach his mother. He pushed on up the hillside, stumbling frequently on the steep slope but never losing his balance completely. His mother's terrified face still filled his vision. His ears rang with her agonized scream.

The flickering yellow glow grew brighter as they neared the top of the ridge and a thick column of dark smoke became visible through the trees. Tal's heart sank. There could be only one cause for so much smoke and such a glow. The village was burning. How Thorogrin could have known he had no idea, nor did he have time to wonder.

As they crested the ridge, the size of the conflagration below stunned them. The entire village was ablaze. Flames danced from every hut, the thatched roofs blazing like giant torches, lighting up the night. The log palisade was a glittering ring of fire. Thorogrin and Tal stopped, momentarily frozen by the scale of the destruction below. Unspoken, each shared the same thought. Such a total inferno could not have been accidental. The huts were spaced well apart for just this reason, to prevent any fire from spreading rapidly before it could be stopped. This had to have been intentional. Someone had set fire to their village.

Thorogrin's despair exploded anew, bursting through the shock that had rooted his feet to the ground.

"Mother!" he wailed, charging down the hillside. He had no fear of the flames and scarcely felt the heat that cut through the night's chill. He saw only his mother trapped within the fire, screaming his name. He had to reach her. Straight toward the burning hell he sped.

Tal chased swiftly after him, afraid his unthinking friend would throw himself uselessly into the flames. He ignored the withering heat that blasted his exposed face and hands as he strained to overtake Thorogrin. The gap between them shortened, but so did the distance between Thorogrin and the flames.

There was no time left. In another moment, Thorogrin would be inside the ring of fire. Tal launched himself in a flying leap at Thorogrin's legs, tackling him just steps from the burning gate. The heat seared his lungs and felt like it would scorch the skin from his bones. He grabbed Thorogrin tightly around the waist and lifted him bodily from the ground. Thorogrin twisted and squirmed like a captured animal, but he was no match for Tal's strength as the older boy lugged him quickly away from the flames.

Only when they reached the relative coolness of the hillside did Tal halt, dropping exhausted to the ground but keeping Thorogrin wrapped safely in his arms until the mad fit that possessed his friend passed.

Thorogrin finally stopped struggling as he regained control of his emotions. All the energy had drained out of him, leaving him exhausted and empty.

"I'm okay now, Tal," he said quietly. "You can let me go."

Tal studied Thorogrins's soot-blackened face. Through the grime and fatigue Tal saw that his friend's eyes were clear. He released his grip.

"Thanks for stopping me," Thorogrin said sadly. "I know we're too late."

Tal nodded in acknowledgment. Neither said another word as they watched their village continue to burn, yet they took comfort in each other's presence. They sat for hours, numb with shock and despair, watching as the fire slowly burned itself out.

The first gray hints of dawn had seeped over the eastern ridge before the fire finally died. As the sky grew lighter, the pall of smoke above the village seemed to darken. It hung over Ishtor like a giant storm cloud, its acrid smell filling the valley. A faint southerly breeze tried to push the black plume to the north, but most of it lingered directly overhead, a somber monument to the destruction below. Wordlessly, the two grief-stricken watchers rose to their feet and started the slow, sad walk down the hillside.

The destruction of the village was total. Only the stone chimneys still stood, outlined against the gray twilight, like silent sentinels in the land of the dead. A thick circle of black and gray ash was all that remained of the palisade. Inside the ring, mounds of ash and rubble marked the remains of the huts. Glowing red embers still winked within the piles, slowly consuming whatever fuel had not yet burned completely.

Thorogrin and Tal trudged numbly through the wreckage. The silence was eerie, complete. All sense of familiarity was gone. This was another world, one that bore no resemblance to the peaceful village in which they had been raised. Several charred bodies, burned beyond recognition, lay just outside the smoking heaps of ash and embers, villagers who had awakened to their burning huts and tried vainly to escape. Most of the villagers had apparently been asleep in their huts, their bodies consumed in the funeral pyres that had been their homes.

Revulsion rose like poisonous bile in Thorogrin's throat as he passed the first of the twisted black corpses. Never in his young life had he imagined, much less seen, anything that compared with the horror through which he now walked. He wanted to run, to speed away from this terrible place and never look back. He forced down the sickness in his stomach and marched onward.

With Tal walking silently at his side, they reached the charred pile of rubble that had once been his home. The pile of glowing embers and smoking ash was indistinguishable from the remains of any other hut, but he knew this one was his. Tears streamed from his eyes, washing tiny white trails down his grime-stained cheeks.

Tal lingered with him for a moment, sharing Thorogrin's grief, before gently squeezing his shoulder and walking slowly away toward his own private sorrow.

Memories washed over Thorogrin as he stood motionless before the ruin. In his mind, the smoldering ashes began to take shape, growing back into his home. He saw his mother standing in the doorway, her golden hair shining in the sunlight as she smiled lovingly down at him. For a while, his young mind found succor in such memories, until finally he was done. The familiar hut turned once more into a pile of rubble. His home was gone, his mother was dead. He had witnessed her end in his dream. There was no need to probe the pile of ashes in front of him, no reason to disturb the pyre that had consumed her.

Aeta had died calling out his name and Mandrar's. She had promised to tell him about his father, a promise she would never be able to fulfill. All knowledge of his father lay buried with his mother's remains, forever beyond his reach. Buried there as well was the child she called Thorogrin, a child of hope. He would never think of himself by that name again. Only Penderyn now remained.

How long he stood there, he didn't know. The harsh clump of approaching footsteps finally pulled him from his thoughts. He swung his head around to see Tal striding purposefully toward him. Daylight had filled the valley, but even before Penderyn saw the grim set of his friend's features, he sensed the anger boiling inside Tal by the fierceness of his walk. Rage had replaced Tal's grief. Penderyn noticed that Tal's hands were covered with fresh brown soil.

"Come with me," Tal growled. Without waiting for a reply, he spun on his heels and turned back the way he had come.

Penderyn scrambled to catch up and fell into step beside him.

They stopped in front of the ruin that had been the twins' home. A body lay twisted on the dirt, far enough from the hut to keep it from being burned. Despite the coating of grime and ash that covered the dead man, Penderyn could see his clothing was not of Ishtor. He looked more closely at the corpse's face. The man was a stranger.

"My father killed him," Tal said grimly. He pushed at the body with his foot, rolling it onto its side. The carved bone hilt of a knife protruded from its bloodstained chest. "That's my father's knife."

Penderyn said nothing. He sensed there was more to come.

"Now I'll show you his reward defending his home," Tal said bitterly.

He led Penderyn out beyond the burned palisade, to a spear whose butt had been driven deeply into the ground. The point was covered with dried blood. Near the spear was a long mound of freshly dug dirt.

"I found my father's body here," Tal said, indicating the mound of dirt. He sucked in a deep breath before continuing. "But his head was there." His voice burned with rage as he pointed to the tip of the spear. "This was his reward for being a warrior and a man. To have his body mutilated and left to rot."

Tal began to tremble with grief and fury. Penderyn watched helplessly, his own smoldering anger rising anew.

"At least I was able to bury him," Tal said finally. "Come, I've one more thing to show you."

He led Penderyn out toward the woods, halting just before entering into the trees. He indicated the thick trunk of the nearest tree. A crude circle, split by a jagged line like a bolt of lightning, had been carved deep into the dark grey bark.

"The killers left their sign."

"We can go after them," Penderyn said angrily, turning toward the path by which the raiders had obviously departed.

Tal grabbed Penderyn gently by the arm, staying him. "Look at the tracks, Penderyn. There are far too many of them. What could we do even if we did overtake them?" He shook his head. "Besides, Dal is waiting for us." He edged forward and traced his finger slowly over the carving. "Vengeance will have to wait."

Penderyn knew Tal was right. He stared hard at the crude design, burning the image into his memory. One day, he would see this mark again—and he would not forget what had happened this night.

CHAPTER 5

While Penderyn and Tal trudged numbly through the charred rubble of their village, a solitary traveler strode determinedly through the gray forest dawn less than two days' journey to the west. Despite his rapid pace, he moved silently, a shadow among shadows, scarcely even noticed by the creatures that shared the woods with him as he glided through the trees, instinctively avoiding any large clearings or exposed hilltops that might reveal his presence to watching eyes. He doubted anyone was around to witness his passage in so isolated a place, but caution had been his watchword for so long now that it was an ingrained habit. Indeed, caution was far more of a mandate than speed, yet still he made good time. The leagues fell away behind him. Despite the many detours he made to insure his invisibility, his path led him unerringly toward his destination—the village of Ishtor.

Ever since he had begun this latest journey two months before, Mandrar had wondered at the wisdom of his decision to return, whether it was too soon, whether his son was still too young.

His son—the thought sent a warm feeling spreading through Mandrar's chest. He hated having to think of the boy in such a generic way, but he did not know his son's name. Twelve long years had come and gone since he had traveled within a hundred leagues of this land. A thousand times he had debated the risks of his present course, but he debated no longer—not after last night, when he had sensed the shattering vibrations of Aeta's pain and despair. He was too late to help her, he knew. Her end had come, and it could not be undone, despite the powers at his command. If only he had begun his journey sooner, perhaps he might have saved her. But such thoughts were of no use. He must concentrate on what still mattered—their son.

The boy had escaped his mother's fate, Mandrar was sure of that. He wondered how much Aeta had told their son about him. However much, the rest was up to him now. He would not be able to stay long with the boy, not if he wanted to insure his son's safety, but there were things he needed to teach him, important things, things upon which a world might depend.

Suddenly, Mandrar froze, yanked from his thoughts and brought to a halt by an unmistakable disruption in the vibrations around him. The feeling crawled over his skin like a thousand toxic insects. The source of the disruption was not yet close, but still near enough for him to feel the evil, to sense the chill dread that sent terrible memories flooding back through his brain. A Blood Hunter, almost beyond comprehension, had come to sleepy, isolated Braemar. Mandrar wondered if his enemies had discovered his whereabouts at long last, or if the creature had come here merely by chance. Or worse, was the demon after something—or someone—else? He shuddered, praying that the cursed Blood Hunter had not somehow learned of his son.

Closing his eyes, he let the demon's fell aura wash over him. The Blood Hunter was still several leagues away. Even from this distance, the foul violation sickened him, but he forced his senses to lock onto it, fixing the direction in his mind. The creature was not behind him, so it could not be pursuing him. The beast was somewhere off to the south, moving diagonally to Mandrar's path. His heart pounded in his chest. The creature was heading toward Ishtor!

Not by chance was the demon-spawn here, Mandrar knew. Ishtor was far too isolated, too distant from anything of importance to bring a Blood Hunter to it, unless the beast was drawn here. Mandrar knew he had no choice. He needed to reveal his presence, needed to make his enemy think any magic it had detected was Mandrar's alone. He spread his arms wide and inhaled deeply, gathering the magical forces around him. Power he had refused to touch in more than a decade flooded through him, building in strength until he could contain it no longer. He flung his arms up above his head and unleashed the magic in one mighty blast. The ground shook as a column of blinding yellow light flashed skyward, lighting up the dawn sky like a second sun.

He lowered his arms and collapsed to his knees, spent. The deed was done; there could be no undoing it. Despite his exhaustion, there would be no rest for him now. He pushed himself to his feet. Once again, he must begin his endless flight. One of his foes was close—perilously close. Others might also be near enough to have sensed the magical blast, but he prayed that was not so. There was no guarantee he would escape his pursuers this time, but at least he would draw them away. He turned and began running swiftly back the way he had come, no longer worrying about stealth. Speed was all that mattered now. He raced west, directly away from Ishtor, his heart weighted by sadness as he plunged through the woods. There would be no father/son talk now, no lessons given. His son was now truly alone.

CHAPTER 6

Something was very wrong.

Dal sensed it the instant he awoke. The cave was swathed in darkness, but the faint grey light leaking through the trees outside told him dawn had already broken. The protective fire in the cave's mouth had burned down to softly glowing embers and a few tiny flickering tongues of dancing yellow flame. Something about the dying fire pained Dal. Sadness pressed down on him like a sodden blanket across his shoulders, a blanket he could not shake off. He knew it had to be Tal. His twin was suffering some deep sorrow. Dal wondered what could be causing his brother so much hurt.

Though they were seldom apart, the twins had long ago learned that they shared a bond that transcended physical distance. Whenever one of them felt strong emotion, the other felt it as well. Their spirits were linked and their feelings shared, no matter what distance lay between them.

Dal's apprehension grew ever stronger as the morning dragged by. He sat restlessly at the edge of the cave, his injured ankle aching dully as he peered into the trees seeking some sign of his comrades' return. While he waited, he felt Tal's grief deepen and then change to bitter rage and hatred. His brother did not easily fall prey to such dark emotions and Dal anguished over what might be happening. Why had Tal and Penderyn not yet returned? Had some ill fate befallen Penderyn? Could that be the source of what Dal was feeling through his brother? He slammed his palm onto to the dirt floor, cursing his helplessness.

Movement in the trees below caught his eye and pulled him from his thoughts. Through the thinning foliage he spotted a black shape moving slowly along the path. All around the strange figure, the leaves and branches seemed to tremble and bend as if before a strong wind, but the rest of the forest was strangely still. It was eerily silent, too, Dal realized. Moments before, the chatter of birds had filled the air, but no longer. A feeling of cold dread stole over him. Instinctively, he edged his way silently back into the shadows, moving as deep into the cave as he could.

The dark form halted at the bottom of the hillside, directly below Dal's hiding place. Dead and dying leaves rustled in the stillness as branches on either side of the path seemed to bend themselves away from the figure, repelled by some unseen force. A loose cloak of coarse black cloth draped the thing, hiding all trace of its true shape, and a thick hood kept its face shrouded in darkness. For a moment it remained motionless, and then the hooded head swung slowly from side to side, as if probing the surrounding woods. What it was searching for Dal had no idea, but he prayed it was not looking for him.

He held his breath and pressed himself against the cavern wall as the creature stared up toward the cave. A pair of glowing yellow eyes shone from beneath the hood and seemed to lock onto his. Dal grew cold, as if a chill wind had suddenly whipped through the cavern, yet the air was still. He tried to turn away, tried to pull his eyes away from the gleaming yellow orbs, but he was unable to move. Paralyzed, his muscles no longer obeyed his brain's commands. He was certain the thing had sensed his presence. He dreaded what might happen next.

Suddenly, the creature snapped its head around and stared off to the northwest. Something or someone had distracted it, grabbing its attention. The spell that kept Dal paralyzed was broken. He followed the thing's gaze, but could see nothing through all the trees. Dal was reminded of a hunting beast as the creature raised its hooded head, seeming to sniff the air. A moment later it raced off into the woods, moving with a loping speed Dal would not have thought possible from its bulky shape. As the creature sped away, the rustling of the leaves and limbs suddenly stopped. The forest was still once again.

Dal limped from the cave. Using his hunting knife, he cut down a small sapling and fashioned a crude crutch from a sturdy Y-shaped bough. With the aid of the crutch, he worked his way carefully down to the trail. He easily found the spot where the frightening creature had stood and studied it carefully. Within a rough circle about five feet across, the edges of the brown autumn leaves on the ground were blackened and curled, almost as if they had been close to a fire. In the same area, the thinner branches of the surrounding brush were all bent away at unnatural angles, as if the limbs themselves had tried to escape the thing's touch.

Dal turned his head and stared into the trees where the creature had disappeared, remembering the hypnotic pull of those gleaming yellow eyes. Whatever the thing was, he truly hoped it had nothing to do with his comrades or with him.

Shaken, he was in no mood to wait alone in the chill, somber forest, so he hobbled slowly up the trail toward Ishtor, leaning heavily on his crutch. As he limped along the path, the woods slowly reawakened. Insects buzzed around his head and the birds had resumed their normal chatter. The sounds comforted him, confirmation that the creature had moved far away. Dal plodded northward for several hours, stopping frequently to rest his ankle. By the time he finally spied Penderyn and Tal striding toward him, the sun was almost directly overhead. His brother and friend appeared unhurt. Relief flooded over him as he rested against his crude crutch and waited for them to reach him.

As they drew nearer, his elation faded. One glance at their haggard faces was proof enough that something was grievously wrong.

There were no secrets between the twins, so Tal left out nothing as he told his brother what they had found. Dal listened in silence, tears running down his cheeks. All thoughts of the creature were driven from his mind. Hot fury filled his head instead. When his brother finished, Dal insisted they return immediately to Ishtor, so he might view the destruction himself. Tal knew better than to try to talk his brother out it.

"I had to see it for myself," Dal said sadly as he turned away from his father's grave and stared at the charred remains of their village. "All this would never have been completely real if I hadn't come back to see it."

Penderyn and Tal nodded silently in understanding. Now it was finished for all of them.

They had no desire to remain among the ruins any longer, so they moved off into the trees to fashion a shelter to live in until Dal's ankle healed. As they walked slowly away from the village, Dal remembered the creature that had stalked him back at the cave. He recounted the tale to his comrades.

"I don't know how it could have seen me, but I had a definite feeling it knew I was there. I couldn't move, couldn't even turn my head away. Maybe I was just too scared, I don't know." Dal shuddered at the memory. "Those yellow eyes, glaring up at me. I'll never forget them."

Penderyn's eyes opened wide at the mention of the creature's eyes. He felt his heart begin to beat faster as the memory flooded into his brain.

"If something hadn't drawn the thing away," Dal continued, "I don't know what would have happened."

"I've seen a demon like that in my dreams," Penderyn said, his voice a frightened whisper. "Even last night, before I saw the fire, before I heard my mother's screams." He trembled as the images came back to him. "First I saw a face, strange to me yet somehow seeming familiar. Then the face faded and was replaced by the glowing eyes."

Penderyn looked somberly at each of his friends. "I don't know why, but I think the creature Dal saw was looking for me."

The twins stared down at him, astonishment etched upon their youthful faces. "What would such a creature want of you?" Tal asked.

"I don't know," Penderyn said uncertainly. "It's just a feeling. I hope I'm wrong." He looked toward Dal. "I wonder what drew it away?"

"I don't know. But I'm grateful something did, whatever it was."

Tal draped his arm around Penderyn's shoulders. "It's gone now, Penderyn," he said reassuringly. "If it ever comes back, Dal and I will be there to face it with you."

Penderyn only nodded, wondering whether that would be nearly enough.

Dal's ankle took a week to heal fully. When it was better, there was nothing to hold the three youths in Ishtor.

Penderyn had been giving their impending departure much thought. He sensed somehow that this choice would be an important one, though he had no idea why he felt that way. It was simply a feeling, a subtle but troubling rumbling, just below the level of his awareness. He had searched his dreams for guidance but could recall none that were of any help. He was not yet twelve years old, he kept thinking—he should not be making decisions such as this. But with his mother dead and his father unknown to him, there was no one to make them for him.

He could leave things up to Tal and Dal, he knew; the twins would take care of him, no doubt, but when he tried to give himself over to that comforting idea something inside him rebelled. Only you know what must be done, some inner voice whispered, and so finally he had made up his mind. He knew Tal and Dal would be surprised by his decision, but he was pretty sure they would go along. At least he hoped they would.

"I think we must leave Braemar," he told the twins as the three of them sat in the flickering light of a small fire in front of the crude shelter that had been their home for the past week.

Tal and Dal looked at him in surprise. Though they hadn't really discussed it, they had assumed they would simply head north to one of the nearest villages. The idea of leaving their homeland had never entered their minds.

"Leave Braemar?" Tal said.

"Why?" asked Dal.

Penderyn poked absently at the fire with a stick. The flames crackled in response and a flurry of glowing orange embers danced up into the darkness. "I'm not sure," he admitted after a moment. "It's just a feeling I have. A feeling that Braemar may no longer be safe for me."

"Is this about the creature Dal saw?" Tal asked. "Do you still think that thing was seeking you?"

By unspoken agreement, they had not talked of the creature since the morning of the fire.

"Perhaps that's a part of it," Penderyn said. "I just feel something inside me telling me to go, before it's too late."

The twins glanced at each other for a moment, reaching a decision without the need for words.

"That settles it, then," Tal said. He clapped a hand onto Penderyn's shoulder. "There's nothing left for us here, so I guess it doesn't really matter where we go."

"One unknown berry is the same as another, grandfather used to say," Dal added with a smile. "Until you bite into one, there's no way to tell how it will taste."

"We trust your instincts, Penderyn," Tal said. "If you think we should leave Braemar, that's good enough for us."

Relief washed over Penderyn. He had not been completely certain the twins would agree to his plan, and was unsure what he would have done if they had not.

"It will be a fine adventure," Dal said enthusiastically. "Perhaps we'll even get to see if there's any truth behind some of the old stories."

They decided to journey south, around the swamp and into a land they knew only by name—Tyrnon. What they might find beyond Braemar's borders they knew not, but their hope was to locate a village to take them in before winter seized the land in its ever-tightening grip. Heading south would delay the season's onset, but could not prevent it. They hoped their skill as hunters would make them welcome in whatever place they finally reached.

"We'd best get to bed then," Tal said. "So we can get an early start."

No one had any objection, so they crawled in to their shelter and were soon fast asleep. Thankfully, no dreams troubled Penderyn's sleep.

They set out soon after dawn. The night's crisp chill still lay upon the valley and the ground was damp with glistening dew. Sadness weighed on their young hearts as they skirted the gray ruins of Ishtor for the final time and departed into the trees. Just before the woods closed around them, Penderyn twisted his head around and took one last look behind him, a final, silent good-bye to the place that had been the only home any of them had ever known.

For a while, none of them spoke as they threaded their way single file along the narrow hunting path they had chosen to take them southward, each preferring to be alone with the memories of the home they were leaving behind. They were young, however, and had already had a week to deal with their sorrows. Gradually, their exuberant natures and the excitement of the adventure in front of them pushed the sorrow back into the deeper recesses of their hearts, even as the steadily rising sun melted the shadows of the woods and dried the dew from the ground.

As the morning warmed, they peeled off their coats and strapped them across the top of the leather packs each carried upon his back. Three hours into their journey, they came upon a bubbling stream that wandered down across the trail from the higher ground to the east.

"This looks like a good spot to rest," Tal said, lifting his pack from his shoulders and dropping it upon the soft grasses growing along the bank of the stream.

Penderyn and Dal followed his lead, and then the three companions knelt at the brook's edge and gulped at the cool, refreshing water, slaking their thirst. When they were satisfied, they sat cross-legged upon the grass, resting.

"How far is it to Tyrnon?" Penderyn asked.

"Four or five days to the river Palorinth, I think," replied Tal. "We've not been that far, but the river marks the border between our lands."

"It may be much farther to find a village, though," Dal said.

"Are the people of Tyrnon very different from us?" Penderyn asked. In his short life he had seen less than a score of people from outside Ishtor, and all of them had come from somewhere in Braemar. He knew of no one from Ishtor who had ever visited the neighboring land.

"A traveler from Tyrnon passed through our village when you were three or four years old," Tal recalled.

"I remember that," Dal mused. "His arrival did not cause nearly the stir that Penderyn's father's appearance did, but it was a rare enough occurrence nonetheless."

"It created plenty of talk, I remember," Tal added, "though in truth he seemed little different to me from the men of our village."

Not for the first time, Penderyn wondered where his father had come from, and what had brought him to Braemar. Even more importantly, why had he left before Penderyn had even been born? His mother had told him very little about his father, only that he had been a wonderful man who could not stay. She had promised she would tell him more when he came of age, but that was never going to happen now.

CHAPTER 7

For an entire fortnight the three comrades trekked southward, seeing no trace of human presence. They fell into a comfortable routine, arising early each morning and beginning their travel in the crisp cold, then enjoying the warmth of the midday sun before halting with enough time before sunset to gather wood and start a fire to warm them through the chill nights. A fierce storm that rolled in from the north delayed them for two days. They rode out the tempest huddled under a crude lean-to they hurriedly constructed when the first of the heavy gray storm clouds roofed the sky above them. Water dripped though the cracks of their shelter, but they managed to collect enough dry wood before the deluge broke to maintain a roaring fire. Their fire kept them warm and mostly dry despite the cold rain that pelted the outside of the lean-to.

A week into their journey, with clear sunlight once again shining upon them, they forded the Palorinth, a broad, slow-flowing ribbon of water. The far side of the river looked little different than the near. The forest was immense and seemingly unending. As the companions pushed further into Tyrnon the land gradually flattened and they made better time crossing the low, rolling hillsides than they had trudging up and down the steeper ridges that crisscrossed Braemar. One thing became abundantly clear to all of them. Ishtor had been far more isolated than they had realized, though in the end, it had not been isolated enough to save their village and their families.

Despite the southward leagues that fell before their steady pace, they could not outpace the descent of winter. The nights grew ever colder, the days shorter and more chill. Their arrows and skill kept them supplied with food and skins to ward off the growing cold, but they knew once the snows arrived, game would be scarce. They needed to find a village soon. If they did not, surviving until spring was going to be very difficult.

Finally, the forest ended. One minute the three comrades were surrounded by trees and the next they were standing transfixed in the shade at the edge of the wood, staring out in wonder at the vista before them. Low, gently sloping hills seemed to roll unendingly to the west, their flanks covered by long, flaxen grasses that rippled in rhythmic waves before the cool north wind. Far to the south, they could just make out the faint, purple hint of a towering mountain range shimmering in the haze. Such a vast, open expanse was as foreign to the forest dweller as the surface of Perator's twin moons would have been. They were accustomed to seeing distances in paces or arrow flights, not the seemingly endless leagues stretching out in front of them. Even so, the wonder of the vast plain paled before the sight that drew their eyes to the east—a walled city of stone thrusting upward from the plain like a jagged mountain.

Penderyn rubbed his eyes. Even from several leagues away, the sheer size of the city was beyond his comprehension. Nothing in his life had given him any frame of reference for such a place. A hundred Ishtors would be swallowed inside the tall stone wall surrounding the city, and the tops of the myriad towers visible beyond the great wall reached a height that was almost unthinkable.

"What can it be?" he muttered in wonder. "A city of giants?"

"Nay, Penderyn. Look there," Tal said, pointing just north of the city, where a group of tiny figures worked in mostly empty fields, collecting the last of the late autumn harvest. "They're men,

Penderyn. Men just like us."

Penderyn refused to believe it. Men they might be, but they were not like him. "What magic they must command, to build such a place!" Tales of magic and adventure welled up in his memory. Stories he had not believed since he was little suddenly became possible. He wondered what miracles they might discover inside those walls.

Dal turned to his brother. "Penderyn may be right," he said. "Who knows what powers exist beyond our valley. At least some of the old legends may be rooted in fact."

"Perhaps," Tal mused. "But we won't find out standing here. Let's go." He strode off toward the city. Penderyn and Dal glanced at each other for a moment and then hurried to join him.

They walked rapidly, eager to meet the inhabitants of this strange new land. To signal their peaceful intentions they kept their bows and spears slung across their backs. As they drew nearer, Penderyn spotted a dirt roadway leading from the city, so they angled toward it. They were almost to the road when the clatter of rushing hoofs erupted behind them. A score of mounted warriors charged toward them, scarlet cloaks billowing behind them as they raced across the plain. Penderyn jerked his bow from his back and began to fit an arrow to the string, but Tal quickly dropped a hand upon his shoulder to stay him.

"Put away your bow," he ordered. "If they mean us harm, three bows will not stop them."

The riders reined to a halt a short distance away, maneuvering into a half circle around the three youths, their long spears pointing threateningly toward the trio. Two of the warriors walked their horses forward.

"Who are you, and why do you come to Kfastia?" asked the younger of the two. He looked to be in his early twenties, but by his bearing they knew he was the leader. Though his voice was strong and commanding, it held no real hint of menace.

"My name is Tal," Tal replied politely. "This is Penderyn, and my brother Dal. Might we have your name, sir?"

"I am Cornon, captain in her Majesty's army," replied the warrior.

"Now answer his question," the second rider growled impatiently. "What are you doing here?"

Cornon glanced sternly at his comrade, but said nothing.

"We seek a place to live," Penderyn explained. "Our village was destroyed by raiders."

Cornon turned toward Penderyn and studied him closely. The surprise on his face was unmistakable. A thoughtful expression crossed his chiseled features.

"Your garb is strange to me," he said at last. "Where was your village?"

"Many leagues to the north," Tal replied. "Our journey has taken almost two fortnights."

"They lie!" challenged the second rider. "Nothing but forest lies to the north. They are spies from Colgoth, seeking to fool us by coming from the woods."

"Silence, Farus," Cornon ordered sternly. He pointed to Penderyn. "Would Halibur send one such as this to spy on us?"

Penderyn grew angry. "I can do anything my friends can do," he said proudly, drawing himself to his full height.

Cornon's features softened. "Lad, you mistake my meaning. No insult was intended, I assure you. How many years do you count?"

"Almost twelve," Penderyn replied.

A surprised murmur rippled through the squad of mounted warriors.

"Twelve years," Cornon repeated, his tone conveying his wonder. "No one in our land has seen fewer than seventeen."

Cornon's words echoed in Penderyn's ears. He was stunned. Kfastia was no different than Ishtor! There were no children here, either. The curse of barrenness gripped this land as well. What *was* the secret behind his birth?

Cornon mistook Penderyn's shock for surprise.

"Your ignorance of our affliction proves you are strangers," he said. "You know not of the curse that slowly destroys our land."

"Sadly, this curse is not yours alone," Tal explained. "My brother and I were the youngest in our village, until Penderyn was born. We are almost seventeen."

Cornon's brow furrowed in puzzlement. Farus looked at him with surprise.

"We had not known this affliction was elsewhere," Cornon said finally. "But rest assured, you will be welcome in Kfastia." He turned to Farus. "Continue the patrol. I'll take our guests into the city."

Cornon dismounted gracefully as Farus led the patrol back to the road.

"Forgive our suspicions. Our land draws near to war. Already some of our outlying cabins have been attacked by raiders. The people grow fearful. Caution is by necessity our watchword."

"May I ask a question before we go?" Penderyn asked. His voice had taken on a grim tone. "The raiders you spoke of—do you know them?"

"We believe so," Cornon replied. "A more complete answer requires a short course on the recent history of our land. I hope you will wait for that. It is too involved to explain quickly."

"There's just one thing I need to know now," Penderyn persisted. He scratched a hated figure into the dirt: the circle cut by a jagged line. "Have you ever seen this mark?"

Cornon studied the pattern silently and then shook his head. "No, the design is unfamiliar to me. What does it mean?"

"It's the symbol of the murderers who destroyed our village. I thought perhaps they might be the ones who burned your farms."

"I'm sorry," Cornon said gently. "But these raiders are our

own problem. I'll explain it all after we get you settled."

As they walked toward the city, Penderyn and the twins barraged Cornon with questions. How was such a place built? Was it carved from a mountain? What magic was used to shape the stone? Did his people still possess their magic?

Cornon smiled at their enthusiasm as he patiently answered what questions he could. He sensed Penderyn's disappointment when he explained there was no magic involved, only long years of work by many laborers under the guidance of skilled artisans.

"The only magic in our history is the Flaming Sword," he said. "And that is long gone. You'll hear more of the sword when I tell you the history of our land."

They entered the city through an immense gateway guarded by a squad of warriors. Two stout wooden doors the height of three full grown men stood open now, but when fastened shut the three friends could see the doors would make a formidable barrier.

"In better times, only two men man this gate," Cornon said resignedly as they passed the warriors. "Too many men are being wasted by the current state of affairs. They could be of better use doing other things."

Inside the walls, the city was even more magnificent than it had appeared from outside. Penderyn's head and eyes were in constant motion as Cornon led them along its broad avenues. He was awestruck by its size and its beauty. Up close, even the smallest buildings seemed huge, and when they moved into the wealthier sections, the grandeur was beyond his imagination. The streets bustled with activity. A constant stream of wagons and carts, some crudely constructed of unfinished wood, others painted in reds or blues or greens, clattered down the center of the avenues, while on either side lines of people hurried by. There seemed to be more people in just a few blocks than the entire population of Ishtor. Many of the city folk stopped and stared at Penderyn as he passed, but he scarcely noticed, his senses too overwhelmed by the vastness and splendor of his surroundings. Despite his maturity, he was in some ways still a child, with a child's sense of marvel and wonder. No matter what Cornon maintained, to him there was magic aplenty in this place.

They passed through an unguarded gateway into a wide flagstone courtyard filled with carefully trimmed green shrubs and lifelike marble sculptures. Three round pools of clear water reflected the beauty of the surroundings.

"This is my parents' home," Cornon said, a trace of amusement in his voice.

"We're going to stay here?" Penderyn asked in disbelief as he stared at the magnificent stone building in front of them, one of the largest they had yet seen.

"Are you sure there's room?" Dal joked.

"I think we can squeeze you in," Cornon replied with a smile.

"Your family must be important," Tal observed.

"We are of the Majhari," Cornon said. "You'll understand when you've learned more about our land."

"I understand one thing already," Penderyn said, shaking his head. "And that's how little I understand about all this."

Cornon laughed. "Come; let's go find my mother and father."

CHAPTER 8

The resemblance between Cornon and his father Valdor was a strong one. Both had the same dark, curly hair, although Valdor's was flecked with grey, and sharp, chiseled features that softened measurably when they smiled. The same proud, confident bearing was evident in both, but was even more pronounced in Valdor. Penderyn could tell he was looking at a man used to commanding the respect of others—and a man who probably deserved it.

Cornon's mother looked small next to her husband and son, but she was almost as tall as Tal and Dal. She wore her brown hair in a long braid behind her head, and her dark green eyes displayed character and intelligence. After a brief introduction, she insisted her guests refresh themselves at once. Penderyn and the twins found themselves being led away to the guest chambers while Cornon remained and recounted their story to his father.

Each boy was given his own room complete with a marble bath filled with steaming hot water. Penderyn had never seen anything like the huge bath. In Ishtor, cleaning had been done in the stream or with a bucket. He thought he had never felt anything as wonderful as when he eased himself down into the water. The hot water began immediately to melt the soreness from his travel weary muscles. A layer of dirt floated up from his body and formed a film on the water's surface.

When he finally climbed out of the bath, his fingers were wrinkled like prunes, but he had never felt better. Weeks of travel had been washed from his skin and his muscles. He donned a clean white tunic left for him by a servant and then walked down the hallway to the first door he found. Before he could knock, Tal opened the door, smiling. He looked as relaxed and clean as Penderyn felt.

"Did you ever imagine a bath could be so fun?" Tal asked. "I could get used to this."

Penderyn held out his wrinkled fingers. "I didn't want to get out, but I was afraid my whole body might look like this if I stayed in much longer."

Dal joined them a moment later and a servant escorted the three of them to a large dining hall where Cornon, Valdor and Thrisa awaited them.

The room was the largest in the house—it could have held at least two of Ishtor's cabins within its confines—with a vaulted stone ceiling twenty-five feet high. The light brown walls were decorated with brightly colored tapestries depicting many strange creatures. Penderyn recognized some from their descriptions in old stories and legends; others were completely unknown to him. He wondered if any these fantastic beasts really existed. A picture of a giant terriwarg on the far wall made him think perhaps they did.

Six places were set at the end of a long wooden table that could easily have accommodated four times that number. When everyone was seated, a pair of young boys served a light midday meal of bread, fruit and dried meat.

"Tell us first about the raiders who have been burning your farms," Penderyn asked between bites, still hoping to learn something about the murderers who had destroyed Ishtor.

"To understand our current problems, you must know something about the history and the geography of our land," Valdor said. "Kfastia is one of four cities that make up Calistan; the others are Colgoth and Dewellyn, located to our northeast, and Legas, to the west. Kfastia is the largest of the four, Legas the smallest."

"It's a good thing you emerged from the forest where you did," Cornon added. "Had your path led just a few leagues to the east, you would have come to Colgoth instead of Kfastia. As you will soon see, that would have meant trouble for us."

"Your comrade thought we were spies from Colgoth," recalled Tal. "Yet you're part of the same country. I don't understand."

Valdor's face tightened. "There are those who wish to change things," he said. "Let me continue with my story and it will become clearer.

"Many hundreds of years ago, there was no Calistan. A number of small tribes, more often than not at war with one another, dwelt here. The two most powerful clans were the Caliden and the Stanahym. Since no tribe was strong enough to conquer the others, alliances shifted back and forth as old quarrels faded and new ones were born.

"Finally, there arose among the Palladin a leader named Sumar, which means The Chosen One. Long had there been a legend among the tribes that one day a mighty warrior with a flaming sword would unite the land and make it prosper. Sumar decided to become that warrior. With ten of his most trusted comrades, he set out to find the flaming sword. Those ten became known as the Majhari."

"Then one of your ancestors went on the quest," Penderyn interjected excitedly, remembering that Cornon had told him his family was of the Majhari.

"I am descended from Merwyn, Sumar's closest friend," Valdor said. "As Cornon has no doubt told you, the Majhari still retain exalted positions. But let me return to my story.

"The details of Sumar's quest have been handed down in our greatest songs and stories. There's no need to go in to them now; suffice it to say that he finally discovered a wondrous gem. Even in the dark, the jewel shone with a fiery red glow. Sumar had it fashioned into the hilt of his sword, thus becoming the wielder of the Flaming Sword.

"Instead of using his newfound power to conquer, Sumar united the neighboring tribes with promises of peace and friendship. They were only too willing to join the bearer of the Flaming Sword. The Stanahym grew nervous at this gathering power and tried to form their own alliances. Rather than fight them, Sumar went to the Stanahym in peace and offered them an honored place in his new kingdom. The country became known as Calistan.

"The energy once wasted on war was now free for more productive uses. Cities were built; first Kfastia, to be the capital city, and then Colgoth, almost equal in splendor and size. Over the years, the old tribal distinctions blurred through intermarriage, until finally we became one people.

"For hundreds of years Calistan grew and prospered in peace. The rule passed through Sumar's descendents, until our ruler became known simply as the Sumar. Now all that is threatened."

"What happened?" asked Penderyn.

"Calistan is once more divided," Cornon replied bitterly.

"Our land is not so overtly divided as before," Valdor said. "Nonetheless, there are those who wish to see changes made."

"Halibur." Cornon spat out the name as if it burned his tongue.

"Halibur is chief among them," agreed Valdor.

"Who's he?" asked Dal.

"Halibur is the Lord of Colgoth. He seeks to claim the title of Sumar as well and be ruler of all Calistan."

"But who's the Sumar now?" asked Tal.

"No one," Valdor replied. "In his stead we have our first Sumara. Calistan is ruled by Arista, widow of the Sumar Kalin, who died three years ago. The position is rightfully hers."

"But Halibur disputes that right?" asked Penderyn, beginning to grow somewhat confused.

"Arista's right to the throne is clear. But Halibur still desires a change. He was cousin to Kalin, and as Lord of Colgoth has many followers. He uses other considerations as well to push his claim. You see, Kalin and Arista had no children, so there is no heir to the throne. More importantly, the last child born before the curse was Halibur's son Calob. Halibur tries to use this as proof of the gods' favor. There has been no open break as yet, but his arguments have been enough to sway Danustiri, the Lord of Dewellyn, to his side."

"That's why your arrival is so important, Penderyn," Cornon explained. "You are five years younger than Calob. Your presence in Kfastia can be used to show that the gods favor Arista."

Penderyn shook his head. All this was very confusing to someone who had grown up in a small, isolated village. He turned to the one thing still foremost in his mind.

"Is Halibur behind the attacks on your farms?" he asked.

"We don't have any proof of it," Cornon replied, "but there's little doubt. He seeks to stir unrest."

"And he grows bolder as time passes," Valdor added. "One day he will break with Arista completely." He paused for a moment, contemplating his youthful guest. "Your presence here complicates matters for him, Penderyn. If he doesn't already know you're here, he'll know soon enough. You need to be very careful. Halibur is not one to let an obstacle stand in his way for long. You'll be a thorn in his side, and he will attempt to remedy that, one way or another."

"I thought with the forest behind us, I could finally sleep in peace," Penderyn said, only half jokingly.

"A city can be more dangerous than any forest, remember that," Valdor warned. "But you'll be safe here." He pushed his chair back from the table. "I must leave now. I have a meeting at the palace. Tomorrow, you three have an audience with Arista. She wishes to welcome the one the city is already calling The Last Born."

CHAPTER 9

The first thing Penderyn saw was the mosaic.

The image dominated the room. It showed a huge warrior, twenty feet tall, brandishing a flaming red sword. Bright blue eyes seemed to lock onto Penderyn's as he followed Valdor and Cornon across the throne room. His heart raced. Was this some artist's clever trick, or had Sumar singled him out in some mysterious way? He stared harder at the mosaic, his imagination working feverishly as it conjured up images of young Penderyn, the mighty warrior, leading his followers to victory against overwhelming odds.

The sound of his name startled him. For a brief moment he thought it might be Sumar calling to him, but then he remembered where he was. Valdor was introducing him to Arista. With an effort, Penderyn pulled his gaze from Sumar's image and turned his eyes to the Sumara.

Arista's soft, gentle beauty took him by surprise; he had expected a sterner, more powerful figure. The handsome woman who rose from her throne to greet them did not look at all like the ruler of such a great city. Long brown hair topped by a simple silver crown flowed loosely across her slender shoulders and framed a delicate, oval face. Her smile seemed warm and genuine, and her dark eyes were filled with compassion. Only when he looked more closely could Penderyn see the faint creases of worry that lined her forehead and narrowed the corners of her eyes. In those eyes he discerned concern as well as compassion. It was clear Arista's troubles were lying increasingly heavy upon her.

Arista smiled as she descended the dais from her throne.

"Welcome to Kfastia, travelers," she said warmly. "I am sorry for your loss. Please make our city your home for as long as you desire."

She stopped upon the bottom step and addressed the twins.

"Welcome, Tal and Dal." She looked from one to the other several times, trying to find some way to distinguish them from one another. "We will have to provide you with different colored cloaks if I'm to tell you apart," she said finally. "Until then, I won't even try."

She moved in front of Penderyn and laid her hand gently upon his shoulder. He saw the hope in her eyes as she looked down at him.

"I'm especially glad to have you here, young Penderyn. And not only because of our current troubles. It's been too long since anyone of your youth has graced our city. I hope your arrival is an omen of better days to come."

The emotion in Arista's voice tugged at Penderyn's heart. He wanted to help, to do something to lessen her burden. His thoughts turned to his mother. He had been unable to save her; he hoped the same thing wasn't going to happen here.

"I hope I can help in some way," he said. "Whatever I can do, you have but to command me."

Arista smiled. "Your tongue belies your youth, Penderyn. I pray that I shall not have to ask anything of you. My hope is that your presence alone will quell some of the unrest which afflicts our land."

"We can hope," Valdor said grimly, "but I doubt Penderyn's presence will stem the cold ambition in Halibur's heart. At best, it will make him change his tactics."

A tall man in a dark blue hooded robe entered the throne room, interrupting their discussion. The hood kept the man's face in shadow, so that his features could not be clearly seen. A simple cord of rope held the robe tight around his waist, but any claim to monastic simplicity was belied by a triangular gold pendant hanging around his neck. He crossed directly to the dais and bowed his head to Arista.

"Greetings, Your Majesty," he said in a soft voice. "I thought I should meet our guest. The whole city is talking of him." He looked at Penderyn. "So this is the one the people are calling the Last Born."

Penderyn felt uneasy under the man's gaze. Something in the shadowed eyes made him very nervous.

"I am Chirops, High Priest of Kfastia," the man said. "Let me add my welcome to Arista's."

Penderyn did not reply. Even the priest's voice disturbed him, though he could name no definite reason for the feeling.

"Do the gods now favor me, Chirops?" Arista asked. "Since fate has brought Penderyn to Kfastia rather than Colgoth, perhaps you were wrong in advising me to consider Halibur's claim to the throne."

Chirops turned to Arista. He folded his hands in front of his waist. "The gods have not yet revealed to me the meaning of the Last Born's arrival," he said evenly. He fingered the medallion on his chest for a moment before continuing. "When they have, you may be certain I will advise my Sumara accordingly."

The High Priest turned his gaze once more upon Penderyn. "I have advice for you though, Last Born," he said. "Be very careful, for I'm certain there are those who would wish you ill."

Despite the even tone of the priest's voice, the words struck Penderyn like a veiled threat. He was about to respond when Valdor spoke.

"He'll be well looked after, Chirops," Valdor promised. "By those who care more for his welfare than our High Priest does."

Chirops did not hide his dislike for Valdor from his face or his voice. "Your words sound like a warning, Valdor, aimed at a man who is merely a humble servant of the gods. Take care your insolence does not bring their wrath down upon you."

"I'm at peace with my gods," Valdor replied evenly. "I do not fear them."

Chirops seemed about to reply, but then mastered his anger. "I must return to the temple to pray. Last Born, I hope the gods bestow their blessings upon you." He turned and strode from the room.

"I don't like him," Dal said. "Does he profess to speak for the gods?"

"He is High Priest of Kfastia," replied Arista. "Had you no priests in your land?"

"We had no one like Chirops in our village, I'm happy to say," Tal replied. "What exactly do priests do?"

"Our priests pray to the gods for us," Arista explained. "They interpret their signs and reveal their will. As High Priest, Chirops is the voice of the gods."

Tal shook his head. "When we wish to speak to the gods we do so ourselves. When we hunt, we seek the blessings of Ragda. Before we sow our seeds, we ask for Celena's favor. The gods show their pleasure or displeasure by our results."

Valdor smiled. "In some ways, your village was far more advanced than Kfastia. I for one could do without the priests."

"Then why have them?" Penderyn asked innocently.

"Because the people believe in them," replied Arista. "As do I."

Penderyn looked up at Arista in surprise. If the Sumara believed Chirops spoke for the gods, there must be more going on here than he understood.

Arista recognized the surprise on the faces of her guests. "Not all our priests are like Chirops. Most are good and kindly men who give comfort to our people. They have served us well for hundreds of years." She shook her head sadly. "Only recently has their power begun to grow. The people see the barrenness of our women as a sign of the gods' disfavor. And there is also our weather, which each year seems to grow more severe, making our crops less bountiful. More and more we turn to our priests for answers."

"Chirops has seized upon the situation to further his ambitions," Valdor said. "He feeds on the peoples' fear."

Arista paced worriedly before her throne. "In my heart, I believe as Valdor does. But I cannot be sure. I cannot risk the welfare of my people by forsaking the gods."

"Not the gods, Arista," Valdor said. "Only Chirops."

The Sumara looked at her three guests and smiled. "Valdor is one of the few who dares to speak to Chirops that way. I envy him his courage, but my heart is still torn by uncertainty."

"Your office places restraints on you that I do not feel," Valdor said consolingly. "One day you will see your duty clearly, Arista. And I will be there to support you, have no fear."

"You can count on us as well," Penderyn assured her.

Arista smiled. "Thank you, all of you. Today my heart is lighter than it's been for some time."

"I feel sorry for Arista," Penderyn said as he and the twins followed Cornon from the palace. "I could tell how heavily her troubles weigh upon her."

"She cares deeply for our people and our land," Cornon replied. "The wealth and power that come with her position mean little to her. If she felt Calistan would prosper under Halibur's rule, she would abdicate immediately. But she knows he's driven only by ambition. It's power he seeks, nothing more."

"Isn't there anything we can do to help her?" Penderyn asked.

"If you could lift the barrenness from our women or increase the yields from our fields, Halibur's support would crumble as quickly as a stale piece of cornbread," Cornon said. "Short of that,

I'm not sure what anyone can do."

Penderyn's heart sank. The city seemed less wondrous and exciting to him now. Even the weather seemed to be plotting against him. The cool, early winter sun failed to warm him, and its slanting rays could not remove the dark shadows that painted the edges of the streets and alleys.

The north wind had risen, too. It funneled through the streets and whipped irritating clouds of dust into their faces as they walked into its frosty teeth. The people on the street hurried about their business, scarcely bothering to look up as they passed. In just one day, Penderyn's new home had begun to grow dark and oppressive.

Cornon saw the sadness darkening his young friend's face. "Cheer up, Penderyn. You've helped Arista already, just by your presence. No longer can Halibur claim his son is a sign of the gods' favor. And Chirops has been forced to retreat from his support of Halibur and to rethink his position." He smiled at the thought of the High Priest's discomfiture. "That's not too bad for one day's work."

"Chirops doesn't strike me as the type to stay on the defensive for long," Tal mused.

"No, he's not," Cornon admitted. "We must be careful. Penderyn is a problem for him. He will be tempted to do something about it."

"I'm not afraid of him," Penderyn said.

"Nor am I," replied Cornon. "But we are in the minority. Chirops has grown very powerful. With each new misfortune that befalls our land, his strength increases."

"If Penderyn is in danger, we'd best learn how to use your weapons to defend ourselves," Tal said. "Arrows and spears would be of little use within the city."

"I know just the fellow to handle that chore," Cornon said, smiling. "A warrior acknowledged as one of the finest swordsmen in all Kfastia."

Penderyn liked the idea of learning how to handle a sword.

"Who is he, and when can we begin?" he asked eagerly.

"You're looking at him," Cornon said, grinning. "And we can begin today."

Penderyn beamed with excitement. He liked Cornon a lot and was glad the young captain would be their teacher.

"I have one more question, if you don't mind," Penderyn said.

"My duties include educating you as well as protecting you," Cornon said. "Arista wants you to feel at home in Kfastia. What do you wish to know?"

"The Flaming Sword," Penderyn said. "Can we see it? Surely it must be one of Calistan's greatest treasures."

Cornon shook his head. "I'm afraid not. No one knows what became of the Sword."

The three newcomers looked at him incredulously.

"How can that be?" Dal asked. "I thought it would be a treasured symbol."

"In his later years, after Calistan was solidly united and Kfastia well on its way to completion, Sumar embarked upon another journey. He told no one of his reason or his destination, not even the Majhari. Before he left he passed the throne to his son. Sumar never returned. His fate and that of the Sword are unknown."

"Maybe once the jewel served its purpose it had to be returned," Penderyn offered.

"Perhaps," Cornon replied. "We'll never know for certain."

He laid his hand on Penderyn's shoulder. "Are you finished with your questions, Last Born?" he asked.

"For now," Penderyn replied, smiling. "For now."

CHAPTER 10

The days flew by.

Penderyn, Tal and Dal were busy from dawn until dusk. They spent hours exploring the city with Cornon and his friend Olidar, learning as much as they could about their new homeland. Their hosts took them through Kfastia's public marketplace, where they marveled over the variety of finely crafted goods available, and to the huge granaries, where food was stored against the impending shortages of winter. They visited the armory and experimented with the many unfamiliar weapons stored in the giant warehouse. Cornon also led them on a tour of the city's defenses, from the top of the outer wall where long unused defensive weapons were now being readied, to the tall watchtowers where vigilant sentries scanned the surrounding plain.

They made frequent visits to the palace, for Arista took great interest in the welfare of her city's newest citizens. A strong fondness developed between Penderyn and the Sumara. He was touched by her warmth and compassion and found her to be genuinely interested in him as a young boy, not just as a symbol of the gods' favor. She in turn enjoyed his youthful exuberance and curiosity. Seldom did Penderyn's presence fail to lift her spirits at least a little.

As Valdor's guests they also met the remainder of the Majhari, who now numbered only six. Four of the original families had died out over the centuries; the remaining six formed a council of the Sumara's closest advisors. Two of them, Aurelus and Jaspar, were frequent visitors to Valdor's home and became quite familiar with the three youths. Jaspar was Olidar's father, so he also received daily reports of their doings from his son.

They devoted several hours each day to lessons in swordplay. Penderyn listened closely to Cornon, but no matter how hard he tried and how much he worked, his size and strength kept him at a distinct disadvantage. Though his comrades continually encouraged him, with each failure he cursed his youthfulness anew.

"Don't be so hard on yourself," Cornon counseled him after Penderyn suffered another quick defeat at Tal's hand. "You're still growing. In a few years, I guarantee you'll be at least as skilled as your friends."

Penderyn knew what Cornon was trying to do, but the captain's words failed to cheer him. He didn't want to wait a few years. He wanted to be treated as an equal now.

Dal sensed his friend's mood. "Don't let Penderyn's size fool you, Cornon. His age isn't the only thing special about him."

Penderyn looked up sharply, fastening his gaze on Dal. They had agreed no mention would be made of his dreams, especially since his visions had been strangely absent since the night of the fire. He hoped Dal was not about to forget himself.

Dal knew better than to talk about Penderyn's strange ability and nodded to his friend not to worry. He recounted the story of Penderyn's heroism in the swamp but made no mention of the dream that had guided him. Cornon and Olidar listened in fascination, but had difficulty picturing the scene. It was hard to imagine an even younger Penderyn than the one now before them slaying the huge beast Dal described.

"It seems there's more to you than we thought, Penderyn," Cornon said when Dal was done. "I do not know what your final destiny might be, but I'm glad your path has brought you to Kfastia."

Penderyn looked away, feeling both proud and helpless. More

than ever, he wanted to do something for these people who had been so kind to him. But he had no idea what the future held. He didn't want to raise false hope, so he revealed nothing of his strange power. Until his dreams returned, the secret would be kept between himself and the twins. If and when the visions came back, he would decide what to reveal then.

There were those in the city who were not quite as glad as Cornon about Penderyn's arrival. The Last Born's presence had quieted the uneasy situation in Kfastia and forced Chirops and his followers to forestall their open support of Halibur. Chirops was patient, however. The wily High Priest did not expect any lasting change simply due to the youth's presence. There would still be no children born, the winter would grow increasingly harsh, and hunger would tighten the peoples' belts. When no miracles were forthcoming, the citizens would lose their enchantment with the Penderyn, and Chirops would again be free to sow his seeds of discontent. For now, though, he would simply watch and wait, favoring neither side overtly.

Halibur had also been forced to quiet his disruptions. Daily he cursed the arrival of the Last Born, but there was nothing he could do for now. Even his secret raids had stopped. The increased vigilance of Kfastia's army made additional attacks risky, so he pulled his hired raiders back and bided his time, hoping the difficulties of winter would soon grow severe enough to further his cause.

Chirops and Halibur did not have long to wait. Winter intensified its grip on the land more quickly and more harshly than ever before. Temperatures plummeted below freezing and stayed there, and frequent blizzards pummeled Calistan for days at a time. Game grew scarce and food supplies dropped. As their hunger increased, the rumblings of the people grew louder. Arista ordered the city's storehouses to be opened, but only minimal rations were distributed. There were still many weeks of winter ahead.

Rumors of huge feasts eaten nightly in the palace and among the nobility spread through the less wealthy sections of Kfastia. The stories fueled the ire of the common people, who had scarcely enough food to survive. In truth, the wealthy fared little better than the average citizen, for most had contributed the bulk of their stores to the communal storehouses.

There was no way to convince the people of that, however, especially since new rumors were constantly started and fanned by Halibur's agents. Mobs gathered despite the cold. Several attempts were made to storm the granaries, forcing the army to intervene to keep the food stores safe. So far, the sight of armed warriors had been enough to quell the disturbances, and no injuries had been caused as yet. But as winter deepened, the mobs grew larger and angrier; everyone knew it was only a matter of time until a tragedy occurred.

One evening, after the largest gathering of protesters yet, Aurelus and Jaspar visited Valdor to discuss the mounting insurrection. The three Majhari sat before the fireplace with Thrisa, Cornon and Olidar. Penderyn, Tal and Dal were allowed to join them. The men warmed themselves with hot rum, while Penderyn sipped happily at a steaming mug of cider.

"We're fortunate Chirops has not yet taken an overt position against Arista," Aurelus said.

"More people visit the temples every day, though," Jaspar said. "And they do not go there just to pray. They seek to discover some cause for their woes."

"Chirops has instructed his priests to tell the people that the gods are angry with Calistan, but that they've not yet sent a sign to reveal the cause of their anger," Aurelus continued.

"Chirops is a snake, but an exceedingly clever one," Valdor said with grudging admiration. "He does nothing to stem the rising discontent, yet has not committed himself to either side. By seeming to stay neutral, he leaves himself free to take advantage of any change in the winds of fortune."

Cornon pounded the wooden arm of his chair in frustration. "Is there nothing we can do?"

"Against Chirops, no," Valdor replied regretfully. "Not until he commits himself. But we're taking steps against those who seek to discredit our Sumara." He allowed himself a trace of a smile. "We're fighting fire with fire, spreading the idea that perhaps the gods are angry because the people of Calistan have grown disloyal to their Sumara."

"And it seems to be working, a little at least," Jaspar said. "Activity against Arista has leveled off while the people await a clearer sign of the gods' will."

"That can't last forever," Penderyn complained, unable to restrain himself any longer. He knew how deeply the unrest troubled Arista and how hard she worked to help her people. He wanted to do more to aid her.

"No, it can't," Valdor admitted. "But each day that passes is one less day of winter ahead. Every day nearer to spring is an advantage for us."

"Trouble simmers more easily among the cold and hungry than among the warm and content," Thrisa added.

"Chirops knows that as well as we do," Cornon pointed out.

"Yes, he does," his father replied. "But he'll have to commit himself to Halibur if he wishes to do anything about it."

"And at least then everyone will know where he stands," Aurelus said. "There are many priests who'll not follow him if he moves against Arista."

"Then there's nothing we can do now?" Penderyn asked resignedly.

Valdor shook his head. "Nothing but wait," he said.

Penderyn hated having to wait. He wanted desperately to do

something to help Arista, to quiet the turmoil which beset her city. He thought of the lines of worry that seemed to sink deeper into the Sumara's face with each passing day. He felt that somehow he possessed the means to help. He could sense it, feel it, but he could not bring it into focus. Whatever it might be continued to elude his grasp.

That night, for the first time in his life, Penderyn prayed for a dream. Lying under the warm covers of his bed, he concentrated as hard as he could, thinking only of his need, trying to will himself to dream.

But no dream came.

He was bitterly disappointed when he awoke. He lay in bed and silently cursed whatever fates controlled his power. First they tormented him with visions of his mother's death, and now they mocked him by taking away his power when he wanted it most.

Finally, he pushed the covers aside and climbed from his bed, shaking his head in resignation as he crossed to the window. He unfastened the wooden shutters and let the cold morning air rush across his face. The sky was filled with dark gray clouds, which seemed to grow blacker by the moment. Penderyn grinned ruefully to himself. Another storm was brewing, and the day matched his somber mood perfectly.

The storm started slowly. Widely scattered snowflakes floated gently from the grey curtain overhead and landed like soft, windblown spores. For a few moments, the snow created an idyllic winter scene, laying a fresh coating of white over the soiled snow of previous storms.

The peaceful beauty did not last, however. The snowflakes grew steadily larger and began to fall more rapidly, driven by a frigid north wind that whistled through the streets and alleys like a howling beast. The snow drifted high in doorways and corners as visibility dropped to almost nothing. The temperature plummeted.

By noon the streets were deserted, with the populace huddling in the protection of their homes. Still the fury of the blizzard increased, until it raged with greater intensity than any storm that had yet struck the beleaguered land.

While the storm raged outside, Penderyn and Cornon dueled vigorously back and forth across the black and white marble floor of the entrance hall. Tal, Dal and Olidar watched the swordplay with interest. Penderyn was definitely improving, but of course was no match for the skill of Cornon. Still, the twins rooted for their young friend to strike at least one successful blow.

Despite the chill in the huge room, Penderyn's brow was moist with sweat as he attempted to pierce his tutor's guard. He used every lunge and feint he'd been taught, but to no avail. No matter how quickly he moved his blade, Cornon's sword seemed always to be waiting for him.

"That's enough for now," Cornon said at last, sensing that Penderyn's strength was finally waning. "This old arm of mine is growing tired."

Penderyn knew that Cornon was not really tired, but was glad for the break anyhow. He rested the point of his sword on the floor and wiped his brow.

"You almost had him that time, Penderyn," Olidar said encouragingly. "When you get a little bigger, Cornon will be sorry he ever picked on you."

Penderyn was about to reply when a loud thumping at the door startled them.

"Who could be foolish enough to venture out in a storm like this?" Dal wondered aloud.

They all moved toward the door. Each had the same thought—that some kind of emergency had befallen the city.

Penderyn reached the doorway first and yanked the thick wooden door open. The chill blast of frigid air and blowing snow that swept over them went almost unnoticed as they gasped in shock at the figure standing outside.

Their visitor looked like a snowman. His hooded cloak was completely covered with a layer of frozen snow. At least three inches of the clinging white powder was piled on his shoulders and atop his head. Tiny icicles hung from his bushy eyebrows and dangled from the long gray hair that poked outside his hood. His weathered face was lined with wrinkles, but the leathery skin seemed untouched by the cold. He carried no gear except a gnarled wooden staff.

"May I come in?" he asked simply when his stunned hosts failed to speak.

CHAPTER 11

"Of course. Come in," Cornon said, recovering from his surprise. He took the old man's elbow and led him inside. "I'm sorry. You must be freezing."

The stranger smiled. "It is a bit chill out there." As he spoke he rapped his staff against his chest, knocking the frozen snow to the floor and revealing a brown cloak that was worn and frayed. Several crude attempts at mending the garment were plainly visible.

The companions watched in silence while their visitor gently plucked the ice from his eyebrows. He seemed unaware of their curious stares.

"Who are you?" Cornon asked finally. "You can't have come far in this storm, but I thought I knew everyone who lives nearby. Yet I do not recognize you."

"That does seem to present a puzzle, doesn't it?" the old man replied. His mouth curved into a warm smile and his gray eyes twinkled with a mischievous gleam. "One of your assumptions must therefore be mistaken."

He spoke in such a pleasant, friendly tone that his hosts were not at all annoyed by his manner. Penderyn found himself liking the old guy immediately.

"Which assumption is wrong then?" he asked.

Their visitor grinned. "Believe it or not, I have been out in the storm since it began."

"That's impossible," Olidar said in disbelief. "You can't see one step ahead of you in this blizzard."

"Yet here I stand," the stranger said simply.

Penderyn moved to the old man's side.

"You saw the snow on his cloak," he said. "It was several inches thick. And look at these icicles," he continued, indicating the slender needles that still hung from their visitor's hair. "He must have been out there for some time, to collect so much snow and ice."

The stranger nodded with pleasure. "You've a pair of discerning eyes, young man, and apparently a wit to match."

Tal stepped in front of the old man and looked at him more closely.

"You say you've been traveling through this storm for hours," he said, "in a cloak I must say has seen better days. Yet you show no traces of frostbite. How can that be?"

"A simple trick I picked up years ago," the man replied. "Occasionally, it comes in quite handy."

"You have magic?" Penderyn asked excitedly.

"Only a small bit. Useful only against minor annoyances, such as the cold."

"This cold would be a bit more than a 'minor annoyance' to us, I assure you," Cornon said, grinning. He extended his hand. "I'm Cornon. You're welcome to stay with us until the storm subsides."

"Thank you, Cornon. That's quite hospitable of you. My name is Jarrowon."

The others introduced themselves one by one. Jarrowon clasped hands with each of them. He held Penderyn's hand a bit longer than the others, gazing deeply into his eyes as he did so.

"I'm especially glad to find you, Penderyn," Jarrowon said as he released Penderyn's hand.

"Where have you come from?" Cornon asked when the introductions were finished. "And what brings you here in such awful weather?"

"I come from no one place," Jarrowon replied. "I am a lore master. It is my doom and my pleasure to wander the land, studying and learning what I can. As to my purpose here, that's easily answered." He turned to Penderyn. "I came to see the Last Born."

Penderyn's eyes widened in surprise. He wondered what the old man meant by that.

"I've come to aid you in whatever small way I may, Penderyn," Jarrowon continued. "I hope you will accept my help."

Penderyn shifted his feet uncomfortably as he gazed up into Jarrowon's dark eyes. He had no idea what the lore master meant, but he sensed that the old man knew something of the destiny that had troubled him so much of late.

"What kind of help do I need?" he asked finally, trying to hide the anxiety in his voice. He was not certain he succeeded.

"Alas, how I may help, I don't yet know," Jarrowon admitted. "But there are trials ahead in which you will be sorely tested. My hope is that I can be of some guidance."

"How do you know what lies ahead for Penderyn?" Tal asked suspiciously.

"Through the lore which I have spent my life studying. The same lore which told me I would find him here."

"Finding Penderyn was no difficult trick," Olidar said. "All Calistan knows he's here. It wouldn't take long to learn, even for a stranger."

Jarrowon appeared unfazed by Olidar's skepticism. "Though it may not seem a difficult task to you, it is one at which I have labored for many years. Countless leagues have I traveled seeking the Last Born, following signs that were not always clear. Only recently was I led to your land."

"What kind of signs?" Penderyn asked.

"Portents of varying kinds," Jarrowon replied. "But they are no longer important, for that part of my task is done. It is the future which must concern us now."

"What do you know of my future?"

The lore master looked down into Penderyn's upturned face, seeing both the eagerness and the hesitancy in his eyes. The boy was so young. Was he ready to shoulder the burdens the fates had decreed for him?

Jarrowon sighed. It was not his choice to make. Penderyn's destiny was fixed, his fate foretold. All the lore master could do was to guide him.

"Your fate has been foretold in an ancient prophecy called *The Rhynn of the Last Born*," Jarrowon replied at last. "Listen, and hear your fate, Penderyn, for I have no doubt that you are the Last Born of whom the prophecy speaks."

He began to recite in a low, rhythmic tone:
Look to the sky for the moons' golden glow;
Their twin lights shall signal the deepening woe.
False day shall fade and night shall grow longer
As Dark assails Light to see who is the stronger.
On the wings of the Darkness fearsome allies shall ride,
Huge-handed Cold, with grave Hunger astride.
Close on their heels the dread demon Greed
Shall enter men's hearts to sow its foul seeds
And bring forth its children, hatred and war,
To rot at the lands like a festering sore.
But foulest of all, most grim of all ills,
Men and women grow old, but wombs cease to fill.

As Jarrowon chanted the Rhynn, Penderyn felt his heart begin to beat faster. He didn't yet see what the thing had to do with him, but the words were certainly scary. What made the whole thing even more frightening was that much of it was already happening. The moons had grown dimmer, and even before his birth wombs had ceased to fill. He wasn't sure he wanted to hear any more, but the lore master droned on:

> *Spirits will weaken as woe blankets the land,*
> *Yet all is not lost, for hope stands at hand.*
> *The Last Born shall rise, despite the foul curse,*
> *And hold the world's fate, for better or worse.*
> *Great is the power his birth will provide;*
> *But a double-edged sword he'll carry inside.*
> *Salvation or doom, blessing or bane;*
> *Heal the world's wounds, or increase its pain.*
> *With each passing triumph his power will grow,*
> *And so too the danger of joy turning to woe.*
> *Such is his fate, his path is not free,*
> *So it is written, so it must be.*

An eerie feeling possessed Penderyn as he listened. Was the prophecy really talking about him? He didn't see how. Sure, he had some kind of power in his dreams, but he didn't think that was nearly enough to fit all the other stuff. *Hold the world's fate... great is his power... salvation or doom... heal the world's wounds....* All of that seemed to him point to someone with much greater powers than he possessed. But if the Rhynn was not about him, then what was Jarrowon doing here? The lore master seemed pretty certain. And if he was indeed correct, then it seemed far more lay ahead of Penderyn than merely his present role in Calistan.

For a brief moment, he wished Jarrowon had never found him, but he quickly dismissed the thought. The lore master's presence had nothing to do with the destiny that may have been ordained for him. He was glad he would at least have Jarrowon's advice when it came time to face whatever might lie ahead.

When Jarrowon finished, no one spoke for several moments as they all struggled to comprehend the meaning behind the words of the Rhynn. Finally, Penderyn broke the silence.

"Salvation or doom, blessing or bane," he repeated solemnly.

"How can I know which it might be? I may destroy what I wish to save."

"Your burden is a heavy one, Last Born," Jarrowon said. "It is not one I would choose to give you. Yet you must follow your path as best you can. You are Perator's hope. If you seek to avoid your destiny, you risk fulfilling the dark side of your fate."

"How do we know the Rhynn speaks truly in either case?" Dal asked. "Where did it come from? What's the source of its prophecy?"

"The Rhynn was buried in lore thousands of years old," Jarrowon explained. "Its source has long since been forgotten. Yet it is among the most powerful lore there is. Do we dare to doubt it, especially as the signs it foretells become increasingly true with each passing season? Already the mocrah has dimmed."

He strode to the door and threw it open. Cold air and snow blasted into the room.

"And here is further proof!" he cried, shouting to make himself heard above the howling wind. He pushed the door closed, but already the room had grown cold. "Has Calistan ever known a winter like this?" he asked as the others hugged their arms across their chests to ward off the chill.

"And most important of all, the Rhynn has foretold the barrenness which afflicts not only your land, but every land through which I have journeyed. Nowhere have I seen anyone younger than Tal and Dal, none save Penderyn alone. I have no doubt that he is indeed the Last Born."

Jarrowon's impassioned words convinced them. Everyone looked toward Penderyn.

"None of this changes anything between us," Tal assured him. "No matter where your road leads, Dal and I will be by your side you."

Penderyn's heart was warmed by Tal's words. "I never doubted that for an instant," he said. "But what is my path?" He turned to Jarrowon. "Do you know, lore master? Is that why you're here, to lead me to my fate?"

Jarrowon shook his head. "I do not yet know your road," he said. "I hope to learn something from you that might help me guide you."

Penderyn thought of his dreams. "Perhaps there is something," he said softly. "But do you know what power lies behind the misfortunes which assail us?"

"My lore does not say," Jarrowon admitted. "But I fear it originates in the land of Malagorn."

His listeners looked at one another with questioning faces. None of them had ever heard of such a place.

"Where's that?" Cornon asked. "I've not heard of it before this.

"Malagorn lies far to the west," Jarrowon said, "on the far side of the world. It is a land of darkness, never brightened by the sun."

"No sun?" Dal said, trying to comprehend the idea. "How can that be?"

The lore master found himself surrounded by puzzled looks. "There is much we must discuss, my friends. Much that I must tell you, and much I must learn from Penderyn. But I am weary. My journey has been long and difficult, and I must rest. We can speak of these things tomorrow. I am not a young man," he added with a smile.

"Of course," Cornon replied. "I've forgotten my manners. I should have given you the hospitality of this house before we wearied you with talk. Come with me."

"You've already given me plenty to think about," Penderyn added. "Tomorrow will come soon enough, I think."

That night, Penderyn dreamed for the first time in many weeks.

These dreams were not clear, sharp visions like the one that foretold his mother's death. That one had seemed so clear and so real. Instead, these dreams were a jumble of blurred images straining to come into focus, but before they could grow clear they were swept away by other images competing for his attention. He saw strange beasts and men, towering mountains and dark forests. None were clear enough to recognize; no single feature tied them together. Whether any of them were related to each other was impossible to tell.

When he woke, he felt strangely rested and relaxed. Somehow, the turmoil of his dreams had not interfered with his body's rest. Before rising from the comfort of his bed, he tried to recall the images, to bring some part of them into focus so he might understand their meaning, but his recollections were blurred and indistinct, just like the dreams. He recognized nothing, so he gave up trying.

Despite the disappointment, the return of his dreams boosted his spirits. At least he knew now that his power had not deserted him completely. He looked forward to the new day and to his talks with Jarrowon—perhaps the lore master would shed some light upon his power. He threw on a robe and hurried from his room.

He found Jarrowon seated at the table in the dining hall, dressed in the same worn brown cloak as the day before. The hood was thrown back, allowing his long gray hair to fall loosely over his shoulders. He seemed quite comfortable in the thick cloak, despite the fire that crackled in the stone hearth at the end of the room.

Jarrowon did not look up when Penderyn entered. The lore master was bent over a cloth scroll, his head shifting slowly back and forth as his eyes followed the long, thin fingers of his right hand across the parchment. Whatever he was reading was clearly very old—Penderyn could see that the edges of the cloth had turned brown and the fabric was stiff and wrinkled. A small pile of similar scrolls lay nearby. Penderyn wondered what they all contained.

He watched silently as Jarrowon finished reading. For a moment the lore master sat motionless, his hands clasped under his chin. Penderyn was startled when Jarrowon addressed him without looking up. He hadn't known the lore master was aware of his presence.

"Good morning, Penderyn," Jarrowon said as he carefully rolled up the final parchment. "I'm sorry I kept you waiting, but I wanted to finish reading before I broke my concentration."

"What were you reading?"

"A most informative and interesting history of Calistan. Since this is my first visit to this land, Valdor was kind enough to provide me with these writings from his family archives." He gently tied a worn gray ribbon around the old scroll and placed it with the others. "I never pass up a chance to expand my knowledge."

"You must know a great deal, then," Penderyn said.

"More than most," Jarrowon admitted. "But less than some, I'm sure."

"I wish I knew more things," Penderyn said wistfully. "All I know is of a village that no longer exists, plus a bit about Calistan."

Jarrowon smiled. "You are still shy of your twelfth birthday," he reminded Penderyn. "I knew very little myself at your age." His tone grew more serious. "I have little doubt you'll be learning quite a bit in the days ahead. So much that you may soon long for your days of ignorance."

Penderyn thought back to the prophecies of the Rhynn of the Last Born. Jarrowon was probably right, he thought grimly.

CHAPTER 12

Dal feigned anger when he and Tal arrived to find Penderyn and Jarrowon already seated at the table. "I hope you two didn't start without us," he said. "You'll not get rid of us so easily."

"Sleepyheads miss out," Penderyn teased, though in truth it was not long past dawn. "Don't worry, we've been waiting for you. We've decided you two might prove useful—if we can break you of your slothful habits."

The twins exchanged glances, but neither had a ready reply.

"We stand rebuked," Dal said humbly.

"The others will be joining us shortly," Jarrowon said. "Penderyn has decided your hosts should know everything."

Almost on cue, Valdor and Thrisa arrived, holding hands as they walked into the room. A few minutes later, Cornon and Olidar joined them. When everyone was seated, Jarrowon began.

"I said last night that I suspected our unseen enemy might dwell in Malagorn, the land of darkness. That none of you has ever heard of it does not surprise me. Malagorn lies many, many leagues away, on the far side of Perator. Little is known of this foreboding land, but I will pass on what knowledge I possess, for I am one of the few who has walked under its foul cloak of darkness and returned to tell of it."

Penderyn leaned forward. He could feel his heartbeat beginning to race. A glance around the table showed him everyone else seemed equally enthralled, though perhaps not quite as anxious.

The lore master cradled the tips of his bony fingers under his wrinkled chin. His eyelids drooped half-closed, bringing his gray brows so low it was difficult to tell whether his eyes remained open. For a moment he was silent, recalling the events of his frightening journey.

"It was many years ago that I ventured into Malagorn," he began finally, "long before the *mocrah* began to dim. In my long years of roaming Perator, I had heard tales of a forbidden land where darkness was broken only by the *mocrah*, a land inhabited by strange and terrible creatures. I journeyed west, determined to discover the truth of these tales. The farther west I ventured, the more stories I began to hear. I also noticed that the days grew shorter, though summer was approaching. Eventually I came to the land of Argoneth, whose legends were filled with tales of Malagorn.

"In Argoneth I met a wizened old scholar named Colo." Jarrowon smiled at the recollection. "If he were sitting here today, Colo would make even me look young. Colo's passion was Malagorn, though it would be some time before I learned why. We spent many delightful weeks trading tales of Malagorn, though most of the stories I had collected he brushed aside as untrue. There were few firsthand tales of Malagorn, he told me, for those brave or foolish enough to venture into its darkness seldom returned. Most who did survive came back half-crazed with fear and horror and could not be fully believed. When I asked how he knew so much, he merely grinned and continued on with his tales.

"One day, Colo took me to the top of the tallest tower in the city. He pointed to a range of snow-capped mountains that stretched across the western horizon. 'They are called the Mountains of Shadow,' he said. 'Beyond those peaks, the light of day never reaches.' He directed my gaze to a rounded summit that seemed strangely out of place among the sharp, jagged peaks of its neighbors. 'And that is the Klama's Hump,' he explained. 'At its southern flank lies the only passage through the mountains. Several days of climbing the Hump brings you to the Caverns of Blackness.' He went on to recount the journey in such detail I realized he had to be speaking from memory. I knew then that Colo had been to Malagorn."

Jarrowon paused so his listeners could digest what he had been telling them.

Penderyn realized he was sitting on the edge of his chair. He slid back a bit and tried to appear more relaxed than he felt.

"What happened next?" he asked.

"Colo saw on my face that I had guessed his secret. 'Yes, I have survived a journey to Malagorn,' he said in answer to my unspoken awareness. 'Though it was more than half a century ago, I remember it as if it were yesterday, for in that cursed land I lost much of what was dear to me.' He shook his head in sad remembrance. 'Two sons I left behind, two strong young sons who had only recently crossed the threshold of manhood. Two score others lost their lives as well. Only I escaped. Why I should be so fortunate, I have no idea.'

"That was all Colo told me that afternoon atop the tower, though I urged him to continue. The memory had wearied him, he said, but he promised to continue his story the following day. Alas, tomorrow never came for Colo, for that night death claimed him in his sleep."

Jarrowon fell silent for a moment. His spellbound listeners leaned back from the table, stretching their tense neck and shoulder muscles.

"You can probably guess what happened next," Jarrowon said with a smile as his audience relaxed. "But telling tales is thirsty work. Let's break for some refreshment before I recount the story of my own journey into Malagorn."

No one demurred, so Thrisa departed to fetch drink for her guests. The others got up to walk and stretch their legs while they waited.

When they had all slaked their thirst, Jarrowon settled back and continued his story.

"I was saddened by Colo's death, for I had become quite fond of the talkative old fellow, but I did not grieve overmuch. His life had been long and full, and his end had been peaceful. His final tale had fanned my curiosity, and I resolved to undertake a journey of my own as soon as possible. I was unwilling to risk the lives of any others, for I had seen the sadness in Colo's heart when he spoke of his lost sons and companions. I decided I would go into Malagorn alone."

Jarrowon recounted the story of his journey through the Caverns of Blackness in great detail. Should any of his comrades have need to journey to Malagorn without his guidance, he wanted them to be able to find their way.

"How much time I spent beneath the mountains was impossible to know, for there was no way to mark the passing of the hours, or even the days. I would guess I journeyed six to eight days within the depths of those seemingly endless caverns."

"How did you light your way?" Cornon asked. "Alone, you could not have carried enough torches to last anywhere near that long."

Jarrowon reached for the old wooden staff that leaned against his chair.

"With this," he said. He raised the staff and uttered several strange sounding words in a tongue Penderyn had never heard. The tip of the staff began to glow. Slowly the brightness increased, until it burned with an even yellow light unlike any he'd ever seen.

"What wonderful magic!" Penderyn marveled. "Look, the wood's not even burning!"

"Only another minor trick, I'm afraid," said Jarrowon. "Though one that was to prove quite useful. But I didn't mean to distract us from the matter at hand." He extinguished the spell and returned the staff to its place alongside him.

"When I finally emerged from the blackness of the caverns, I found it to be only slightly less dark outside. I had no way of knowing what time it was. Sometime in the early evening, I surmised, for though the sky was filled with stars, I saw no sign of Primus or Ferus. Not until Primus finally appeared many hours later did I realize how wrong I'd been. As hard as it was for me to believe, I'd actually left the caverns in the middle of the afternoon! Where there is no sun, the sky is always filled with stars.

"What manner of covering can block the sun yet let the stars show through?" Thrisa asked.

"The sun is not blocked by anything, save our own world," Jarrowon explained. "Some property of Perator's orbit keeps Malagorn facing perpetually away from the sun. The days are short even in Argoneth, and the Mountains of Shadow block whatever meager daylight Malagorn might otherwise receive."

"And yet the paths of our moons must be such that they do cross Malagorn," mused Valdor.

"Exactly. The *mocrah* is the only 'day' that Malagorn knows."

"A land without sunlight," Tal said, shaking his head. "I can scarcely imagine such a place."

"I, for one, don't want to imagine such a place," Dal said.

"Malagorn is a far more forbidding place than I ever dreamed," Jarrowon said gravely. "The foothills beyond the cavern were nothing more than jumbled heaps of barren rock. Deep ravines and sheer cliffs crisscrossed the area. Piles of gray stone and black slag covered much of what little level ground there was. Finding a path through such a place was no easy task.

"There were no trees in anywhere in those foothills, and of the few species of plants that have adapted to Malagorn's total lack of sunlight, none would look familiar to you. Indeed, most are carnivorous and are as dangerous as the beasts that prowl the darkness."

"Plants that eat you?" Penderyn said with disgust. "How horrible."

"I saw one such plant ensnare a beast almost as large as a gryth," Jarrowon said. "The creature's shrieks filled the darkness for hours while it was slowly digested alive." He shook his head at the memory. "Should you ever venture into Malagorn, give a wide berth to any plants you find," he warned.

"But let me continue with my story. I moved through the maze-like hills very carefully, marking my way with magic from my staff. I dared risk no light, for I knew not who or what it might attract. I was forced to rely on the faint glimmer from the stars.

"Never have I felt as naked and alone as in that desolate land. The darkness was no cloak, for whatever creatures dwelt in such a place would surely have no need of light to find me. There were few places to hide, and I doubted my magic could protect me for long.

"Still, fortune was with me that first day. I use the term day loosely; only the *mocrah* allowed me to mark the passage of time. I crossed the foothills without incident and came to a wide, dirt plain whose barren surface was broken only by scattered outcrops of rock. I had thought the foothills bleak, but this desolate wasteland was even more foreboding.

"Uncertain whether to risk crossing such an open space, I remained hidden within the edge of the hills, waiting for the *mocrah* to give me a better view of what might lie ahead. As I sat huddled against a small cliff, shielded in part by an overhanging ledge, I heard padded footfalls scuffling softly upon the rock near my hiding place. I froze, afraid the slightest movement would reveal my presence, but I was too late. I had already been discovered.

"In seconds, I was surrounded by a score of gigantic creatures. Even cloaked by the shadowy darkness, they were the most frightening beings I had ever seen. They were man-like in form, but just barely. The smallest stood at least seven feet tall; several towered a foot above that. Four muscular arms extended from their thick, furry torsos. Their broad, rounded heads were completely hairless, covered instead with wrinkled skin that appeared tough as leather. Two long incisors curved down from their thick lips. The creatures had no noses, only wide, flaring nostrils in the center of their faces. Huge, lidless eyes stared hungrily at me from each horrid face.

"I recognized the beasts immediately from Colo's tales. They were gorlaks, flesh-eating creatures who had massacred his entire party. The gorlaks are cruel, evil beings spawned by the darkness. They prefer to torment and torture their prey, believing that fear lends taste to the flesh. Fortunately, this habit of theirs proved to be my salvation."

"How did you get away," Penderyn asked, back on the edge of his seat again.

"Instead of rushing me quickly and tearing me to pieces as they might easily have done, they moved closer slowly, leering down at me with horrible grins and growling threateningly. For a moment, their torments were successful and I found myself paralyzed with fear. I knew I had not the power to stop these gigantic creatures."

Penderyn was unable to restrain his excitement. "What did you do? Tell us how you escaped."

Jarrowon smiled. "After cowering in fear for a few moments, I was struck by a sudden inspiration." Even now there was a thankful tone in the lore master's voice. "Rather than waste my meager magic trying to stop the gorlaks, I closed my eyes and channeled all my power into the same illumination spell I just showed you, only magnified tenfold. Bright yellow light burst from my staff like a miniature sun, blinding the sensitive eyes of the gorlaks. While they stumbled around in confusion, howling with pain and rage, I darted between them and raced into the hills, following my markers toward the Caverns of Blackness. How long the gorlaks were disabled by my spell I have no way of knowing, but I did not feel safe until at last I emerged from the mountains into Argoneth. Never was I so happy to see the sun, I tell you."

He leaned back in his chair. "That, my friends, is the story of my brief sojourn into Malagorn, a land I am not overeager to visit again."

"I hope your guess is wrong, Jarrowon," Penderyn said quietly. "And that our unknown foe does not reside in Malagorn."

"Time alone will tell," the lore master replied. "I sensed no magic while I was there, but my stay was brief. Who can say what other horrors Malagorn's eternal darkness hides."

"Which brings us to an important point," Valdor said. "How *will* you know where to seek our enemy?"

"I'm hoping the Last Born will provide a clue," Jarrowon said. He turned to Penderyn. "You said yesterday that you had something to tell us."

Penderyn sat silently for a moment, gathering his thoughts. When he began, he spoke first to his hosts. "Please believe I have not held back what I'm about to say for any lack of trust or affection," he said, "but only because of my own uncertainty." He paused, looking to each of his new friends. "Since I was a young child, a strange power has haunted my dreams. Whether this power is a blessing or a curse, I wonder still."

All listened in fascination as he told the story of his dreams. He began with the first nightmare when he was five, about his mother's death, how real and lifelike it was, and how Aeta had explained to her frightened child about the power inside them both, a power beyond either of their control. Then he recounted his vision in the swamp, the forgotten dream that had reared into his consciousness in time to save Tal and Dal from the terriwarg. Finally, he told them of that awful night when his dream about his mother's fiery death had come horribly true.

"That nightmare was the last time I dreamt," he said, his voice filled with sadness. "I didn't know whether my power was gone or simply dormant, so I decided not to speak of it. But last night, I dreamed again. The images were blurred and unrecognizable, but they were there nonetheless."

"Perhaps your dreams will hold the key we seek," Jarrowon mused. He leaned forward and cradled his fingers under his chin. He closed his eyes, lost in thought. The others waited silently, not wanting to disturb the lore master's concentration.

"We must somehow help you learn to control your gift," he said at last. "Tell me about your mother."

Penderyn felt renewed pain as he described Aeta, but he told Jarrowon everything he could remember.

"There are tales that speak of a golden race who can see the future," Jarrowon said when Penderyn had finished. "They are called the Eirydi. They are said to dwell in the north, though no one knows exactly where. Perhaps the golden description originated with the color of their hair. Your mother may have been of that race, though how she came to Ishtor I cannot begin to guess. I think our goal is clear, though, even if the path is not. We must seek the Eirydi, to see if you may learn to control your dreams. Perhaps then your visions will tell us what we wish to know."

"But how will we find them?" Penderyn asked. "You said no one knows where they live."

"By long search if necessary," Jarrowon replied. "There's one thing we know. If your mother was indeed of the Eirydi, then they must dwell somewhere in this sector of Perator. It's doubtful that whatever separated Aeta from her people took her more than a few hundred leagues from her birthplace."

"That's still quite an area to search," Valdor said. "I suppose there is no other choice, though."

"Not unless Penderyn's dreams provide us with some clue," Jarrowon said.

"I wish I could tell you they will," Penderyn said without enthusiasm. "But last night's visions were certainly no help."

"There's no hurry, Last Born," Jarrowon said soothingly. "We cannot begin our search until after winter is ended. Perhaps by then your dreams will have grown more clear."

CHAPTER 13

Winter dragged inexorably on, colder and snowier than anyone could remember. The few scattered days of sunshine and relative warmth were overmatched by the seemingly endless string of storms that swept out of the north, burying Kfastia in snow. Narrow pathways walled by banks of snow taller than a man were all that remained of the city's once broad avenues. The roadways were barely wide enough for a single cart—whenever two wagons moving in opposite directions encountered one another, one had to back up until it reached a cross street and could get out of the other's way. With tempers frayed by cold and reduced rations, quarrels and fights among the drivers were common. At the end of each storm, hardy warriors began anew their never-ending task of moving and stamping the frozen snow to keep even these meager passages open.

Finally, after almost four months of continuous onslaught, the storms began to decrease in frequency and intensity. The calendar had turned to spring in name only—it was still another month before the warming temperatures melted enough snow to make riding practical. As soon as they could do so safely, Cornon and Olidar began teaching their three young friends to ride, in preparation for the journey that would commence as soon as Jarrowon deemed the weather suitable.

Penderyn was given a small, gray mount, which he promptly named Surefoot, for though it was smaller than most of its fellows, the horse was uncommonly nimble. With each passing day of practice, the boyish warrior and his horse became more of a unit, until Surefoot was often able to guess Penderyn's next move before he signaled it.

Jarrowon questioned Penderyn often about his dreams, but the infrequent visions remained as puzzling as ever. Even so, the lore master made him repeat everything he could remember, in hopes something would connect with his vast store of lore and provide some clue. So far, it was to no avail—whatever the meaning of Penderyn's dreams, they remained beyond comprehension.

At last, Jarrowon decided it was time to begin their journey. Though the nights remained bitter cold, the lore master was confident the last of the winter storms was past. In addition to Penderyn and Jarrowon, the company would consist of Tal and Dal, of course, along with Cornon and Olidar. The two Kfastians were somewhat torn about leaving their city in its time of trouble, but Valdor convinced them the departure of two warriors among thousands was unlikely to make a difference, while their presence with Penderyn could prove vital.

The evening before their departure, the company dined in the palace as Arista's guests. Though she remained cheerful, Penderyn was saddened by the effects the long winter had wreaked upon the Sumara. Her face was more deeply lined than ever, and her shoulders seemed to slump under an invisible weight. Penderyn was tempted to postpone their journey, knowing his presence was at least some small support against the growing threat of Halibur.

Almost as if she had read his mind, Arista turned to him and smiled. "Do not worry about our small problems while you're away," she said. "You will have enough to concern you with your own quest. Remember, the success of your mission may prove far more important than anything that might happen here in Calistan."

Arista laid her soft hand lightly upon Penderyn's forearm. "I shall miss you, so hurry back." She leaned over and kissed him gently on his cheek. "But not before you've completed your task," she added sternly.

"I'll do my best," Penderyn promised solemnly.

He was engulfed by darkness. Within the darkness, he saw shapes darker still. They were huge black shapes, looming against the darkness. Slowly, the darkness lightened. The shapes grew even blacker and a faint glow rose behind them. Dawn, he thought... and mountains. The dark shapes were mountains, immense and solid. One mountain began to grow lighter somehow. He saw an arch, letting dawn's golden light filter through. Suddenly, the rock burst into flame. Fire filled the archway. No, not fire. It was the sun, shining through the arch. For a moment, the rock seemed to burn, but then the fire was gone.

Penderyn awoke abruptly, his heart pounding. His room was dark, but he gave no thought to the hour. Jarrowon must hear of this dream while it still remained fresh in his mind. He donned his cloak against the chill and hurried to the lore master's chamber.

Penderyn was surprised to see a faint light flickering beneath the door. He knocked softly. A moment later Jarrowon opened the door, dressed as always in his worn brown cloak. The light inside shone from two candles, one on either side of a wide desk. Spread open atop the desk was an ancient parchment Jarrowon had been studying.

"I thought you'd be sleeping," Penderyn said in surprise.

"I wanted to finish reading these before we departed," the lore master said. "Come in. Your visit at this hour suggests to me that you've had a dream."

Penderyn nodded. "The vision was clear this time," he said excitedly, "though it has no meaning to me. I wanted to tell you while I still remembered it clearly."

Jarrowon motioned to the chair by the desk. "Sit down and tell me what you saw." The lore master returned to his seat behind the desk.

Penderyn drew his chair close and recounted the brief dream, describing the details as accurately as he could remember. Jarrowon's dark eyes glinted with recognition as he listened.

"You have indeed provided us with our first clue," he said when Penderyn had finished. "Listen."

If what is to be you think you would know,
To She Who Knows All is where you must go.
If to see what's to come your heart truly yearns,
Look to the place where the round mountain burns.

"The round mountain burns," Penderyn repeated excitedly. "Do you know of such a place?"

"Not exactly. The rhyme is from a very old writing. I never connected She Who Knows All to the Eirydi, but it seems possible. Though they remain hidden, perhaps they still share their power through an oracle. According to the writing, She Who Knows All is a sculpted stone head."

"How can we find it?"

"I know the land where this rhyme originated," Jarrowon said. "Once there, we have only to look for your arch filled with fire."

Penderyn smiled. Finally, one of his dreams seemed to have come through when he needed it. How much more, he wondered, would he be able to accomplish once he learned the secrets to controlling his power?

The early morning air chilled their cheeks and hands as the six comrades rode unhurriedly from Kfastia. White puffs of breath floated from their mouths and were quickly swallowed by the damp air. Off to their right, tattered rows of thin orange clouds slowly paled to pink and then white as the eastern sky turned a deepening blue. Overhead, the sky was clear. Before long the spring sun would drain the chill from the air; for now, they kept warm inside woolen cloaks.

Cornon and Olidar rode in the lead, followed by Penderyn and Jarrowon. Tal and Dal brought up the rear. Only Valdor and Thrisa had seen them off, for the company wished their departure to attract as little attention as possible. All except Jarrowon wore the uniform of the royal army, though for now the scarlet tunics were hidden beneath their cloaks. Arista had appointed Penderyn, Tal and Dal honorary members of her personal guard and had ordered uniforms made for them. In addition to their swords, each carried a sharp dagger that fit snugly inside their sturdy leather boots. They retained their bows and arrows, while Cornon and Olidar had long spears fastened to their saddles. Only Jarrowon was unarmed, save for his wooden staff, which he had attached to his saddle in place of a spear.

The grass covered plain was soft and wet from the recently melted snow, but the horses traversed the soggy ground without much problem. Galloping might have been a challenge, but their journey was a long one and so they rode their mounts at a walk. Before long, they entered the woods, not far from the spot where Penderyn and the twins had emerged almost six months earlier.

Once inside the forest, they followed a seldom used trail to the northwest. In places, pockets of snow shielded from the sun's probing rays still brightened the forest floor. As the morning progressed it grew warmer, until all save Jarrowon had removed their cloaks. Penderyn smiled as he glanced at the lore master.

"Don't you ever take that thing off?" he asked.

"I've worn it so long I'm afraid my old bones would fall apart if I removed it," Jarrowon said, laughing.

Penderyn grinned. Their journey might become perilous later on, but for now he was riding with good friends through a peaceful, leafless forest on the warmest morning in months. After being cooped up in the city for the winter, this was wonderful. He was determined to enjoy it while he could.

For three days they rode northwest, seeking a trail that would take them more directly north. They didn't mind the slight detour, for the farther west they went, the less chance they had of encountering any of Halibur's raiders. On the afternoon of their third day, they found what they were looking for, a narrow game trail that bent off into the hills to the north.

The path forced them to ride single file, making conversation difficult. Penderyn felt a strange combination of joy and sadness as they passed silently through the wooded hills, so similar to those of Ishtor. The familiar sounds and feel of the forest were comforting after so many months within Kfastia's walls, but they also tugged at his heart with bittersweet memories of the happy, peaceful life that had been so suddenly taken from him. He thought wistfully of those bygone days and then of the long, unknown road ahead, wondering if he ever again feel so content and at home.

They stopped for the night in a small clearing beneath the gracefully spreading branches of a giant modoc. Hundreds of dark red buds tipped the sinewy gray boughs; soon the tiny buds would burst open into the wide red leaves that made the modoc so different from its green cousins. Penderyn loved these singular trees, scattered as they were through the forests. He had always felt like a kindred spirit to these isolated giants—like him, they were similar yet very different from those around them.

Jarrowon watched his young comrade gaze affectionately upward into the giant tree.

"Did you know the modoc is the most ancient of all trees?"

Penderyn shook his head.

"Each one is thousands of years old. It's said that once whole forests of them stretched league after league across hill and vale. But their time is passing. Now they are the scattered monarchs of the forest, waiting untroubled for whatever is to come."

"There was one not too far from Ishtor," Penderyn said. "I used to climb it whenever I could. Somehow, climbing it never tired or frightened me, no matter how high I climbed. I always felt at home in its branches. Perhaps it's the kinship between us, that they are the last of their kind, like I may be of mine."

"Let us hope not," the lore master said, "for we humans are a short-lived folk. The modocs will remain for many centuries. If you are truly the last of our race, then our end is near at hand."

Despite the urgency that drove the company, their journey continued to be a pleasant one. Spring blossomed around them as they rode, sowing its warmth not only into the reawakening land, but into their hearts as well. New leaves sprouted from the barren branches of trees and shrubs, turning the woods green again, while colorful wildflowers began painting the sides of the trail in blues and yellows and reds. Melodic whistles filled the air as returning birds called for mates, while the undergrowth was alive with the rustling of tiny creatures. Streams and springs bubbled all about, overflowing with cold, delicious water from the freshly melted snow.

Eventually, the forest gave way to more open terrain, allowing the company to increase their pace. They saw no signs of habitation in this land of gentle hills and scattered trees: no fields, no roads, not even any tracks. Riding through league after empty league, Penderyn began to appreciate the vastness of the world.

When Cornon spotted a solitary rider watching them from atop a nearby hill, they became instantly alert, reining their mounts to a halt and watching the stranger carefully. He sat motionless astride his mount, a dark figure outlined against the bright afternoon sky.

In a few moments he was joined by a second rider, and then another and another until at least a dozen lined the hilltop. With the sun behind the riders, it was difficult to see them clearly, but there was no mistaking the flashing of blades in the sunlight when they unsheathed their swords. A shouted command broke the stillness, and the riders charged down the ridge, filling the air with whoops and hollers meant to frighten their outnumbered victims.

The company was not intimidated. Flight did not seem to be an option, so they quickly prepared to fight.

Tal and Dal whipped their bows from their backs. Penderyn nervously followed suit, trying to pretend this was just another hunt. Drawing a deep breath, he tried to keep his fingers from shaking while he took careful aim. He knew there would be time for just one shot. He was determined to make his count.

When the attackers rode within range, three arrows streaked in unison toward the villains. The boys' aim was true—all three arrows buried themselves in the breast of an enemy. Even before the arrows struck home, the three youths dropped their bows and drew their swords.

Cornon and Olidar also wasted no time. With the speed and smoothness gained through long hours of drill, they unfastened the long spears from their saddles with their right hands while unsheathing their swords with their left. When the attackers were nearly upon them, they hurled the spears. Two more riders fell from their mounts, pierced by the Kfastian's spears. The odds had now become far more even.

The remainder of the unkempt lot fell upon the company. Penderyn found himself confronted by a burly, bearded ruffian who sneered down at him with disdain. The brute attacked wildly, attempting to overcome Penderyn by size and strength alone.

In the heat of his first real fight, Penderyn promptly forgot all his lessons in swordplay. This was no practice match; this was real, with his life hanging in the balance. Fear gripped him, numbing his brain. He defended himself instinctively, aware only of the flashing blade slashing down at him. By reflex alone he managed to parry the first few strokes, but each blow came closer to ending the unequal contest. Penderyn's arm soon ached from his awkward blocks. As weary muscles dragged Penderyn's weapon down, the villain's sword swung toward the opening. Penderyn tried to will his leaden arm to move, but he knew he was too late. He could only watch as the sword slashed toward him, seeming to descend toward his unprotected head in slow motion.

Suddenly, his attacker's sneer twisted into a grimace of pain as Cornon's blade sliced through his side. Warm blood spurted across Penderyn's arm as the bandit's sword dropped from his lifeless hand. The man slumped ingloriously from his horse.

In another moment, the battle was over. Six bandits lay dead upon the ground. A seventh was galloping up the hillside in hasty retreat.

"He must not escape!" Cornon shouted. "These villains may have friends nearby." He wheeled his mount around to begin pursuit.

Tal leaped from his horse and retrieved his bow. He fit an arrow to the bowstring and took careful aim before letting fly. His aim was perfect; the final bandit toppled lifelessly from his horse, an arrow protruding from the center of his back.

"Great shot, Tal!" Penderyn exclaimed.

"Has anyone been hurt?" Jarrowon asked worriedly. He looked first to Penderyn and was relieved to find the Last Born unharmed.

"I've got a bit of a scratch," Dal said sheepishly. He held out his left arm to the lore master. The sleeve was wet with blood.

Penderyn and Tal moved closer.

"Don't worry, it's not much," Dal assured them while Jarrowon pulled the torn fabric aside to examine the wound.

A long red slice curved across Dal's forearm. Blood oozed from the gash as Jarrowon gently examined it.

"The blade didn't cut too deeply," the lore master said. He reached into his cloak and drew out a small pouch. "This will keep any infection away." He sprinkled some powdered herbs into the wound, and then tore several strips from the ripped sleeve and wrapped them tightly around Dal's arm, forming a crude bandage.

"Try not to use your arm," he instructed when he finished tying the bandage. "Too much pressure will reopen the wound."

Dal nodded in understanding as he gingerly held his arm across his chest. "What are you two staring at?" he said to Tal and Penderyn, who were still watching him with concern.

Tal grinned. "I'm just trying to see how long it will be before your arm heals," he said good-naturedly, "so we can give you a few more lessons in swordplay."

Their joking was interrupted by Cornon, who knelt beside one of the fallen attackers. "Come look at this," he called.

His comrades hurried over.

Cornon pulled the dead man's tunic aside, exposing his right shoulder. "Here," he said as they peered down at the body.

Penderyn gasped. The man's shoulder had been scarred with a familiar design: a circle pierced by a jagged line!

Penderyn began to shake. His breathing grew labored and his fists clenched and unclenched at his sides. Nerves and muscles already stimulated by the battle were now overloaded. Hatred, anger, grief, blame and despair all whirled inside him, tugging at his heart and his soul. His emotions demanded too much of him—more than he could pay. The world seemed to fade away and he felt as if he was about to collapse.

Through the turmoil, he felt something reaching for him, trying to anchor him. He realized it was the sound of his name, repeated over and over again, calling to him. He fastened his thoughts to it.

Finally, he opened his eyes and found himself looking up into the dark eyes of Jarrowon. The lore master held him firmly by the shoulders and was gently repeating his name. Strength seemed to flow into him through Jarrowon's wrinkled hands.

"It's all right, Penderyn," Jarrowon whispered gently. "It's over."

Penderyn sucked in a deep breath. He still couldn't speak.

"I know about the design," Jarrowon said. "Tal told me about it when the seizure gripped you."

"All of them bear the mark," Tal added, motioning to the other dead bandits.

Penderyn turned away, ashamed. What must his friends think of him now? He needed to redeem himself.

"We'll follow their trail, then," he said determinedly. "Perhaps we can find the rest of this murderous band."

Jarrowon laid his hand on Penderyn's shoulder. "No, Last Born, I'm afraid that we cannot do. Our quest is too important. Your vengeance must await another day. We have to continue our journey."

Penderyn stared silently at the old lore master for several moments before nodding resignedly in understanding.

"I suggest we distance ourselves quickly from this place," Cornon said. "We don't know how many more of these cutthroats are about. They'll not be happy when they discover these bodies."

The company climbed back astride their mounts. As they rode hurriedly away, Penderyn wondered who these murderers were and where they came from. Neither Cornon nor Jarrowon had ever seen the strange insignia before, but Penderyn knew the bandits could not have survived the winter without some sort of permanent base. He hoped they would remain in the area until his quest was finished, for Cornon had promised Kfastia's help in wiping them out completely. Only then would he be able to put aside the grief and anguish that tormented him.

CHAPTER 14

As the afternoon faded toward dusk, Jarrowon led the company to a small, wooded valley he had spied to the northeast that offered some concealment for the night. Until now, they had always ridden until dark, but the lore master was worried about Penderyn. The Last Born seemed listless, bereft of his usual enthusiasm. His seizure had clearly drained him. He needed rest.

Inside the woods, the twilight thickened. The six companions entered a small clearing sheltered by tall, thick evergreens. Though the place seemed perfect for their needs, Jarrowon kept going, ignoring the questioning looks on the faces of his comrades. He peered into the woods as he rode, seeking a telltale patch of red in the deepening gloom. Finally he found it.

"We'll camp here," he said, halting beneath the curving limbs of a modoc.

Penderyn smiled as he gazed into the familiar tangle of gray branches. A trace of color began to return to his wan cheeks.

While the others set about preparing the camp and dinner, Penderyn leaned his back against the modoc's smooth trunk and closed his eyes. Somehow, the tree's comforting presence soothed his troubled spirit. Its strength and serenity seemed to flow into him and he dropped off into a deep, relaxing sleep.

When he awoke, he found himself wrapped in a warm blanket one of his comrades must have placed around him while he slept. The camp was bathed in twilight; he guessed dawn must be very near. He looked to his companions, all of them stretched out around the small fire one of them had built earlier in the evening. Surprisingly, they were all still asleep. He'd expected at least a few of them would be up by now, preparing for the day's journey. An orange tongue of flame leaped up from the fire as a log split in half and fell into the embers. Clearly, wood had been added not too long ago. Penderyn noticed that Olidar was nowhere in sight. He wondered if perhaps the Kfastian had fallen asleep at his watch. Maybe that was why he hadn't awakened the rest of them yet.

Penderyn gazed up at the sky. Through the gaps in the modoc's early spring foliage, he saw two golden lights—Primus and Ferus. Everything suddenly became clear. He had awakened not to dawn, but to the pale light of the *mocrah*.

He listened to the quiet sounds of the false day. Above him the rustle of wings swept through the modoc, and somewhere to his right he heard the scurrying steps of a small rodent. An insect buzzed swiftly by his ear.

A soft green glow among the trees caught his eye. The strange light seemed to be suspended in the air, a few feet above the ground. The light was oval in shape, taller than it was wide. He watched it float slowly toward him, curving gracefully around the trees and branches in its way. He sensed no danger, only gentle warmth. Three feet in front of him, the glowing cloud stopped. It hovered in front of his face, mystifying and beautiful.

Close up, he could see it was not one light as he had originally thought. Instead, thousands of tiny green lights flowed swiftly within some invisible boundary, dancing like fireflies inside a giant jar.

While he watched, the cloud slowly changed its shape, growing taller and narrower. He noticed he could see through it, to the trees behind. As the flowing lights grew brighter, the cloud seemed to grow more solid. It began to assume a form, manlike, but far thinner than any man could be. A face slowly materialized at the top. Within the face, the lights continued to flow, but the features somehow remained stable. They were youthful, masculine.

"Greetings, Penderyn. I am Alythym." Penderyn was unsure whether he actually heard the soft, gentle voice or if it merely sounded within his head. Before he could reply, Alythym's features began to change. The differences were subtle, but the new face was decidedly feminine.

"And I am Elaemir." This second voice was similar to the first, but he knew it was female. As before, it seemed to arise from within his head. *"Alythym and I are brother and sister. Our vibrations are nearly identical. Only by merging them do we have the strength to appear to you. That is why it was we who were sent."*

Penderyn did not reply. He wondered if this was another of his dreams.

"You do not dream, Last Born. We are real." It was Alythym again. *"We have been sent to help you in whatever way our fading power allows."*

The face shifted again. *"My brother and I can only materialize for a brief time. Still, we will do what we can for you in the time ahead."*

Penderyn watched as Elaemir's face dissolved into Alythym's. "Who...what are you?" he asked hesitantly. He found it disconcerting enough to speak to a cloud of moving lights, let alone one that constantly transformed from Alythym to Elaemir and then back again. "Can just one of you speak, please?"

"I'm sorry," Alythym said. *"We can each maintain our form for only a few moments. As we weaken, the other must take* over." Penderyn felt a tinge of sadness in Alythym's voice. *"It was not always so."*

"Our strength derives primarily from the mocrah.*"* Elaemir said. *"The light of the sun is too strong, the darkness too weak."*

The lights were beginning to dim.

"As the mocrah *has weakened, so have we."* It was Alythym again already. The shifts were coming more rapidly now, the voices growing fainter.

"We are of the Luminari," Elaemir said.

"The Light within all things."

"Our strength fades."

"We will come again..."

"When we are able."

"Ask Jarrowon..."

"He knows..."

"Of us..."

The lights faded away. Penderyn rubbed his eyes, still not sure what he had just experienced. He looked toward his companions, still stretched out in their blankets. Whatever had just happened, it had not disturbed them.

Olidar entered the clearing and walked toward the fire, his watch ended. He saw Penderyn awake by the modoc.

He squatted beside Penderyn. "Are you all right? You've a strange look upon your face."

"I'm fine, I think." Penderyn glanced around the clearing once more. "Tell me, did you see anything unusual in the past few minutes?"

Olidar's brow furrowed. He shook his head. "No, nothing. Everything seems quiet. Is something wrong? Should I awaken the others?"

Penderyn hesitated. "No, let them sleep. It's nothing that won't wait until morning."

Jarrowon bent over the still sleeping Penderyn and smiled. The boy's features were no longer drawn and tight. Even in the pale light of dawn he could see that the Last Born's color had returned to normal. He gently shook Penderyn's shoulder.

"Wake up, Penderyn," he said softly. "It's time for a bite to eat, then we're on our way again."

Penderyn open his eyes and yawned. When he looked about the campsite, he was surprised to see his companions had already finished preparing breakfast and readied the horses.

"Look who's the late sleeper now," Dal teased. His voice turned more serious. "How do you feel?"

Penderyn stood and stretched his arms. "Rested and ready." A puzzled look crossed his brow as he remembered his strange visitors from the night before. Had they been real, or were they just another of his dreams? Either way, he sensed it was important. He studied the ground where he had slept, but found no trace of their presence.

"What is it, Last Born?" Jarrowon asked.

"I...I'm not sure. Last night... I don't know if it was one of my dreams... or if it really happened."

"If what happened?" Tal asked.

Penderyn hesitated, trying to remember everything he had seen.

"You acted a bit strangely last night," Olidar told him. "During the *mocrah*."

Penderyn nodded. He remembered asking Olidar if he had seen anything. That part, at least, had been real. He turned to Jarrowon. "They said to ask you."

The lore master's eyes narrowed. "Who said? Ask me what?"

"Alythym and Elaemir. They said you knew them...or knew of them. I'm not sure."

Jarrowon thought for a moment and then shook his head. "No, I have never heard those names. Start at the beginning, Last Born. What do you remember?"

Penderyn recounted his strange vision. The more he spoke of it, the more unbelievable it seemed.

"Alythym told me I wasn't dreaming," he said when he had finished. "It didn't feel like a dream. Not like any others I've had, at any rate."

He watched Jarrowon, awaiting his reply. The lore master's eyes seemed far away.

"*Luminari*," Jarrowon said quietly, his voice filled with wonder. "Yes, I do know of them, though I've never been fortunate enough to encounter one. The *Luminari* are beings from the dawn of time, embodiments of the light that is within all things. Rarely do they take form and appear to mortal man. It's said their power is behind much of the magic in our world." He shook his head sadly. "If even the *Luminari* grow weak, Perator's ill is grave indeed."

He turned back to Penderyn. "Whether you dreamed it or not, Last Born, I cannot say. Either way, it seems you are to have help unlooked for."

Penderyn smiled. Whatever might lie ahead, on this journey and after, he felt less troubled now than he had for some time.

CHAPTER 15

Ten days later, early in the afternoon of another beautiful spring day, the company reined their mounts to a halt atop a small hill. In the distance, they could see a range of jagged, snow-capped mountains stretching across the horizon.

"The Riftwill Tages," Jarrowon announced. "According to legend, She Who Knows All dwells somewhere within those mountains."

His companions smiled. Spurred by Penderyn's vision of the *Luminari*, they had been riding as hard as they dared push the horses. Now at last they were nearing the land they sought.

"We'll soon be looking for Penderyn's burning arch," Dal said happily.

Cornon shook his head skeptically. "There are a lot of mountains out there. Unless the gods smile on us, we may be searching for some time."

"We won't have to trust in the gods alone," Jarrowon replied, "though their help will certainly be most welcome. There are other landmarks to guide our way. We must seek a mountain with a triple peak at its summit. When we find it, we'll know exactly where to enter the mountains."

Two days later, they spied the distinctive mountain. Its three narrow peaks stretched upward like the gigantic spires of some mighty fortress, giving the mountain its name—The Giant's Castle. The icy summits glistened in the sun, beckoning the six riders as they turned their horses toward the rocky slopes.

"According to my lore," Jarrowon said, "a pass cuts through the mountains just to the west of The Giant's Castle. Once within the range, we must search for the second marker, a river that emerges from the face of the mountain."

They found the trail into the mountains exactly where Jarrowon predicted. Confident they were on the right path to their goal, they forged onward.

The pass climbed steadily upward, but at a gentle enough slope to cause no difficulty for the horses. On either side, walls of rock rose steeply above the narrow defile, keeping the company in shadows for most of the first few hours. Small, scattered weeds and bushes clung even to these vertical faces, their roots holding fast to narrow ledges and thin cracks where bits of soil had collected. Tiny gray and black birds darted from shrub to shrub, disturbed by the clatter of hoof beats that echoed through the pass.

After a while, the way widened. The wall of rock to their left began to fall away, until it disappeared entirely, leaving the path flanked now by a deep ravine. Far below, the riders saw the churning white water of a mountain stream racing between narrow stands of evergreens. The river looked like an inviting place to refill their water bags, but there was no way down the nearly vertical cliff.

All that day and the next they followed this twisting, climbing path ever deeper into the mountains. The river remained to their left, its constant presence lending strength to their hope that they would soon find the strange waterfall they sought as their next landmark.

On the third day, they found it. They halted their mounts and gazed in awe at the beautiful natural wonder. The water emerged from some underground channel two thirds of the way up a towering cliff, plummeting in a narrow white ribbon for several hundred feet until it splashed into a wide pool at the bottom of the ravine. A rainbow hued veil of mist, formed where the spray crashed against outcroppings of rock, danced around the falls in a shimmering curtain of ever-changing colors.

Jarrowon was the first to break the silence. "The tales speak of the beauty of this waterfall, naming it the Rainbow Veil, but they do not begin do it justice."

"That such beauty existed, I scarcely imagined," Cornon said reverently. "Whatever else may happen, I'm glad Penderyn's quest has given me the chance to witness such a sight."

"Those who seek She Who Knows All are indeed well rewarded, even if their questions remain unanswered," Olidar said.

"Let's hope this is just the beginning of our good fortune," Jarrowon said, smiling. "Our way lies here." He indicated a path down into the gorge.

Cornon guided his horse toward the narrow trail and his companions fell in behind him.

To Penderyn's eye, the path looked like it had been cut out of the rock, though he could not imagine what kind of power and skill it would take to fashion such a traverse.

"Do you know who made this path?" he asked Jarrowon, who rode just ahead of him.

Jarrowon twisted his head around. "My lore does not say. But your eye is good, Last Born. I do not think this way was made by nature, or by game. Perhaps its origins are tied to the oracle."

Penderyn hoped so, for that meant they should be drawing close.

They awoke the next morning to a dark, gray dawn. A thick layer of heavy black clouds had roofed the mountains overnight, reducing the gorge to a small, sealed tunnel. A cold wind gusted across their faces.

"We'd best try to find some kind of shelter," Jarrowon suggested as the dark ceiling dropped ever lower. "Unless I'm mistaken, it will not be long before these clouds unleash their flood."

The storm started slowly. Widely scattered drops splattered against the rocks as the party searched for shelter. Tal spied a shallow hollow in the cliff with a small, overhanging ledge above it. Finding nowhere else that would afford even such minimal protection, they crowded into the opening, huddling against the rock and holding their horses between themselves and the rain.

They took shelter just in time. Moments later, the storm unleashed its full fury. The rain descended in heavy sheets, driven furiously by the swirling wind. Even under the overhang and shielded by the horses, they could not escape the chilling water. Before long, their cloaks were drenched.

"Can't you do something, Jarrowon?" Penderyn asked. He shivered as the cold sank deeper into his bones. "Your magic protected you against the blizzard."

"You overestimate my powers, Last Born. I cannot stop the weather; I can only protect myself from the storm. I'm afraid all I can do for the rest of you is to dry your cloaks from time to time."

"That'll be better than nothing," Tal said, hugging his arms across his chest.

The lore master touched each of his companions with his staff, mumbling a few strange words as he did so. Their cloaks dried instantly, giving them a few precious moments of warmth before the rain soaked their clothes again.

"That's an improvement, at least," Penderyn said. "Thank you, Jarrowon."

Jarrowon repeated his spell often, especially for Penderyn, whose smaller frame afforded him less protection from the cold. Still, they spent a chill, uncomfortable night while the storm raged around them. They managed what sleep they could, but it was not much. Shortly after dawn, the rain finally ended.

Penderyn felt as if he had aged fifty years as he stepped gingerly out onto the trail. Stretching and straightening his cold, stiff joints and muscles as gently as possible, he tried to undo the effects of the miserable night, but with little success. He knew by the slow, awkward movements of his comrades that they fared little better. Only Jarrowon seemed untouched by the effects of the weather.

The sky remained overcast as they continued on their way, but it had brightened into a lighter gray, portending little threat of any more rain. Though the ceiling on their world had lifted somewhat, the upper reaches of the mountains were still hidden from view.

The cold, damp air did little to raise their spirits as they guided their horses carefully over the wet, slippery rock, but the steep gorge to their left kept them from becoming impatient with the slowness of their pace. The penalty for a misstep was all too clear.

As they walked, Penderyn gazed up often at the sunless sky. Even if they found an arch today, there would be no way to tell whether it was the one they sought. Only when the clouds lifted could dawn confirm whether it was the arch he had seen in his dream. From the thickness of the gray canopy above, he doubted that was going to happen any time soon.

Jarrowon was the first to spot it.

He pointed to the immense stone bridge that curved across the canyon several hundred feet above the trail. Even from half a league away, the giant formation dominated the view. Through its wide, round arch they could see the summit of a far off mountain and a patch of gray sky. Penderyn's companions looked at him questioningly.

The Last Born studied the formation, comparing it to the image in his dream. The two seemed similar enough, but he could not be certain. Only when he saw the sun burning beneath the arch would he know for sure.

"I think that's it," he said. "But I must see it burn to be certain."

"Then we shall wait here until you do," Jarrowon said. "If not tomorrow morning, then the next. These infernal clouds must lift sometime."

Tal studied their barren surroundings. This would not be a comfortable place to camp.

"I'm going to make sure you don't oversleep tomorrow, Penderyn," he promised with a smile. "I'd hate to spend an extra night here because you missed the dawn."

"Don't worry," Penderyn replied. "I'm as anxious to see the sun as you are."

But the next day's dawn passed unseen, hidden behind the blanket of clouds. There was nothing the company could do but wait.

With each passing night, Penderyn's sleep grew more troubled as he and his comrades endured a seemingly endless succession of dark, overcast days. He felt as if he had dreamed, but he could not recall anything of the visions after he awoke. His frustration grew. He sensed that something was trying to reach him, but like the sun, it remained hidden behind some impenetrable barrier.

Finally, he turned to Jarrowon for advice.

"Try not to worry about it," the lore master counseled. "Such things usually come unbidden, but when sought for become most elusive."

Penderyn tried to push the matter from his mind, but with little else to do in their remote campsite, it was not an easy task. He prayed the clouds would give way soon, and at last his prayers were answered.

The company lined the trail expectantly as the eastern sky slowly brightened. For the first time in almost a week, the sky was free of clouds. Penderyn found himself holding his breath as the first faint signs of yellow and pink appeared under the giant arch. He forced himself to breathe as he silently watched a scene he had viewed once before slowly come to life.

With each passing moment, more and more of the fiery red sun became visible under the arch, until finally the flaming sphere filled the opening completely. For a few seconds, the dark stone seemed ablaze in fire, just as he had dreamed it.

His comrades turned to him expectantly.

"That was it," he said, smiling. "Exactly as I saw it in my dream."

Dal clapped him on the shoulder. "That's the best news I've heard in some time," he said.

The company quickly gathered their belongings and mounted their horses.

As they rode toward the arch, Penderyn began to feel a gnawing in the back of his mind, similar in some way to the disturbance that had troubled his sleep. It felt like a faint voice calling to him through a fog; he could not quite understand the words or even be sure where the voice was coming from, but he knew it was important. He could feel its urgency. Recalling Jarrowon's advice, he tried to think of other things.

Suddenly, an image burst into his mind. The vision was clear and sharp. He saw himself silhouetted against the sky atop the arch. His comrades were nowhere to be seen. He was alone.

The image faded as suddenly as it had appeared. Now a voice whispered in his head. A soft, caring, voice that sounded hauntingly familiar.

Your goal draws near, Penderyn. But you must travel the rest of this path alone. Only then will you reach the place you seek. Trust me, my son.

The voice was his mother's! Somehow, she was reaching out to him from beyond the grave. His heart ached at the familiar sound of her voice, but he pushed his grief aside. He knew he must heed her words. He reined Surefoot to a halt.

"Wait," he called to his companions.

"What is it, Last Born?" Jarrowon asked, alarmed by the strange look he saw upon Penderyn's face.

"I must go on alone."

His comrades stared at him. For a moment they were too shocked to speak.

"What are you talking about?" Tal asked. "We're in this together."

"You can't go without us," protested Dal.

"I have to," Penderyn replied adamantly. He explained his vision and repeated his mother's words. "I will not forsake my mother's warning. My dreams have not failed me yet."

Even as he spoke, he recalled his mother's earliest advice: never to put too much trust in his dreams. He forced the thought aside. If his friends sensed his doubts, they would never allow him to go on alone.

The twins turned to Jarrowon for support. The lore master said nothing for several minutes.

"It is the Last Born's road that we follow," he said at last. "If Penderyn feels he must travel this part alone, we must respect his wishes." He stared intently into Penderyn's eyes. "Are you certain of this, Last Born?"

Penderyn wanted anything but to go on alone. His heart trembled at the thought of venturing deeper into these unknown mountains without the companionship of his friends, but he knew he must heed his vision.

"Yes," he replied. "I'm sure."

"Then so be it," Jarrowon said. "We shall wait one fortnight. If you have not returned by then, we will follow you. Agreed?"

Penderyn nodded. He pointed to the top of the arch. "My way lies there. Across the arch."

He embraced each of his comrades, keeping Tal and Dal for last. Sadness engulfed him as he hugged the twins tightly. The three of them had not been apart since the night their village was destroyed.

"Don't worry, I'll be all right," he told his companions when he was done. "And when I return, perhaps I will have the key to my dreams."

CHAPTER 16

Penderyn stood atop the giant arch and waved to his comrades far below. The climb had been surprisingly easy. He had followed a narrow ledge that slanted up the wall of the gorge and then finished the ascent by climbing a cliff lined with easy hand and footholds. Despite the height he felt no danger; the huge natural bridge was far wider than he was tall, and he kept well back from the edge.

The view from his lofty perch was breathtaking. Scores of forbidding mountains stretched before him, their barren slopes a panorama of dark gray rock laced with streaks of white snow. The summits were just the opposite, wide expanses of snow, dotted with crags of gray where the wind had exposed the rock. Only at the very lowest elevations were there any sizable areas of vegetation to relieve the starkness of the landscape. The vastness of this stone wilderness made him feel very much alone.

He looked back down at his comrades. Their presence reassured him. He knew he had but to signal, and they would hurry to join him. But he could not. This part of his road, at least, was his alone. He waved one last time and then strode resolutely across the bridge.

The hours passed slowly as he moved carefully along this new trail. Sometimes his way climbed steeply upward, other times it sloped downward, but on the whole he felt he was descending. As morning gave way to afternoon, the path began to drop more sharply, carrying him down into the lower elevations. Shrubs and small trees began to flank the narrow trail.

The thickening vegetation encouraged him. If the Eirydi did indeed live somewhere in this region, they were far more likely to dwell in some hidden valley than among the inhospitable upper slopes. Perhaps he would soon find their home.

His hopes were dashed when the trail ended abruptly at the base of sheer granite cliff. He stared at the exposed rock in disbelief. There was nowhere to go. Towering walls of stone blocked him on three sides; the only way out was the way he had come. His trail had led him to a dead end!

He rubbed his palms over the offending rock in front of him. How could this be? He had been so confident, so sure he was nearing his goal. His vision had led him to the top of the arch, and this trail had brought him here. There had been no other paths, no way to go but the one he had followed. What had he done wrong? He should have brought Jarrowon along, at least. Surely the lore master would know what to do.

He slumped wearily to the ground and rested against the cliff. Closing his eyes, he tried to think. More tired from his day's travel than he realized, he nodded off to sleep.

A warm, gentle sensation caressed his skin and awakened him. He opened his eyes to a whirling mass of tiny green lights. He smiled. The *Luminari* had returned.

Alythm's face appeared in the glow.

"Come, Last Born. All is not lost."

The shimmering figure floated slowly back into the twilight. Penderyn rose hurriedly to his feet and followed, surprised at how long he had slept. The *Luminari* settled in front of a thick clump of waxy-leafed bushes at the base of the cliff. Elaemir took form.

"Here lies the way you seek, Penderyn."

The face shifted to Alythym's.

"Take care, Last Born," he warned. *"For there is danger ahead."*

"Not all danger comes from without," Elaemir added. *"Be strong."*

What did she mean not all danger came from without? Penderyn wanted to ask her to explain, but already the sparkles were growing dim. Alythym reappeared.

"Remember, your mother..."

"The key..."

The lights winked out. Penderyn was alone again. He studied the clump of bushes the *Luminari* had indicated for a moment and then bent one of the thick branches to the side. Behind it he saw an opening into the cliff.

It was black as pitch inside, but he thought he saw the faint glimmer of twilight at the far end. His magical friends had revealed a tunnel through the mountain!

Before he entered the cave, he scratched a crude arrow into the rock beside the entrance with his sword. If he didn't return in the fortnight allowed, at least his friends would know which way he had gone. He squirmed through the opening and found he could stand erect inside the passage. Already he had forgotten the *Luminari's* enigmatic words of warning. Too anxious to wait for morning, he moved carefully ahead into the darkness, making his way blindly toward the faint light ahead. He took small steps, testing the unseen ground in front of him with his foot before committing his weight to it and keeping one hand against the stone wall of the tunnel for balance.

It was impossible to judge distance inside the cavern, but despite the slowness of his pace, the far opening grew steadily larger. He could tell he did not have far to go.

Less than twenty feet from the opening, something dropped on him without warning from above, knocking him off his feet. He tried to draw his sword, but his arms were pinned firmly to his side. He kicked and twisted, but could not escape the clutching grasp. An angry grunt echoed through the cavern as his foot connected with a solid form and then his skull exploded in a flash of pain. Blackness claimed him.

Penderyn awoke on a cold stone floor, his hands bound tightly behind his back. He had no idea where he was or how he had gotten here. He tried to move his legs, but found they were tied together at the ankles. When he tried to twist himself up into a sitting position, a searing wave of pain shot through his head. He collapsed back to the floor.

He lay motionless with his eyes clenched shut, waiting for the agony to subside. When at last he could think clearly, he opened his eyes and surveyed his surroundings.

He was in a small, square room about eight feet across. The walls, ceiling and floor were all rough gray stone, with no windows anywhere. The only light came from a small torch fastened to the wall next to the entrance. No door blocked the opening, but beyond it he saw only darkness. Whether it opened into another room or to the night outside he had no way of determining. He heard no sounds; either his captors were sleeping, or he was very much alone.

Once again he attempted to gain a sitting position, moving slowly and carefully this time. He eased himself across the floor to the nearest wall and then used his shoulder to inch himself upward along the rough stone. Finally he made it. He leaned his back against the wall and waited, wondering who his captors were and what they had in store for him.

How long he sat alone in his dim, cold prison he had no way of knowing, but it seemed like forever before he saw the flickering glow of a torch approaching through the darkness outside the doorway.

Two men entered the room. One was tall and slender, the other much more burly. The heavier one carried the torch.

The first thing Penderyn noticed was their hair. Even in the torchlight, he could see the bright golden locks that hung to their shoulders. He was immediately reminded of his mother. Could these be the Eirydi?

Hope flared inside him. Why they had treated him this way, he didn't know, but once he explained his mission he was certain all would be well. He opened his mouth to speak, but was interrupted before he had scarcely begun.

"Silence!" roared the man holding the torch. "It is not permitted for you to speak."

Penderyn was stunned by the fury in the man's voice. His captors didn't look evil or cruel. What could he have done to anger them so?

The second man raised a finger to his lips, signaling Penderyn to be silent. He turned to his comrade.

"Talga, inform the queen that the prisoner is awake," he ordered. "I'll bring him along shortly."

Talga glowered down at Penderyn before spinning on his heels and departing.

"Forgive Talga's manner," the other man said in a friendly tone when they were alone. "He follows our laws much too closely, I'm afraid. My name is Orith."

Penderyn studied his captor. Orith had a smooth, friendly looking face. He appeared to be in his mid-twenties.

"I'm Penderyn. I mean no harm to your people. Why was I attacked? And why am I held prisoner."

Orith knelt and took a look at the bump on Penderyn's head.

"I'm sorry about that," he said regretfully. "In the darkness, I had no way of knowing you were so young." He smiled. "You fought like a gryth. I suspect that's another reason behind Talga's manner. His stomach still aches where you kicked him."

Penderyn laughed despite himself, remembering how his foot had connected with something solid in the darkness. "Tell Talga I'm sorry, but I wasn't expecting such a reception. Why am I treated like an enemy?"

Orith's face saddened and his tone turned serious. "It is another of our laws, I'm afraid. You will hear more when I bring you before the queen." He bent and began to untie Penderyn's legs. "Why have you come to our valley?"

"I seek the Eirydi, in search of answers to certain questions which beset me," Penderyn replied. He watched Orith's face closely. "Have I found them?"

"We are the Eirydi," Orith admitted. "But I'm afraid you will not like the answers you will find here. You should have asked your questions through the Oracle, like others do."

"My questions are not like those of others."

Orith finished untying Penderyn's legs and gently helped him to his feet. "You'll have a chance to explain your visit to our queen," he said, but his voice did not sound very hopeful. "Come."

Orith removed the torch from the wall and led Penderyn into a narrow corridor. The dim passage seemed more like a cave than a hallway. They passed several openings in the wall, but all were too dark inside for Penderyn to see anything. He guessed they must be rooms similar to his own.

When they emerged into the daylight he saw he had indeed been inside a cave, one which exited onto a small ledge on the face of a wide cliff. Peering carefully over the edge, he saw a drop of more than a hundred feet. Below him stretched a narrow green valley enclosed by towering walls of rock. The still waters of a large lake filled much of the near end of the valley and reflected the jagged gray and white peaks like a beautiful tapestry.

"We call our valley Gaelin Mirrosil, the isle of green," Orith explained as Penderyn stared into the distance. "For many ages it has been our only home."

As Penderyn followed Orith along the ledge, he discovered the cliff was pockmarked with caves. Several ledges similar to the one they traversed cut across the rock. The different levels were connected by sturdy wooden ladders, turning the mountain's face into virtual city.

Each time they passed one of the tall ladders, Penderyn breathed a sigh of relief. He didn't relish the thought of climbing one with his hands tied behind his back. He hoped Orith would untie him if it came time to climb.

Orith halted in front of the largest opening they had passed thus far. "This is the home of Erowil, our queen," he said before they entered. "With her lies your fate."

The royal cavern was wider and more brightly lit than the others Penderyn had seen. Almost circular in shape, it had a round, dome-like ceiling some twenty-five feet above the smooth stone floor. Several passages exited from the back of the chamber, leading no doubt to the private quarters of the queen and her attendants. At the far end of this amphitheater he saw the queen herself, seated upon a raised throne of polished wood.

Orith led him across the cavern, stopping at the foot of the throne. Erowil was growing old, Penderyn saw. What must once have been a beautiful face was now creased by lines, and the graying hair piled atop her head showed only traces of the golden hue of her race. He sensed an aura of sadness around her.

"Here is the prisoner, Your Majesty," Orith said. He bowed slightly and then stepped to the side, where he took a position next to Talga.

An expression of surprise flashed across Erowil's face. "He is so young," she said in tone that revealed she had not been aware of their prisoner's youth. "What is your name?" she asked.

"I'm called Penderyn, Your Majesty."

"I'm sorry your path brought you to our valley, Penderyn," Erowil said softly. "Especially since you are so young. But our laws are clear. Any who chance upon our land must die, lest they betray our presence to the outside world."

Her words echoed inside Penderyn's head. He couldn't

believe what he had just heard. He had come all this way, only to be sentenced to death merely for entering this land.

"I don't understand," he said at last. "I've done nothing to harm you. I seek your help, on a matter vital to all of Perator."

Erowil raised her hand, signaling him to be silent.

"You've done nothing yet," she admitted. "But we must make certain it remains that way. It saddens me to pronounce your fate. Perhaps you'll understand our law if I tell you our story.

"Long ago, our people lived free among the cities of Perator. Wherever we visited, we were welcomed and honored. Our aid was sought by rich and poor alike, for we made no distinction about who we helped. Then came a day when an evil and ambitious king decided he alone should possess our power. He imprisoned our people in his castle and cruelly tortured them if they refused his orders.

"A group of our ancestors managed at last to escape from the evil king. They fled across the land until they reached these mountains. Here, guided by their dreams, they discovered this hidden valley. For centuries we have remained in hiding, free from the greed and ambitions of others. Our name has become but a legend of the past.

"Still, we help those we deem worthy through the voice of the Oracle, but our existence must remain a secret. The law has been passed down through the ages. Any outsider who discovers our land must die."

Orith stepped forward. "You have the power to waive that law, my Queen."

"You need not remind me, Orith," Erowil said sadly. "I was merciful once and was betrayed. I shall not make that mistake again."

"Please, Your Majesty," Penderyn begged. "You have to listen to me. Your people were wronged. I understand your mistrust of outsiders." He remembered the words of Alythym and

Elaemir. "But I am not an outsider. I too am visited by dreams that see the future. I believe my mother was of the Eirydi."

An astonished murmur ran through the cavern. Erowil rose from her throne and took two faltering steps toward him. When she spoke, her voice quaked. "Come nearer," she ordered.

Penderyn stepped closer. Erowil reached out and cradled his cheeks in her palms. She studied him closely, trying to look past the bright copper hair so different from that of her race. Tears brimmed in her eyes.

Suddenly, she turned away.

"No!" she sobbed. "I will not be deceived again." She climbed back to her throne and sat. "The sentence stands," she announced, her voice choked with emotion. "Your death shall be quick and merciful. At dawn tomorrow."

"I'm sorry, Penderyn," Orith said as he led Penderyn from the chamber.

"I don't understand," Penderyn said. "What upset Erowil so? It doesn't make sense. I've done nothing."

"Erowil is tormented by something that happened many years ago, before I was born," Orith said. "She had only recently become queen when an outsider named Horglim discovered our valley. He was kind and friendly, and Erowil grew fond of him. She could not bring herself to order his death, so she spared his life on the condition that he remain with us for the rest of his days. Horglim readily agreed.

"Eventually he and Erowil fell in love and were married. A year later, Erowil gave birth to a daughter, Feyitha. When Feyitha was five years old, Horglim disappeared from the valley, taking her with him. No one knows why. Erowil was heartbroken. To this day, she grieves for her lost daughter. If your mother was in fact of our blood, she could only have been Feyitha."

"If that's true, I can understand the grief my arrival stirs in her," Penderyn said. "But how can she order my death?"

Orith shook his head. "She was merciful once and was badly hurt. Perhaps she fears you were sent here by Horglim, to somehow betray her again. I do not know."

"If my mother truly was Erowil's daughter, then the queen has ordered the death of her own flesh and blood."

"That's why she will not let herself believe that you are her grandson." Orith sighed. "I'll try to talk to her, but I have little hope I can change her mind. I'm sorry, Penderyn."

Penderyn watched as the light from Orith's torch faded from the corridor. He slumped to the floor. He sat alone in the dimness of his prison, his only company the flickering torch Orith had lit upon the wall. Though Orith had left his legs untied, he knew there was no escape. He could easily make it back to the ledge, but where could he go from there? To attempt to climb the ladders with his hands tied behind his back would only send him crashing to the bottom of the cliff, to an even quicker death than the one ordered by Erowil.

His thoughts turned to his companions, waiting patiently on the other side of the mountain. Had it been only yesterday that he had left them? He had been so confident and full of hope, never guessing it would be their final farewell. When he failed to return they would follow him, but by then he would be long dead.

He cursed his decision to come alone. Why had he listened to his dream? His mother had warned him to only trust his dreams when there was no other way. Why hadn't he heeded her advice? But his vision had been so lifelike, and his mother's voice so real. If only it had been some other voice, he might not have listened. But it was too late now. Tomorrow he would die, and the quest of the Last Born would be ended before it had barely begun.

CHAPTER 17

Penderyn opened his eyes and found himself enveloped by total darkness. For a moment he forgot where he was, but the rope that bound his hands behind his back quickly reminded him. He was a prisoner, condemned to die by a law he hadn't even known existed. There was nothing he could do until someone came for him, so he eased himself into a sitting position against the wall and waited.

He must have slept for several hours at least, he decided, because the torch Orith had left behind had burned down to a barely visible smoldering orange nub. How long until the light of dawn filtered back here into his prison he didn't know, but he was in no hurry to see its arrival.

He had not dreamed that he could remember, and he smiled despite himself at the capriciousness of fate. Here among the Eirydi, from whom he had sought to learn the key to his power, his sleep had been empty of any visions. Even the confused, mist-shrouded images which so often disturbed his sleep of late had been absent.

No sounds from the night outside penetrated his prison—the silence was as total as the darkness. Where there was no sensation, his senses sought to create it. His pulse pounded in his ears; tiny lights seemed to streak before his eyes. He thought the *Luminari* had come to aid him, but he quickly realized it was only a trick of his deprived eyesight.

His heart sank. His eyes ached from staring into the utter darkness, so he let them close.

He began to drift off. He felt weightless, floating in a timeless void, cast loose in some empty limbo between worlds where nothing existed but his thoughts. Slowly, dim figures began to emerge from the blackness....

A bright light against his eyelids awakened him. He opened his eyes to see Orith standing in the doorway.

"It is time, my friend," Orith said regretfully.

Penderyn did not reply. He remained silent as Orith helped him to his feet and led him from his prison.

The first faint touches of daylight were only just beginning to paint the sky above the valley as Penderyn followed Orith across the ledge toward the throne room. The busy chirpings of awakening birds danced upward through the still morning air. The floor of the valley remained dark, with the forest as yet indistinguishable from the rock that surrounded it, save only that perhaps it was a shade darker. All these things were lost on Penderyn. His thoughts were elsewhere.

The vacant stare on Penderyn's youthful face puzzled Orith. Fear, sadness, anxiety, resignation—all these he would have understood. The utter absence of expression he did not.

When they reached the throne room, Erowil was already seated upon her wooden throne. Her face was also an expressionless mask. Orith looked from the queen to Penderyn. The similarity was startling.

In a voice devoid of feeling, Erowil pronounced Penderyn's fate once again. "Young Penderyn, please understand we of the Eirydi bear you no malice. But we are bound by our laws, handed down through the centuries to protect our people and our land. Your arrival has broken such a law, however unwittingly, and the sentence is clear. As I promised, your death shall swift and painless. So do I, Erowil, Queen of the Eirydi, decree. Have you any final words?"

"Yes. I do." Penderyn drew himself erect and looked steadily into Erowil's eyes.

The queen gasped under his stare. She seemed to shrink back into the wood of her throne. Penderyn seemed changed—older, larger. An aura of power radiated from him.

When he spoke, his voice was strong and compelling.

"I did not come to Gaelin Mirrosil seeking gain or reward, but rather because I am part of a fate that was written long before any of us were born. I did not choose this destiny, but I have no choice but to follow it. Upon my head may lie the future of all Perator. Even the Eirydi, hidden here in this valley far from other peoples, cannot escape the doom that threatens our world. Already your people have felt the curse of barrenness. How long has it been since the cries of a child have echoed through your caverns?"

Erowil's face whitened. Whispers hissed through the throne room. Penderyn seemed to notice neither.

"This affliction is not yours alone. It besets all of Perator. I am the Last Born. Upon me falls the doom of opposing our unseen enemy."

The murmurings rose in volume. All within the cavern felt the power in Penderyn's voice.

"But I do not ask you to spare my life on the basis of such a story, however important it may be. I do not ask you to break the laws of your ancestors. I came here to learn to control the power in my dreams; dreams which I see because the blood of the Eirydi flows in my veins."

Erowil was visibly shaken. "Your words are moving, Penderyn," she said weakly. "Even I feel the strength behind them. What am I to do? Shall my sentence be the death knell of all Perator? Yet you yourself say you should not be spared because of the tale you have woven. Guide me, Last Born. What would you have me do?"

Penderyn's voice softened, yet lost none of its power. "It is not enough that you should spare my life," he said. "You must help me, for without your help, I shall never be able to control my dreams. Any doubt I had that you can help me is gone. I am one of you."

He stared hard into Erowil's eyes. The queen winced.

"Open your mind to me, Erowil. See my dream."

There is a young woman, with long blond hair—Erowil, looking as she looked thirty years ago. She is seated upon a wooden throne. A frightened cry breaks the stillness and a child races toward her. The young queen hugs the crying child. The child buries her face in her mother's breast. Sobs wrack her slender frame. Erowil stokes the child's golden hair, comforting her.

"That child you see was my mother," Penderyn declared. "She is the daughter taken from you when she was still a child."

Erowil's pale skin had grown even whiter. She slumped in her throne. "How did you do that?" she whispered in a voice that seemed about to crack. "None of us possesses such power. How am I to believe you are of our race, when you can do things we cannot?" She turned her gaze slowly toward Orith. "Anyone could have told you of my daughter, so cruelly taken from me."

Penderyn's voice drew Erowil's eyes back to him.

"Yes, I was told of your loss, that is true. I do not deny it. But there is more. Your daughter ran to you that day for a reason. She sought the comfort of your arms because of a dream she had that frightened her. It was a dream of being trapped in a fire. She told you how she felt the flames burning against her skin."

Erowil's strength drained from her body as she relived the moment. Penderyn continued.

"That same dream was my first dream as well, though I never knew until this morning that my mother had seen it also. She spared me that knowledge."

The cavern had grown completely silent. Erowil gathered her strength and rose unsteadily to her feet.

"Everything was as you say," she said slowly. "No one but my daughter and I knew of that moment. I never told anyone." The queen descended falteringly from the dais and opened her arms to Penderyn. A smile replaced the grief on her face. "You have proven your birthright, Penderyn. Come to me, grandson."

For a moment, Penderyn stood motionless. Whatever power had aided him this last hour faded away unnoticed, replaced by the joyful feeling of knowing he had family once again. He moved into Erowil's waiting arms. Tears streamed down both their faces as grandmother and grandson embraced for the first time.

When at last they ended their embrace, Erowil led him from the throne room to one of her private chambers so they could be alone. Her people smiled happily as they passed. Such joy had too been long absent from their queen's face.

"We've so much to talk about, Penderyn," Erowil said eagerly. "I want to know all about Feyitha, and about you, of course. How long can you stay with us?"

Penderyn sighed. "Only a fortnight, I'm afraid. My friends are waiting for me in the mountains."

"We can have them brought here," Erowil suggested.

Penderyn thought about it for a moment, but then shook his head. His comrades would be fine where they were.

"No, I'll not ask you to waive your law for my comrades. I trust them all with my life, but I think the fewer who know your secret, the safer you'll be. Besides, there are matters in our homeland which compel us to return soon."

"Then I'll not press you stay longer than your fortnight," Erowil said. "We'll have time enough to talk, and for us to help you begin to learn the secrets of controlling your dreams." She smiled and shook her head. "The days will pass too quickly, I'm afraid."

She looked him directly in the eyes, and her voice turned serious. "I must warn you, grandson, mastery of your dreams is no easy task, even with years of practice. I have dreamed for half a century now, and even I don't have complete control over my power."

Penderyn frowned in disappointment. In the face of Erowil's words, what could he hope to accomplish in less than a fortnight?

Erowil patted his hand reassuringly. "Don't worry, we'll have time enough to show you many things. When you leave, I'm certain you will have learned at least a small measure of control. After that, your skills will improve with time and practice."

Penderyn nodded, relieved by Erowil's reassurances. "I'll try to be satisfied with that, though I'm certain my patience will be sorely tried. Already I've grown tired of the mist that so often veils my dreams."

"Even uncontrolled, your power led you to our land," Erowil reminded him. "And it saved you from the foolish actions of an old queen, who still grieves over a hurt thirty years old."

"From a queen who did what she thought best for her people," Penderyn corrected.

Erowil smiled and hugged her grandson one more time. They spent the remainder of the day in happy conversation, learning as much as possible about one another. Tomorrow they would begin work on Penderyn's dreams, but for this day they were simply a boy and his grandmother with much to talk about.

Penderyn's training began immediately after breakfast the next day. Erowil brought him to a small, quiet chamber deep within the mountain where they might work undisturbed. Two wooden chairs faced each other in the center of the room—the only furnishings in this cavern. The seats were padded with thin yellow cushions stuffed with soft feathers. Two pairs of slow burning candles mounted on the walls illuminated the room with their flickering light.

Erowil indicated one of the chairs to Penderyn and lowered herself into the other.

"Did you dream last night?" she asked.

Penderyn shook his head. "Not that I can remember. Last night was one of the few times since Jarrowon's arrival that I saw no images at all, however unclear." He wondered if his power was once again slipping away, as it had for several months after his mother's death. He prayed not, now that he had finally found people who could help him.

"Don't worry," Erowil said. "All of us have periods without dreams. This is the time of the *solana*, dreams that are stored in your unconscious until they are triggered by some external event. Your vision in the swamp when you slew the terriwarg was undoubtedly a *solana*."

Penderyn listened intently to Erowil's every word, determined to learn as much as possible in the time he had.

"There are two basic parts to controlling your power. The first is to be able to see your visions clearly and to recall them in detail when you awaken, so that you may interpret them correctly. The second aspect is more difficult, for it involves summoning a dream about a specific subject. Even the most skilled of us are not always successful at this. Sometimes what you wish to know may simply be beyond the realm of your power. Also, there are many obstacles that can block your attempt."

Erowil paused for moment, smiling at the eagerness she saw in her grandson's eyes. "At times you may curse these limitations in your power, but remember that the true curse would be to know the future in its entirety, for what mind could stand under the weight of such knowledge?"

Penderyn nodded. Absolute knowledge of the future would be a terrible burden indeed.

"Remember also that your dreams are merely guides, not infallible laws. But like the signposts that lead a traveler along strange roads, your dreams are most useful when they are clearly seen. This is where we shall begin.

"When the images in your sleep are unclear or seem veiled by a mist, sometimes the harder you concentrate, the more elusive they become. At such times we use the *iffirium*, which means "empty mind." The *iffirium* involves ridding your mind of all conscious thought, for it is from your desires and emotions that the mist most often springs. By making your mind go blank, your visions may float more easily to the surface, like reflections upon still waters."

Penderyn tried to empty his mind of thoughts, but found it impossible. Erowil could see by the expression on his face what he was trying to do.

"No, no," she said, chuckling. "You can't just tell yourself to think no thoughts, for that in itself is a thought. Let me explain."

For the next few hours, Erowil demonstrated how to achieve the trance-like state through a kind of meditation. Complete relaxation, deep breathing and the use of a soft rhythmic chant to push conscious thoughts away were all necessary to reach the *iffirium*.

Penderyn listened closely to Erowil's instructions and tried diligently to follow her example, but he was unable to achieve a complete *iffirium*.

"You're trying too hard," Erowil explained after his fourth unsuccessful attempt. "You cannot force the *iffirium* on yourself. Allow it to slip gently over you, like an unseen breeze."

She stood up. "I think we done enough for today," she decided. "Too much work at the beginning can defeat our purpose. Relax for the rest of the day and try not to think about what we've been doing. Orith is anxious to see you. Have him show you our valley. Tomorrow, we will continue our work."

Almost a week of training went by before Penderyn could consistently drop into the *iffirium*. Each day, as he grew accustomed to the work, more and more hours were devoted to his training. Still, there was always some time to spend with Orith, relaxing and having fun. They enjoyed walking together through the beautiful valley, with Penderyn as enthusiastic in learning about this new land as Orith was in describing it. Erowil was pleased by the fondness she saw growing between the two and gradually had Orith assume some of Penderyn's training as well.

Once Penderyn gained some proficiency with the *iffirium*, they began instructing him in the suggestive devices the Eirydi used to program their minds before entering the trance state. Many more hours of lessons passed before he gained some mastery over these, but his teachers would not let him become discouraged. In truth, his progress was beyond what they had expected.

Penderyn was amazed by the clarity of the images he saw when in the embrace of the *iffirium*, even though they were still just random pictures that as yet had no meaning. With each day he grew more positive about controlling his dream power, until he dared to let himself think that one day it might indeed be the key he and Jarrowon had been hoping for.

"The task we begin today is far more difficult than anything we've done do far," Erowil warned. They were seated in the same chamber where Penderyn's lessons had begun, ready to embark on the second phase of his training. "Even I, Queen of the Eirydi, am not always successful in calling forth a dream on a chosen matter."

Penderyn recognized the tone of frustration that crept into his grandmother's voice.

"Never have my limitations been clearer to me than this last week," she continued. "Each night, I have exhausted myself trying to summon a vision of your future, yet I've seen nothing. Your fate is hidden from me, and from others of my people who I've asked to try as well. I can only hope that somehow you yourself will find the key to unlock what lies before you."

"Already I believe I've seen glimpses of my destiny," Penderyn said. "Perhaps what I'm learning will enable me to see these things more clearly." He paused for a moment. "If not, I will have to follow my path in darkness, but follow it I shall."

Erowil's heart swelled with love and pride at her grandson's noble bearing. Her anguish over the loss of her daughter, already lessened by Penderyn's arrival, was reduced still further, for Feyitha's road had led her to give birth to this brave young lad. Even her anger toward Horglim softened. Perhaps he had somehow known that their daughter's destiny lay elsewhere, though he had no dream power of his own. She puzzled over the matter for a moment before returning her attention to Penderyn.

"To summon a dream about a specific matter is completely opposite what you have learned so far," she explained. "Instead of emptying your mind, you must concentrate totally upon the subject you wish to see. Your every thought must lock on one key element of that subject, whether it is a person, a place or an incident. Nothing can be allowed to distract you; all your energy must focus on the thing you have chosen. You must not even think of falling asleep. Then and only then will you have a chance to see what you desire."

"Is that the main reason for failure, then?" Penderyn asked. "That one's concentration was not complete when sleep arrived?"

Erowil shook her head. "That is but one of many obstacles. Sometimes you fail because you made the wrong choice of the key element. You can try changing that element. Perhaps a different person or incident will be the key that will unlock the dream you seek. Unfortunately, there's no way to know what to choose except by trial."

"And if many changes still fail to bring forth the dream I seek?"

Erowil flashed a thin smile. "Then the knowledge you seek may simply not be available to you. In that case, you must meet your fate as other men do, blindly and unforewarned."

But he was not as other men, Penderyn thought to himself. Already he had been given a glimpse of what lay ahead through the Rhynn of the Last Born. Salvation or Doom—those were his birthrights. He prayed his power would provide him further clues, for he was unsure he had the courage or wisdom to succeed unaided.

CHAPTER 18

"You've come a long way, Penderyn," Erowil said as she and Orith reviewed his progress in the quiet chamber behind the throne room. The three of them had just returned from Orith's cavern, where the Last Born had achieved his biggest success so far.

Penderyn smiled, delighted that his grandmother thought so highly of him.

"Your dream about where Orith would hide your arrow was exactly right," the queen continued.

"You told me he would put it somewhere in his bedchamber," Penderyn said modestly. "It wasn't all that hard to find."

Orith smiled at his young friend. "It wasn't finding the arrow that was important, Penderyn. It was seeing me hide it in your dream that mattered."

"I know it seems only a little thing," Erowil added, "since you knew what he would be hiding and which room he would choose. But it was an important first step. You summoned a dream about an event that had not yet occurred. Orith could have put the arrow anywhere in his chamber, yet you dreamed of him placing it under his bedding."

Penderyn finally realized why they were both so pleased. His feat had seemed so simple he had missed the real point. He had just called forth his first dream!

"You're right!" he said excitedly. "I can do it!"

Erowil and Orith smiled knowingly at each other.

"Don't get too carried away," Orith cautioned. "It isn't always so easy. The real future is far more complex than our little practice."

"Still, we're pleased you've come this far," Erowil said. "And we have two more days to work with you. But now it's time for bed."

Penderyn kissed his grandmother and said goodnight to Orith.

"Don't forget the dream I asked you to try tonight," Orith reminded him. "It will be more difficult with a place you have never seen."

Penderyn nodded and hurried from the room, anxious put his newfound skill to the test.

"He's done remarkably well for so short a time," Erowil said proudly when Penderyn was gone. She was surprised to see a very serious expression on Orith's face and looked at him questioningly.

"Maybe too well," Orith replied, somewhat ominously.

Erowil looked at him sharply. "What is it?" she asked worriedly. "What are you saying?"

"I'm not quite sure. This morning, I had planned to hide Penderyn's arrow in amongst my own. Yet I ended up putting it beneath my bedding, rather than where I had intended." Orith frowned. "There have been times I've sensed an unfamiliar facet to his power, a hint of strength far greater than anything we possess."

"I know," Erowil said. "I have felt it, too. That morning he convinced me he was one of us, he projected *his* dream into my head. None of us has that ability. And when our minds linked, I sensed powerful magic. And yet, I have no doubt that he's my grandson."

"Nor do I," replied Orith. "He's one of us, but more somehow. How this has affected his power, I hope to find out."

Erowil looked at him suspiciously, becoming protective of her grandson. "What are you going to do?" she asked.

Orith smiled at her protectiveness. "Don't worry, my Queen.

I'm as fond of him as you are. I want to help him all we can. But to do that, we must learn everything we can in the time remaining."

He paused for a moment, wondering if he should let Erowil in on what he was planning.

"I described the old spring where we used to swim when I was child to Penderyn. I told him we would be visiting it tomorrow. He's never been there. I asked him to try to summon a dream about it."

"I know the place," Erowil recalled with a fond smile. "I used to swim there too, long before you were born. But that spring has been dry for years."

"You and I both know that, but Penderyn doesn't."

Erowil looked at him questioningly, but said nothing.

Penderyn's face was flush with excitement when he joined Erowil and Orith in the throne room the next morning.

"I did it," he announced proudly. "I summoned a dream about our visit to the spring today." He turned to Erowil. "I didn't know you were coming grandmother, until I saw you in my dream."

Erowil and Orith exchanged wondering glances.

"Well, you're right, Penderyn," Erowil replied. "I will be coming. What else did you see?"

"Oh, no," he said with a laugh, seeming very much a child again. "That would spoil the fun. You'll have to trust me to tell you later if my dream was correct."

"Very well," Erowil said. "But you must promise not to be disappointed if you are wrong."

Penderyn's grin vanished momentarily. He looked toward Orith, and his smile reappeared.

"I hope I'm not," he said happily.

They descended from the cliff by way of a crude stairway cut into a tunnel at the rear of Erowil's caverns. When they emerged onto the valley floor, Orith took the lead, guiding them along a well-worn path that circled the eastern shore of the lake. In deference to Erowil, he set a more leisurely pace than when he and Penderyn walked about the valley alone.

Penderyn found it difficult to restrain his excitement and chaffed at the slowness of the pace. He was eager to see if this second attempt at seeing the future, a much more difficult assignment than his first, would be as successful.

They soon turned off the main trail onto a path that was badly overgrown. Penderyn was puzzled. This new path looked as if it had once been as wide as the first, but the invading branches of small trees and thick shrubs had narrowed it considerably. He would have thought that the path leading to the beautiful, refreshing spring he had dreamed of would be much more worn by use.

"We're almost there," Orith announced as he bent a thorny branch and held it to the side while Erowil and Penderyn passed by. "The spring is just around that next bend, Penderyn."

Erowil smiled as they entered the clearing. She hadn't been here in many years, but it was just as she remembered it from her childhood, though more overgrown, of course. The almost triangular opening in forest was flanked on two sides by tall, straight evergreens whose thick canopy kept the forest floor fairly clear of underbrush. She breathed deeply of their strong, fresh scent. Soft piles of needles covered the dirt beneath their feet.

The third side of the triangle was formed by a tall cliff whose dark grey face was lined with cracks and ledges easy for children to climb. At the base of the cliff sat the spring. The queen remembered how much fun it was to dive from those ledges into that cool, clear water.

A sudden chill shook her body as she realized what she was seeing. This could not be. The spring had been dry for years. She turned quickly to Penderyn. Her grandson was watching Orith stride rapidly across the clearing to the spring. She followed his gaze.

Penderyn struggled to hold back the laughter that threatened to burst from his slender frame. He watched closely as Orith stepped onto a flat rock at the edge of the spring and bent to scoop some of the water into his hand. Suddenly the rock gave way, and Orith tumbled into the water with a loud splash.

"That's it!" Penderyn laughed excitedly. "That's what I dreamed!" He turned to his grandmother. "That's why I couldn't tell you what I saw. Orith might have been too careful, and he wouldn't have fallen in."

Erowil smiled, but Penderyn saw a strange look in her eyes. He wondered if he'd done something wrong.

They watched Orith climb from the spring and shake as much water as possible from his clothes and hair.

"I was here late yesterday," he said in response to Erowil's inquiring look when he rejoined them. "It was dry."

Penderyn was puzzled. What was Orith talking about? It had been Orith who described this spot to him, with its beautiful spring. What did he mean it had been dry?

Orith placed a damp hand on Penderyn's shoulder. "We'd better sit down and talk about this," he said.

"I'm sorry," Penderyn said worriedly. "I didn't think you'd be upset with me for not warning you."

Erowil smiled. "We're not angry with you, Penderyn. We just do not understand what just happened. You see, this spring has been dry for years."

Penderyn looked confusedly from Erowil to Orith.

"I described the spring as it used to be," Orith said. "It was a test. Erowil and I have both sensed that your power differs in some ways from ours. If what I suspect is true, then your dreams not only foresee the future, they sometimes create it."

Penderyn did not understand. How could a mere dream create the future? Maybe the gods ordained what was to be, but not young boys. It just wasn't possible. Last night's dream had seemed no different than any of his others. Did that mean that all his dreams had caused what he had foreseen? His head began to spin as he recalled his dream about his mother's death.

"Nooooo!" he screamed, sobbing uncontrollably.

Erowil hugged him tightly to her breast. "It's all right, Penderyn," she soothed. "We're here with you. It's all right."

He remained wrapped in her embrace for several moments. Gradually his sobbing diminished, until at last he was able to stop. Erowil gently wiped the tears from his face.

"What is it, Penderyn?" she asked softly. "What troubles you so?"

"My mother," he replied haltingly. "If my dreams create the future, then I..." He could not finish the awful thought.

Erowil cradled his cheeks in her palms and looked directly into his eyes. Her voice was firm, certain. "No, my grandson, you were not responsible for Aeta's fate. She had the same vision herself, long before you were born. You showed me her dream, remember?"

Penderyn breathed out a big sigh of relief. He did remember. His dream could not have been the cause of his mother's death.

"Not all your dreams create," Orith explained. "Most are like ours, merely indications of what may come."

"But how can I know the difference?"

"I do not know," Orith admitted. "I do not know."

They returned to the cliff city in silence, each of their minds filled with thoughts about their startling discovery. Penderyn struggled to understand the meaning and consequences of what he had learned, while Erowil and Orith wondered if there was anything they could do to help him with this immense new power. None of them were very successful in their endeavors.

"Sit down, Penderyn," Erowil instructed when they reached the cavern where most of Penderyn's training had taken place.

The room somehow seemed smaller to Penderyn as he took a seat on one of the padded chairs. Erowil seated herself opposite him. Orith stood by her side.

"I am afraid we may not be able to help you control this new aspect of your power," Erowil said after a moment. "I do not see how any of our methods apply."

She looked questioningly toward Orith, who shook his head.

"Nor can I," Orith said resignedly.

Penderyn looked at them blankly. He did not understand. The Eirydi were masters of dreams. Why couldn't they help him?

Erowil and Orith sensed his confusion.

"I'll try to explain," the queen began. "When we summon a dream, we are gathering vibrations and energy that already exist. We merely collect the strands and focus them. If we are successful, then our minds can visualize these pre-existing strands. That's what you've been learning to do this past week. But sometimes, your dreams are different. Somehow, they create their own energy and then transmit it into the collection of vibrations that make up all possible futures. How you can do this, I have no idea. We can only direct our dreams toward the energies we wish to gather; how to direct your dreams to create new energy is beyond our knowledge."

"What we have taught you can direct your dreams toward a specific subject," Orith added, "but it cannot tell them to create new energies. That is something you will have to learn to do on your own. Until then, we believe it will only happen by chance."

Penderyn nodded, understanding some, but not all of what they were saying.

How ironic, he thought, that when he finally began to learn to control one power, he discovered a new, greater power that remained beyond his control. There was nothing he could do about it, though. He would have to try to push it from his mind for now and learn what he could from the Eirydi in the day that was left to him.

Penderyn found it hard to believe his two weeks were already over. In a short while he would be leaving Gaelin Mirrosil, perhaps forever. All that remained was to make his farewells to Erowil, Orith and the other friends he had made among the Eirydi.

He had learned much in his fortnight here. He was able to slip into the *iffirium* almost at will now, and had made progress in directing his dreams as well. Though it would take much practice before he was skilled at this, he knew he had the basic knowledge he needed. It was what he and his comrades had hoped for when they set out from Kfastia more than a month before.

When he entered the throne room, Erowil and Orith were awaiting him. Orith was dressed and armed for one of his frequent hunts into the valley, and Penderyn was glad that his friend had delayed his hunt until they had the chance to say farewell.

Erowil descended quickly from her throne. Though her lips were curved into a smile, Penderyn saw the deep emotion etched into her features as she hurried toward him and embraced him tightly. Neither spoke as they hugged. Penderyn's eyes began to mist as he held his grandmother. She had given him a kind of love he had not felt since his mother's death.

Finally, Erowil broke the embrace. Her eyes were filled with tears. She wiped the tears away and tried to smile. When she spoke, her voice was choked with emotion.

"Your stay with us has been all too brief, my grandson. But you have breathed new life into my heart and finally allowed me to put to sleep the ghosts of my past. For that alone I shall be eternally grateful." Her voice grew stronger as she continued. "Though you must bid us farewell to follow your destiny, know that you will always be in my heart and in my prayers."

"And you will never be far from me, grandmother," Penderyn replied. "Thoughts of you will be always in my mind, as will the lessons you've taught me."

Erowil leaned forward and kissed him on the cheek. "Others have grown fond of you as well," she said with a smile. "One so much that he has made a rare request. Stand forth, Orith, and speak your request."

As Orith approached them, Penderyn wondered what kind of request his friend was going to make.

"My queen has graciously given me leave to make this offer," Orith said. "Should you wish it, I would like to come with you when you leave Gaelin Mirrosil."

Stunned voices whispered through the throne room. No one had left the valley in centuries, save for Feyitha and Horglim.

Penderyn could scarcely believe what he had heard. A big smile lit up his face.

"That's wonderful," he said. "Never did I dare hope that you might join me. I thought you were dressed for another hunt."

"Now you will have someone to confide in who understands your power," Erowil said. "I ask only that you reveal Orith's true nature to none but those you trust completely. Let the world continue to think that the Eirydi are but a legend of the past."

"I will guard his secret closely," Penderyn promised.

"Now, it's time for you to leave us," Erowil said. "Come, let your grandmother kiss you one last time, and then be on your way. Long good-byes do not make farewells any less painful."

Penderyn and Erowil embraced once more, squeezing each other tightly. Finally, Erowil ended the embrace and pushed Penderyn gently toward the cavern's entrance.

"Farewell, grandson," she said. "I shall pray that the gods watch over you."

Penderyn walked slowly toward the daylight. When he reached the outside of the cavern he turned and waved. "Good-bye, grandmother," he called.

Eyes still misty, he stepped onto ledge and followed Orith to the secret tunnel out of the valley.

They stopped in front of the opening and took one last look back at Gaelin Mirrosil. Penderyn was saddened by the realization that he might never again visit this lovely land. He imagined the thoughts that must be going through Orith's mind as he prepared to leave his homeland for the very first time.

"Let's go, my friend," Orith said finally, "while I'm still able to. My resolve weakens by the moment."

Without waiting for a reply, he spun around and entered the dim cavern. Penderyn followed quickly behind him.

CHAPTER 19

Penderyn took the lead when he and Orith emerged from the hidden tunnel. Now that Gaelin Mirrosil lay behind them, his sadness at departing gave way to mounting excitement about rejoining his comrades. His eagerness propelled him rapidly up the steep, rocky trail.

"I'm very glad your legs are shorter than mine, Penderyn," Orith puffed after a few minutes. "I'm almost running as it is to keep up."

Penderyn paused for a rest. "I'm sorry," he said, grinning. "My eagerness seems to have lent wings to my feet." His chest heaved as he gulped at the thin mountain air. "Unfortunately, it hasn't increased the size of my lungs."

"I was beginning to wonder about that," Orith replied, smiling despite his own labored breathing.

"I'll slow down," Penderyn said between breaths. "We'll find my friends soon, I'm sure, and I'll want to have breath enough to greet them."

They resumed their journey at a more moderate pace. Even so, Penderyn almost crashed into Tal and Dal when the twins came hurrying around a sharp bend in the trail. He had not expected to see them here, on this side of the arch.

"You two seem in an awful hurry," he said cheerfully. "If you're on the trail of some pretty maiden, I'm afraid she's given you the slip. We've passed no one on the way up."

The twins laughed.

"In that case, we'll settle for you," Tal said. "After two weeks, even you look good."

"Has it really been two weeks?" Penderyn teased, his voice filled with boyish innocence.

Jarrowon appeared behind the twins, followed by Cornon and Olidar.

"Your friends have made certain of that," the lore master said. "It was all I could do to make them wait the full fortnight. At dawn, we left the horses below the arch and followed your path."

"Not that we were worried about you," Dal said quickly. "But we were growing tired of sitting in these mountains with nothing to do."

Cornon stepped past the twins and clasped Penderyn by the arms. "I'm not ashamed to say I'm glad to see you," he said warmly, "nor that I was beginning to worry as the end of the fortnight drew near."

"And I'm glad to see all of you," Penderyn replied. "I'm sorry I cut it so fine, but there was much to do." In the excitement of seeing his friends, Penderyn realized he had forgotten Orith. He apologized and introduced him to the others.

"Orith is of the Eirydi," he explained. "I've promised we'll keep his identity to ourselves. His people wish their existence to remain a secret."

"Welcome to our company, Orith," Jarrowon said. "From the tales I've heard of your people, I can well understand your desire to remain hidden." He turned to Penderyn. "Since you travel with one of the Eirydi, can I assume your quest was successful?"

"I've learned much these past days," Penderyn replied, "though in some ways I wish I'd learned nothing."

He explained Orith's discovery that his dreams not only saw into the future, but sometimes carried the power to create the future. And that he had no way to control what they created.

His companions looked at him in astonishment. Such power

was difficult to comprehend.

"I can't even tell the difference between the dreams," Penderyn said ruefully. "I may be the cause of more trouble than we know."

Jarrowon draped his arm around Penderyn's shoulders, his heart filled with compassion for the Last Born. More than anyone, the lore master understood the terrible possibilities inherent in such uncontrolled power.

"Power is often a double-edged sword," he said.

Salvation or doom; blessing or bane. The words from the Rhynn of the Last Born echoed in Penderyn's head. He wondered which he was fated to be.

"There's nothing we can do about any of this now," Jarrowon continued. "All we can do is return to Kfastia and hope that Orith can help you learn more about your power."

Cornon took the lead as the company walked single back along the narrow trail toward the arch and the horses waiting below. They were glad to see their mounts had remained close to where they had left them. Within a few minutes, their gear was packed and they were astride their horses.

The hours seemed to drag by endlessly as they journeyed back toward Kfastia, all but Orith wondering anxiously what might have transpired during their long absence. With so many leagues to cover, they couldn't push their mounts too rapidly and had to be satisfied with long hours of riding each day.

Penderyn was reluctant to test his newfound powers by summoning a dream, afraid of what the consequences might be. In the back of his mind, he still wondered what ill fortune he might already have caused. Instead, he contented himself with practicing the *iffirium* each night before he fell asleep, hoping that any unsummoned dreams would be clear. For better or worse, his sleep remained undisturbed by visions.

As his eagerness to reach Kfastia increased, his desire to

know what was happening in his adopted homeland grew with it. He knew Halibur's ambition could not long be held in check and wondered how Arista was faring. Finally, his impatience and anxiety outweighed his reluctance to chance summoning dream. He decided to try his skill.

That night, he spread his bedding a little farther from the others than usual, so he might lie undisturbed. After wrapping himself tightly in his warm woolen blanket, he began to concentrate as Erowil had taught him. He chose Arista as his key, focusing all his thoughts on the Sumara.

At first, the sounds of the night filtered through his concentration. The mournful howl of some far off beast of prey, the crackling and sputtering of their campfire, even the rustling of the cool wind registered in his brain. But he persisted, and gradually his trance deepened, until he no longer felt even the hard, rough ground beneath his back. His physical being ceased to exist. He had become energy, nothing more, focused entirely on Arista.

He awoke to the sounds of Tal adding wood to the fire in preparation for their morning meal. Sitting up in his blanket, he wiped the sleep from his eyes. He had the feeling that something was missing. For a moment it eluded him, but then he remembered. He had tried to summon a dream about Arista. He closed his eyes and searched his memory, but his mind was blank. He had not dreamed at all. He sighed and got to his feet.

Night after night, he tried to summon a dream about what was happening in Kfastia, each time varying the key element as Erowil had suggested. Chirops, Valdor, even Kfastia itself became his focus, but none produced any result.

Frustrated, he tried to think of some new key while he rode, but could not. Finally, he turned to Orith for advice.

"Remember first," Orith reminded him after the Last Born edged his mount alongside and explained his problem, "that the vision you seek may not be within your reach. Also, that you are still new at this most difficult skill."

"Both thoughts have crossed my mind," Penderyn admitted. "But I don't think either is the answer. Somehow I sense that what I seek is there and that I have but to chose the proper key to find it."

"Describe the situation in Kfastia once more for me," Orith said. "Perhaps I'll be able to suggest something you've missed." He listened closely, straining to hear every word over the thudding hoof beats of the horses, as Penderyn explained Arista's troubles.

"It seems there's but one key left to try," he said after a few moments of thought. "The cause of the problem is Halibur. Why not use him?"

"I thought of that, but I've never met Halibur. How can I concentrate on the image of a man I've never seen?"

"Have any of your comrades met him?"

Penderyn's eyes brightened at his friend's question. "Cornon and Olidar must have met him many times," he said excitedly.

"Ask them to describe Halibur for you. If he is indeed the key, then the image from their description will be enough."

Penderyn squeezed Surefoot's flanks with his knees to urge the horse to quicken his pace. When he reached Cornon's side at the head of the company, he explained his need for a description of Halibur. Cornon nodded and called Olidar to join them. Together the two warriors described the Lord of Colgoth in great detail, while Penderyn formed a picture in his mind. When he described the image back to his friends, they smiled.

"It sounds as if you've seen him with your own eyes," Cornon said. "If you're successful with your dream, let us know what you see. We're all anxious about Kfastia."

That night, Penderyn locked his thoughts on Halibur. Slowly his concentration deepened, until his mind blocked out all invading thoughts. He drifted off to sleep with a vision of the Lord of Colgoth before his eyes.

He was enveloped in blackness. Deep and impenetrable. A faint light appeared in the center of the darkness. Slowly it brightened, expanding in size. The glow revealed the outline of a man. The image became steadily clearer. He was dressed for battle, mounted upon a black horse. A flaming red pennant streamed behind him. Finally, his face grew clear. It was Halibur.

The light widened. Halibur was surrounded by warriors. Thousands of them. Some wore uniforms of gray, some of gold. Many wore no uniform. These were cloaked in brown, black, and green. In front of them stood a giant, black-bearded man. An aura of pure evil emanated from him.

The army moved forward, warriors and ruffians alike. In front of them rose the walls of a city—Kfastia! From the city's gate issued a column of scarlet clad warriors. They were hopelessly outnumbered. The armies clashed together. Screams of pain and the ring of metal filled the air. For a moment, the scarlet defenders pushed their foes back, but then the weight of numbers began to tell. Their advance slowed and then stopped. The enemy surrounded them. Defeat was inevitable.

Penderyn awoke with a shudder. His body was chill and drenched with sweat. Anxiously he looked around him, unsure of his surroundings. He saw the glowing embers of the campfire and the still forms of his companions, asleep in their blankets. He realized he'd been dreaming. A dream he himself had summoned. But at what cost?

Doubt and torment flooded over him. Had he witnessed the future? Or had he created it? He cursed his dreams, wondering if the destruction of his adopted city now rested on his shoulders. How much more suffering might he cause with his uncontrolled power?

He tossed fitfully under his blanket. There was no escaping his magic, he knew. But until now his dreams had been few and far between. Dare he risk more misfortune by trying to summon them? He recalled the *Luminari's* warning about danger from within. Had they known about this terrible power hidden inside him? Was a possible glimpse of the future worth the risk of the ill he might create?

The future would come whether he saw it or not; there was no reason to tempt fate by employing a power he could not control. He swore to himself he would not do so again.

He could not ignore what he had already seen, though. He threw his blanket aside and moved to wake his comrades so he could tell them of his grim vision. He woke the twins first and told them what he was about to do. Dal threw some more wood on the fire to ward off the morning cold while Tal and Penderyn woke the others. In just a few minutes, they were all gathered around the fire.

Penderyn's friends listened in stunned silence as he recounted his dream. Cornon's face twisted into an angry scowl as the Last Born described the battle. Both he and Olidar stood up and turned toward their horses.

"We must return with all haste," he said. "We will be needed."

"Wait, Cornon," Jarrowon cautioned. "Too much haste could prove to be our undoing. I think we can spare a few moments to discuss what Penderyn has seen."

Cornon was reluctant to waste any time at all, but recognized the wisdom of the lore master's words. He nodded to Olidar, and the two warriors rejoined their comrades by the fire.

Jarrowon turned to Orith. "You know dreams far better than the Last Born. Must what he has seen come to pass?"

"Each of our dreams is only one possible future," Orith

explained. "There are always others." He hesitated, and then his voice turned grim. "But what is seen is always the most probable."

"Can what was seen be changed?" Jarrowon asked.

"Only the past cannot be changed," Orith replied. "The future is never certain until it happens. But what action might best alter the future is difficult to know."

Penderyn sat quietly, his heart filled with grief, while his comrades discussed the matter. For the moment, they seemed to have forgotten that his dream may not have been an ordinary dream. But he could not forget. He might have created future he had foreseen.

"So our presence could make a difference," Cornon said.

"It might," Orith agreed. "But it might also be the event that triggers Penderyn's vision into being."

For a long moment, no one said anything. There seemed no way to know what action to choose.

"Penderyn, did you see any of us in your vision?" Cornon asked finally.

The sound of his name drew the Penderyn from his silent torment. He shook his head. "No, none of us appeared in my dream. I saw only two faces clearly—Halibur and the black-bearded giant whose evil touched me even in my dream." He described the man again, but no one knew who he might be.

"Then we must go, and go quickly," Jarrowon decided. "With nothing else to guide us, I think it best we be there to do what we may."

They pushed their mounts as rapidly as they dared through the forest, but it still took several days of hard riding before they reached the borders of Calistan. The horses were nearly spent, forcing their anxious riders to slacken the pace.

Near midday, their mounts' coats slick with sweat, they stopped at a small stream to let the horses rest and drink. The weary riders took advantage of the break to slake their thirst with the cold, refreshing water and to wash the sweat and dirt from their faces and arms. Were they not in such a hurry, they might have rinsed their grimy clothes as well, but instead contented themselves with beating the dust from their cloaks and tunics and then spreading them to air upon the branches of the small trees that grew at the stream's edge.

While they refreshed themselves, Tal spotted four Kfastian warriors leading their horses slowly through the woods. The soldiers were studying the ground carefully, apparently tracking someone or something, and they had not yet noticed the company's presence.

Tal called his comrades' attention to the new arrivals. At the sound of his voice, the approaching warriors looked up quickly. They stared at the company in surprise for a moment before leaping astride their horses and disappearing in the direction they had come.

"I don't understand," Cornon said, puzzled by the behavior of his countrymen. "They may not have recognized us from that distance, but they could not have mistaken our uniforms."

"Perhaps the riders were not what they appeared to be," Jarrowon cautioned. "We'd best be ready, just in case."

"They wore Kfastian uniforms," Dal protested. "Who else could they be but soldiers of Kfastia?"

"A man may don the skin of a gryth," Jarrowon replied, "but that does not make him one."

"We'll know soon enough," Penderyn said loudly. "Look there!"

He pointed into the trees, where more than a score of mounted warriors were now visible. All wore the familiar scarlet uniforms, and all had their swords ready as they advanced toward the outnumbered company.

Tal fit an arrow to his bow. Penderyn, Orith and Dal followed his lead.

Tal looked toward Cornon. "If they mean to attack, our only chance is to lower the odds before it comes to swords. It's up to you and Olidar. Do you recognize any of them?"

Cornon peered hard into the trees. "The shadows hide their faces," he said. "I cannot say."

"Me either," Olidar added.

They waited nervously, fingers wrapped tightly around their bows, as Cornon and Olidar tried desperately to recognize any of the oncoming warriors through the shadowy wood. Penderyn could feel his grip beginning to sweat as the soldiers drew closer. Soon it would be too late.

The four archers drew back their bowstrings, awaiting only a command from Cornon to fire, but he remained silent.

"Wait!" he shouted finally. "Put down your bows. I recognize their commander."

His comrades sighed in relief as they as they lowered their weapons. Cornon stepped forward to meet the patrol.

"Traimar, what is the meaning of this?" he demanded.

"I'm sorry, Cornon," Traimar replied. "I did not recognize you." He ordered his men to sheath their weapons.

"Did you not see our uniforms? Have you gone blind since I left?"

"Things are not as you left them, my friend," Traimar replied grimly. "Uniforms are no longer enough to prove friendship. Two days ago, ten of our warriors were ambushed not far from here. Only one man escaped to report the massacre. When we found the bodies, they had been stripped. We were trailing the murderers when we came upon you."

"Does this mean Halibur has begun his attack?" Penderyn asked.

"Not openly," Traimar said, "but there are few who doubt he is behind these raids, which grow bolder and more brazen with each passing day."

"We have returned in time, then," Cornon said. His relief was evident in his voice and on his face, despite the ill news reported by Traimar.

"A party as small as yours would be an inviting target," Traimar warned. "I can spare ten men to join you as an escort."
Cornon nodded, angry that such a state of affairs should have come to be in his country. "Thank you, Traimar. We'll be ready to leave in a few moments."

CHAPTER 20

Penderyn and his companions returned to a changed city. A somber pall of anger and sadness hung over Kfastia as its citizens went quietly about their daily business. The warm spring sun that bathed the city seemed to have no effect on the sullen faces of the people the company passed as they made their way home.

Cornon and Olidar felt the depression most keenly, for the dark mood was emphasized by memories of other, more joyful springs. But the change was not lost on Penderyn or the others, and the Last Born's desire to help his adopted home was fanned anew. Though he had forsaken his dream power, he was tempted to ride to Colgoth and confront Halibur face to face, a foolish and dangerous idea, he knew.

The city's troubles did not dampen the joy with which Valdor and Thrisa welcomed them home, though.

After a series of warm embraces and the introduction of Orith, Thrisa insisted they clean and refresh themselves before doing anything else. Cornon tried to protest, eager to learn what had been going on during their absence, but his mother insisted, declaring that another hour would make no difference to anyone. Cornon turned to his comrades and meekly shrugged his shoulders.

When they had washed and soaked the weariness from their bodies, they gathered at the long wooden table in the dining hall, where cool drink and a light meal awaited them.

Penderyn briefly described his stay among the Eirydi to his hosts, cautioning them to make no mention of the dream seers' existence to anyone else. He told them of the dream that weighed so heavily on all their minds and promised to recount the details of their journey later. First though, they were eager to be brought up to date on the machinations of Halibur.

"Things do not go well," Valdor admitted in a somber tone. "Winter's end brought little of the relief we'd hoped for. The warmer weather brought renewed raids upon our farms and outlying settlements, raids much bolder and closer to the city than before. We were forced to put the army on full alert. Patrols have been increased and squads of warriors are now billeted among the farms. Also, random stops are made of anyone traveling about the region.

"Our measures have stemmed the raids, but the people feel as though they're living in a conquered nation, their every move watched and checked by the army. Halibur is a clever man. His schemes have not allowed the discontent of winter to ebb; instead of hunger and want, he has substituted a far more damaging condition—the loss of freedom."

Penderyn grew angry at Valdor's descriptions. "Can't you do anything to Halibur?" he asked.

Valdor shook his head. "Not yet. He has not even renewed his claims to the throne. His spies spread rumors that our enemies come from foreign lands and raise questions about why our Sumara cannot protect her people. The raiders lend credence to this view by attacking the settlements of all our cities, even Colgoth's."

"Halibur has had his own people killed?" Tal asked incredulously.

"Until last week, yes," Valdor said. "Halibur is a ruthless and diabolical scoundrel. The lives of a few score of his people mean nothing to him."

"You said 'until last week,'" Cornon said. "What happened then?"

"Halibur officially broke from the Sumara, saying that since she could not even protect her city, he would take his own steps to protect his. The action was more symbolic than anything else, since he has not listened to Arista for some time."

"And I suppose now that Halibur has split with Arista, the raids against Colgoth have miraculously stopped," Jarrowon said.

"Exactly. And his supporters are beginning to say that we, too, would be safe if Halibur was the Sumar."

Cornon was furious. "Does he think to deceive us with such obvious treachery?"

"Not us," Valdor replied. "He knows he cannot fool us. His words are aimed at the common people, the farmers and merchants whose only concerns are for the safety of their families and their goods."

"In an ironic way, Halibur is right," Thrisa added. "The raids *would* stop if he were Sumar."

"There has to be something we can do," Penderyn insisted.

"We could attack Colgoth," Valdor replied, "but that would make us appear the aggressor and lessen any chance we have of being supported by Legas or Dewellyn. Their armies may ultimately be the difference, since Kfastia and Colgoth are fairly equal in strength." He shook his head and sighed. "No, our best chance now seems to be to hope that part of your dream does come true. If Halibur attacks, all will know the true aggressor. We'll just have to pray that the end of your dream does not come true as well."

"What of all the warriors I saw who didn't wear Halibur's uniform?" Penderyn asked worriedly.

"If he indeed has secret allies, we'll have to hope there's

strength in righteousness, for we will be outnumbered."

Further discussion was interrupted by the sound of footsteps and voices in the front plaza. With the shutters on the windows thrown open to allow the warm spring air into the room, the company could see soldiers approaching the house. The warriors wore the insignia of the royal guard upon their scarlet tunics. Valdor and his guests hurried to the entrance hall to learn the meaning of this unusual visit.

At the door, the front rank of warriors slid to the side, revealing the yellow-robed figure of Arista. Penderyn stared in surprise. The Sumara had never visited them here.

The Last Born's astonishment was mirrored on the faces of his companions. His fear that something was amiss was reinforced by Valdor's rapid move toward Arista, but the Sumara laid their apprehensions to rest with a warm smile as she stepped into the house. A half dozen of her guards followed her inside; the rest took up positions outside the door. They were taking no chances with their Sumara's safety, even in the house of Valdor.

"I heard that our wanderers had returned," Arista said happily, "so I decided to welcome you back without waiting for you to come visit me. Besides, I don't get out of the palace nearly enough these days."

Arista's jesting tone and warm smile only partially concealed the effects wrought by her recent troubles. Penderyn was shocked to see how deep the lines of worry across the Sumara's brow and around her eyes had become in only two months. Despite her smile, he could see the sadness in her eyes and the traces of fatigue in her bearing. She even seemed to move more slowly than he remembered.

"I can't tell you how glad I am to see you all again," Arista continued. "I get good news so seldom these days, it's a welcome change."

"My father has just been telling us about that," Cornon said, his voice still edged with anger.

Arista waved him off the subject. "There'll be time enough to discuss my problems later. Right now, I want to hear about your journey. Did you learn what you sought to know, Penderyn?"

Penderyn drew in a deep breath. "In some ways, more than I wished," he replied.

Arista heard the torment in her young friend's voice and saw the pain in his eyes.

"Tell me, Penderyn," she said softly.

Penderyn described his stay among the Eirydi and the things he had learned about his power. Arista stopped him when he began to describe his most recent dream.

"We'll worry about that in a bit," she said. "But first, let's see if we can lighten the gloom that darkens your heart." She laid her hands softly upon his shoulders and lowered her head until her eyes were level with his.

"Do not hold yourself responsible for things you cannot control," she counseled. "It will only do you harm. Remember the good things you've learned—how to see your dreams more clearly and how to understand them better. And no longer must you wonder about your heritage, for you know now that the blood of the Eirydi flows in your veins. Think of these things when you despair."

Penderyn forced a smile to his lips. "I'll try, Your Majesty," he promised, "though only half of my questions have been answered. There's still my father to wonder about. But now, I must tell you of my dream."

He described his vision of Halibur's attack in as much detail as he could recall. Arista's expression remained stoic as she listened.

"I shall almost be glad when Halibur finally attacks," she sighed when Penderyn finished. "At least this waiting will be over and the matter settled." The first note of discouragement since she had arrived slipped into her voice. "If I cannot deal with someone like Halibur, perhaps I really am not fit to be Sumara."

The protests voiced by her friends were interrupted by the sudden arrival of a dirty, sweat-soaked warrior. His scarlet cloak was rent in several places and a crude rag bandage around his head was clotted with dried blood. Despite his evident exhaustion, he hurried across the floor to Arista.

The Sumara moved quickly toward him. "Selenus, what is it?"

Thrisa immediately dispatched servants to bring water and fresh bandages for the wounded man. Valdor pulled a chair from against the wall and set it behind Selenus.

"Sit, Selenus," Arista commanded, "then tell us what happened."

The warrior nodded and sank gratefully into the chair. He closed his eyes and took several deep breaths before speaking.

"We were attacked by raiders, Your Majesty. Not three hours out of Kfastia. Jodtho is dead."

His listeners were stunned. Jodtho was one of the Majhari.

Valdor's face was tight with fury. "Halibur has gone too far. Arista, we must act. Now."

Arista paced back and forth, her face twisted in a mixture of grief and anger.

"My heart agrees with you, Valdor," she said at last. "But my head tells me I need proof of Halibur's guilt. I cannot afford to be wrong about this."

"I have the proof you need, my Sumara," Selenus said.

All eyes turned back to the wounded warrior.

"I was returning to the caravan with a scouting patrol when the attack occurred," he explained. "When we heard the sounds of the battle, we spurred our horses. Our rush through the trees brought us headlong into a company of raiders waiting in the woods beyond sight of the battle. Though we were greatly outnumbered, it was too late to do anything but fight.

"My men defended themselves valiantly, but the numbers against us were too great. I fought my way to the man who seemed to be the enemy commander, determined that he at least should pay. During our struggle he threw aside his hood and I recognized his face. It was Bleen, one of Halibur's most trusted lieutenants."

"You are certain?" Arista asked.

"I served six months in Colgoth with our ambassador," Selenus replied. "I know Bleen well."

Arista looked to Valdor, who nodded in grim determination as Selenus continued his story.

"As soon as I recognized Bleen, I knew I had to bring the information to you at all costs. I ordered my remaining men to retreat. Our flight took us near the caravan. Already there were but few of our warriors left alive. A band of raiders tried to head us off, but my comrades dropped back to delay them, allowing me to escape." His voice dropped. "I have little doubt I'm the sole survivor, but at least my men did not die in vain."

"There were more than a hundred warriors with that caravan," Arista said sadly.

"And a Majhari," Valdor added.

"Halibur will deny Bleen's presence," Arista said.

"He'll not be able to deny the wound my sword opened in Bleen's left arm," Selenus said.

"Do you require further proof, Arista?" Valdor asked.

Arista's voice was firm with determination. "No, I do not. Halibur has gone too far this time." She turned to one of her guards. "Dispatch messengers to the Majhari," she ordered. "Tell them the Council meets at the palace in one hour."

The warrior hurried away.

"Send five hundred warriors to search the site of the massacre," she commanded a second guard. "There may be wounded left alive or further proof of Halibur's treachery."

"What was Jodtho doing outside of Kfastia?" Cornon asked when Arista was finished.

"I sent him on a special mission to Legas, to enlist Lord Mylar's support against Halibur. His departure was not widely known, yet he was attacked less than three hours after leaving the city. Unless the raiders came upon them by chance, there is a spy in the palace."

"I don't believe in that kind of chance," Valdor said.

"Nor do I," replied Arista. "Nor do I."

The Sumara turned and headed for the door. Valdor followed behind her.

"What do you think Arista will do?" Penderyn asked Cornon when Arista and Valdor were gone.

"I don't know," Cornon replied after a moment of thought. "The last thing she wants is a civil war, but she may no longer have any choice. She cannot let Halibur go unpunished for this."

"Perhaps this brutal massacre will draw Legas and Dewellyn to Kfastia's side," Jarrowon suggested.

"Perhaps, but Danustiri and Halibur have been keeping close counsel this past year," Cornon reminded them. "Even this may not be enough to turn Danustiri against his ally."

"I hope Arista chooses to attack," Penderyn said. "And the sooner the better."

His comrades turned to him, surprised by his grim frankness.

"Do you realize what you're saying?" Dal asked in disbelief.

"Yes," Penderyn replied. His face had grown very somber. "I have no desire for war, but in my dream Kfastia was attacked by Halibur. If Arista makes the first move, then my dream will have been wrong. Perhaps then the outcome will be different as well."

"I hope we find a better way to prove your vision false, Last Born," Jarrowon said. "In a war such as this, there can be no real victor."

*   *   *

The following days were hectic ones. Arista had stopped short of an immediate declaration of war, deciding that first the city should prepare itself as much as possible. The army's reserves were called to readiness, bringing Kfastia's total strength to more than ten thousand warriors. Hunting parties were sent into the forest to bring as much meat into the city as they could, to be dried and stored in the event of a siege. Those citizens who lived beyond the wall were ordered to be ready to move into Kfastia at a moment's notice.

Arista dispatched another envoy to Legas, guarded this time by five hundred warriors. The envoy carried a message detailing the massacre, including the presence of Bleen among the attackers. She asked for immediate aid, but knowing that Mylar might still be hesitant, implored him at least to prepare for war.

Penderyn, Tal and Dal asked to join the hunting parties so they could use their skills on Kfastia's behalf, but Arista forbade Penderyn from joining such dangerous duty. There was no telling when the raiders might strike next, and she felt the Last Born's life was far too valuable to risk merely to bring a bit more meat into the city's larders. Tal and Dal might go if they wished, but not Penderyn.

Penderyn insisted the twins go without him. He saw no reason they should stay behind just because he did. Cornon assured the twins he would look after Penderyn, and that Orith would remain with him as well. The need for meat was great, and after some hesitation, Tal and Dal agreed.

While the twins hunted, Penderyn and Orith joined Cornon's company of cavalry in their preparations for the coming war. They spent hours each day drilling with other squads upon the plain, and then spent still more time manning the defenses atop the wall. As he had promised Tal and Dal, Cornon was never far from Penderyn's side.

Just four days later, a scouting patrol reported that Halibur's army was marching from Colgoth. Whether this attack was part of his original plan or had been spurred by news of Arista's preparations did not matter. There was no longer any choice for the Sumara.

Calistan was at war.

CHAPTER 21

Penderyn waited anxiously with Jarrowon and Orith atop the parapet above the south gate, scarcely noticing the chill night wind blowing across his bare face and arms as he probed the darkness beyond the wall for some sign of Tal and Dal. He was growing more worried by the moment. The twins should have returned by now. Messengers had been dispatched to call the hunting parties back to the Kfastia as soon as word of Halibur's approach reached the city; all but Tal and Dal's group were safely back.

Already Penderyn could see the fires of Halibur's advance force winking in the blackness to the east; by morning the entire army could be in place. If the twins did not return soon, they might find their entry into the city blocked completely.

Penderyn cursed his helplessness. His friends might already be in trouble, he thought gravely. He began to pace. He wished he could do something beside wait.

"I know how you feel," Jarrowon said in answer to Penderyn's unspoken thoughts, "but there's nothing we can do."

"I should be out there with them," Penderyn replied guiltily, "not safely tucked behind these walls."

"Would our cause be bettered if you were out there as well?" the lore master asked.

Penderyn shook his head. He knew Jarrowon was right, but that didn't change the way he felt.

"Tal and Dal will be careful, even without knowing of Halibur's advance," Orith reminded him. "There's always been danger from the raiders to watch for."

"You should get some sleep, Last Born," Jarrowon advised. "Matters of import are almost certain to unfold tomorrow."

"You expect me to sleep, when I can't even stand still?" Penderyn asked as he resumed his pacing. A moment later he felt Orith's hand on his shoulder.

"Have you forgotten the *iffirium* already?" Orith asked with a smile. "With it, you can always sleep."

Penderyn stopped walking. He had forgotten. If only he could master the rest of his power as well as he had the *iffirium*. Then he could create a dream that would bring Tal and Dal safely back into the city. But he dared not risk the attempt—he was just as likely to dream them into greater disaster than whatever they now faced. But there was another thing he had forgotten: Orith's dream power.

"You're right," he said finally. "The *iffirium*, at least, I can control, though I don't dare try anything more. But your power isn't dangerous, Orith. Maybe you can learn something about Tal and Dal through a dream."

"I'll try," Orith promised.

"Thank you," Penderyn said.

He turned toward the stairs that led down from the parapet. Orith followed.

Jarrowon went with them, but after seeing Penderyn to his bedchamber, the lore master did not continue on to his own room. Instead, he walked slowly back out of the house.

He stood motionless in the dark plaza, arms folded across his chest as he gazed silently into the sky. Only a few stars pierced the ever-darkening canopy. Many sounds carried through the night air as Kfastia prepared for the coming day, but lost in thought, the lore master heard none of them.

Penderyn awoke before dawn, refreshed and alert. At least his power was good for something, he thought as he quickly rolled from under his warm covers into the cool morning air. The *iffirium* had given him a night of unbroken sleep, despite his worries about Tal and Dal, but now that he was awake his anxiety was greater than ever.

He hurriedly donned his scarlet uniform. The bustling sounds filtering into his bedchamber told him the household was already astir, which surprised him not at all. Much would be happening today, but right now he was more concerned with the safety of his friends.

If Tal and Dal had returned during the night, he knew they would have awakened him immediately, no matter what the hour. He didn't even bother to check their rooms as he strode from his chamber down the long marble hallway to see whether Orith had met with any success.

Orith was dressed and waiting for him. The look of disappointment in his eyes when Penderyn appeared told the Last Born all he needed to know.

"I'm sorry, Penderyn," Orith said, shaking his head. "I saw nothing. I'll try again tonight."

"Tonight may be too late," Penderyn said impatiently, angered by his inability to do anything for his friends. "I should have gone to look for them yesterday, while I could still leave the city."

"Scouts who know this land better than you failed to find them," Orith reminded him. "You would have fared no better, and we'd have you trapped out there as well."

Orith was right, Penderyn knew, but he still could not rid himself of his guilt. His thoughts were interrupted by the arrival of Jarrowon.

"I see by your face that you've learned nothing of Tal and Dal," Jarrowon said to Penderyn. "And I can guess you're blaming yourself for not helping them."

"Do you read minds as well as old scrolls, lore master,"

Penderyn asked, unable to keep a trace of anger out of his voice.

Jarrowon pretended not to notice. "Such power is beyond my humble abilities," he said, smiling. "But I do know Arista's mind. She has sent a message requesting our presence."

"And do you know why as well?" Penderyn asked, unwilling to be cheered so easily.

"The Sumara and the Majhari are on their way to the wall," Jarrowon explained. "They wish us to join them. You have seen a vision of this war, Last Born. You can tell Arista whether events unfold as you foresaw them."

Penderyn studied the lore master's wrinkled face. He was not certain this was the real reason for the invitation, suspecting instead that Jarrowon and Arista sought to keep him well away from danger should the battle begin today. But the lore master's face was an unreadable mask. Penderyn would learn nothing there.

"When do we go?" he asked.

"Valdor awaits us."

Penderyn surveyed the sprawling enemy encampment from the battlements above the eastern gate. He never imagined the invading army would be so immense. Their tents formed a sea of brown and gray hundreds of yards wide. They stretched in a long arc that encircled the entire eastern half of Kfastia like a giant, living claw. The nearest of the tents was but half a mile from the wall.

From his vantage point, Penderyn could see patrols of enemy cavalry riding to guard the north and south flanks, and he knew only too well they must also be blockading the city from the west. Kfastia was sealed off. If Tal and Dal's hunting party had escaped capture, there was no way they could enter the city by day. Even under cover of darkness it would be risky to attempt to cross the plain, but perhaps it could be done.

A few feet to Penderyn's right, Arista studied the same scene.

Beside her stood Valdor and General Kriselor, the commander of Kfastia's army, while the rest of the Majhari gathered nearby. Jarrowon and Orith watched on Penderyn's left.

The enemy camp was filled with movement, but there was nothing that looked to be any kind of preparation for an imminent attack.

"They're fortifying their encampment," General Kriselor announced after surveying the activity for a few moments. He smiled grimly. "It would seem they intend to remain awhile."

"What would your plan be if you were Halibur?" Arista asked her general.

"I'd do exactly what he's doing. There's no chance for a surprise attack, so I'd make sure of the strength of my own position. I do not think he'll attack for a few days, at least."

"Perhaps we should attack instead," Jaspar suggested.

"No," Arista said immediately. Her voice was adamant. "I will not strike the first blow. We are comfortable here in our city, while Halibur's men must live in tents. We shall wait."

"But we cannot wait forever," General Kriselor pointed out. "Our stores of food are low after the ravages of the winter. Sooner or later we'll have to break out."

"Your view is a soldier's, and that's how it should be," Arista said. "But I must look at things as a ruler. Halibur's warriors cannot have any love for this war against their countrymen, nor can his subjects in Colgoth have much taste for it. The more time that passes, the more their discontent will grow. I'm prepared to wait as long as possible."

"Your plan is a wise one, Arista," Valdor agreed. "But Halibur also knows these things. I do not think he will wait long."

"If he attacks, we shall fight," Arista replied. "But only after Halibur begins it."

"Someone's coming!" Penderyn announced as he watched a small group of mounted warriors emerge from the enemy camp and ride slowly toward the city.

All eyes turned toward the camp. There was no sign of any unusual movement within its confines, so they fastened their sight on the approaching riders.

"It looks like they wish to talk," General Kriselor said. "Perhaps Halibur wants to pay his respects," he added wryly.

The riders halted several hundred yards from the wall. One of them walked his mount slowly forward, holding a spear aloft in front of him. From its tip a white flag of truce fluttered softly in the breeze.

General Kriselor ordered his archers to stand at ease. The warrior approached to within forty feet of the gate before drawing his horse to a halt.

"Who commands the wall?" he called.

General Kriselor looked to Arista. The Sumara stepped forward.

"I do," she replied.

The messenger was silent for a moment, obviously surprised by Arista's presence. "My captain wishes to speak," he said at last. "Will you honor our flag of truce?"

"Your comrades may come forward," Arista replied. "They shall be under the protection of their Sumara."

The emphasis she placed on the final two words was not lost on the warrior. His head dipped slightly—whether in shame at his position or respect toward Arista the watchers on the wall could not tell. He turned and signaled his companions to approach.

As the warriors drew near, Valdor recognized their leader. His mouth turned down in disgust. "The man Halibur has chosen to speak for him is Bleen," he announced angrily.

General Kriselor grabbed a bow from an archer standing next to him. He aimed an arrow toward Bleen, but Arista grabbed his arm to stay him.

"Would you make a liar of your Sumara, General?" she asked.

General Kriselor lowered the bow. If Bleen noticed the action atop the wall, he gave no sign.

"I bear a message from Halibur, Lord of Colgoth and rightful Sumar of Calistan," he called.

A wave of low murmurings ran atop the wall as the warriors there fumed at the insult to their Sumara.

"Still thy tongue, Bleen," Arista commanded. "Your Sumara does not converse with murderers."

Bleen ignored Arista's command and began to speak again.

"Silence!" Arista shouted before he could voice a single word. Her voice was filled with cold fury. "You live only because I promised my protection. Make one more sound and that promise is revoked!"

Bleen looked about uncertainly. A score of bows were trained upon him. He whispered something to the warrior who bore the flag of truce and then turned and galloped away.

"Have I your permission to speak, Your Majesty?" the warrior asked after Bleen was out of range.

"To you I will listen," Arista replied.

"My lord Halibur's message is this. He wishes to discuss this most unfortunate situation. He proposes that each of you choose an escort of ten men and meet midway across the plain."

"I doubt your lord has any words I wish to hear," Arista replied. "You may tell Halibur this. Since he comes to me with an army camped outside my door, he may speak to me as any enemy might—under the same flag of truce that protects you."

The warrior thought for a moment. "I shall give my lord your reply, Sumara," he said. His use of Arista's title was noticed by all.

"Add this to my message," Arista said. "No flag of truce shall apply to Bleen. The next time he approaches these walls, he shall die. Now go."

The messenger saluted and then turned and rode away with his companions. They joined Bleen where he waited, beyond bowshot of the city. Evidently Arista's message was repeated, for Bleen took one hurried glance toward the wall before galloping away.

"It appears you're right about the mood of Halibur's army," General Kriselor said. "Even his messenger seems unsure of his loyalty."

For almost an hour they waited atop the parapet, wondering how Halibur would respond to Arista's harsh words. Those who knew the Lord of Colgoth best suspected he needed the time merely to cool his temper, for Arista had left little doubt who was in command. General Kriselor and Jaspar voiced the opinion that Halibur would not come forth, that he would be afraid of further humiliation, but Valdor disagreed.

"He'll come," Valdor declared with certainty. "His vanity will not allow him to do otherwise. He will not even consider that Arista could best him. Our serpent won't miss his chance to shake his rattles before our walls."

"Valdor is right," Arista said. "Halibur will come." The Sumara allowed herself a brief smile. "After he cools his rage."

A few moments later a second party, several times larger than the first, rode from the enemy camp. Penderyn watched closely, straining his eyes for any sign of Halibur. He spotted a streaming red pennant, just like the one in his dream, and he knew Valdor and Arista were right. Halibur was coming.

As the riders drew closer, Penderyn recognized Halibur by his neatly trimmed black beard and flowing golden robe. But instead of riding at the head of the party as Penderyn had expected, Halibur had positioned himself in the center of his warriors.

The Last Born glanced toward Arista. Her face betrayed no emotion as she calmly watched her enemy approach.

While they waited, they were joined atop the wall by an unexpected newcomer—High Priest Chirops. The priest's blue robe contrasted sharply with the scarlet uniforms of the warriors who manned the battlements.

Ignoring the looks of disdain with which Valdor and General Kriselor greeted his arrival, Chirops maneuvered himself close to Arista. The Sumara acknowledged his presence with a glance but said nothing. Chirops chose to remain silent as well.

Penderyn sensed the same aura of evil he'd felt the first time he met the High Priest. He forced his eyes from Chirops back to the Halibur, who had halted his company well beyond range of the city's defenders.

"A different man bears the flag now," Valdor remarked with a smile as a single warrior rode forward with a flag of truce. "Perhaps the previous one lacked the proper respect when he reported back to Halibur."

"I hope he has not been harmed," Arista said as the new messenger halted beneath them.

"Lord Halibur requests protection under this flag of truce from the Lord of Kfastia," the messenger called, using the lesser of Arista's titles.

Arista showed no offense. "You may tell Halibur that his Sumara grants his request. He may come forward without fear."

The warrior dipped his flag and spurred his mount back to the waiting company. A moment later Halibur rode forward, surrounded by his escort.

Arista smiled. "It appears the Lord of Colgoth does not fully trust his Sumara."

"Those who cannot be trusted seldom trust others," Jarrowon said.

Everyone atop the battlements noticed that Halibur halted twice as far away from the wall as his messengers.

"Hear me, Arista," he called, his voice loud and commanding. "I come for the sake of peace, to ask you to relinquish your claim to the title of Sumara and give to me what is rightfully mine."

Penderyn saw the anger in the taut faces of Arista's followers. His own rage boiled as well at Halibur's blatant insolence, but Arista seemed unaffected.

"Upon what right do you base your claim, Halibur?" she asked calmly.

Halibur edged his horse closer to the wall, emboldened by the seeming meekness of Arista's reply.

"By right of blood," he declared, "as your late husband Kalin's closest relative." His voice grew softer. "Not for myself do I make this claim. I make it for the people of Calistan, who each day suffer more from foreign raiders and from the anger of the gods. It is for the people that I urge you to renounce your position."

Valdor stepped forward to reply, but a stern look from Arista silenced him.

"Do you, Halibur, claim the favor of the gods?" she asked.

"My priests tell me the gods would look with favor on the changes I propose," Halibur replied with increasing confidence. "I see your High Priest beside you. Why not ask his advice?"

All eyes turned to Chirops.

"Well, Chirops?" Arista asked. "What is your word on this matter?"

"The signs are still unclear," the High Priest responded evenly. "But I believe the Lord of Colgoth is right. It appears the gods may favor his claim."

Even now, Chirops refused to commit himself completely. Only a second stern look from Arista kept Valdor away from the treacherous High Priest, but it was evident to everyone that Valdor would not long be able to restrain his mounting rage.

"You have heard the words of your Priest," Halibur said. "For the sake of our people, will you accept my claim?"

Arista stepped forward to the very edge of the parapet. She seemed to grow in stature as she stared down at the men below her.

The sunlight glinted off her silver crown, the crown Halibur sought to make his own. Never was the majesty more apparent in her bearing.

"It surprises me to hear such noble words issue from so black a heart," she called loudly enough for all to hear. "You think not of our people, Halibur, but only of your own ambition. Though it is true my people suffer, it's not because the gods desire you to rule, of that I'm certain."

Halibur looked about to reply, but Arista held up her hand, silencing him.

"Leave this place, Halibur!" she cried. "Return to your palace! Perhaps there is some trace of the noble blood of my departed husband in your veins that has not been poisoned by your greed and ambition. Go seek that small speck of goodness and cease this folly."

Halibur seemed shaken by Arista's response. "You have made an unfortunate choice," he replied angrily. "You alone shall be responsible for the suffering and death that follow."

"Speak no more," Arista commanded. "This audience is ended. In five minutes, the protection of the truce ends as well."

Halibur glared up at his enemies. Already a hundred archers aimed their bows at him. He barked a gruff command to his escort and rode hurriedly away.

Arista watched him depart and then turned to Chirops. "Do you wish to join him?" she asked icily. "You seem to prefer Halibur to me."

"I favor no one," Chirops replied smoothly. "I am merely a humble servant of the gods. I answered Your Majesty's question as best as my abilities allowed."

Valdor stepped toward the High Priest. "Say rather that you favor yourself," he said angrily. "You are ambitious and you are a coward." He turned to Arista. "That is a most dangerous combination to allow loose within our walls at a time like this,

Your Majesty."

"I will not be insulted by a blasphemer," Chirops said to Arista. "If Your Majesty has no further need of me, I shall return to the temple to pray."

"Pray that you see your duty clearly, Chirops," Arista replied sternly.

Chirops was clearly discomfited by Arista's display of previously hidden strength. He stared silently at her for a moment before turning and walking away.

"That one bears watching," Jarrowon said to Penderyn in a low voice.

The Last Born nodded his agreement. He had been thinking the same thing.

CHAPTER 22

The day before Arista's dramatic confrontation with Halibur, Tal and Dal trailed a small herd of marluks through the wooded hills south of the city. For several hours they silently stalked the graceful, deer-like creatures, roaming much farther from Kfastia than they normally ventured, beyond the reach of the messengers who even now were seeking to warn the hunting party of Halibur's advance.

The marluks were a difficult quarry, blessed with sharp eyes and exceptionally keen ears, so the twins had separated from their less skilled Kfastian comrades to circle around in front of the herd, where they would have a chance at the beasts even if the marluks detected the Kfastians' approach.

When Tal guessed he and Dal were directly ahead of the slowly moving herd, he signaled silently to his brother, motioning toward a small grove of leafy saplings. The twins slipped quietly into the middle of the trees and concealed themselves among the thick foliage.

Scarcely had they settled into their hiding place when the woods erupted with the sound of rushing bodies. The high pitched squeaks of frightened marluks filled the forest as the beasts crashed wildly through the underbrush, fleeing some danger behind them. Tal and Dal quickly readied their bows.

The marluks' mad flight carried them directly toward the waiting twins. For a moment the woods seemed filled with bounding brown and white bodies, but so swiftly did the terrified creatures run that Tal and Dal had time to fire only one arrow apiece before the animals disappeared behind them. Both had aimed skillfully, however; at least there would be two marluks to add to Kfastia's stores of meat.

The twins smiled ruefully at each other as they retrieved their prey. Had their comrades not spooked the herd, they might have brought down a half dozen of the animals. Still, two were better than none.

They heard footsteps in the underbrush behind them. Expecting to see the chagrined faces of their Kfastian comrades, they turned to find themselves facing a score of dirty, murderous-looking rogues, a number of whose bared swords were stained red with still dripping blood. The twins knew now what had caused the marluks to stampede.

"I'm seein' double," laughed one of the men. "Must've taken a blow to me head back there."

"Let's send these two to join their fellows," said a second. He raised his bloody sword, but a tall bandit with a tangled brown beard stepped in front of him. By his manner, the twins knew he was the leader of this band of ruffians.

"Would you kill 'em after they was kind enough to provide us with all this fresh meat?" he laughed. "We'll take 'em to Rorgul. He may enjoy entertaining 'em."

"Aye, Brok, that he might," said another of the scoundrels, his voice filled with anticipation at the thought.

The man called Brok turned to Tal and Dal. "What say you, lads? Will you put up your swords and come quietly?"

Tal and Dal looked at one another. The prospect of being captive to this band of cutthroats was anything but pleasant, but to resist meant certain death. Reluctantly, they dropped their swords. While they lived, there was always the chance for escape.

Two ruffians bound the twins' hands behind their backs with thick leather thongs, which were then fastened to a rope held by a short, stocky bandit named Marl. Marl's cruel mouth spread into a yellow smile as he pushed his prisoners roughly ahead of him.

The villains took them to a crude encampment where more than a score of bedraggled tents were scattered among the trees. Brok ordered them held in a tent fashioned of rotting animal skins near the center of the camp, cautioning Marl to make sure no harm came to them. The man called Rorgul was evidently not at this camp, for Brok dispatched one of his men to report the twins' capture.

Marl pushed them unceremoniously into the dim, foul-smelling tent. He bound their legs together at the ankles and warned them not to make any trouble. When he left, he tied the front flap closed, shutting out what little light had managed to filter in through the thick skins.

Time dragged by with almost unendurable slowness. Their captors ignored them, except for one brief visit each day from Marl, who brought cold, tasteless scraps of food they struggled to eat as best they could with their hands tied behind them. The remainder of their time they passed in stoic silence, listening to the seemingly endless series of shouts and arguments that filled the raider camp, hoping they might hear something that would be of use should they manage to escape.

Sometime in the middle of their third day of captivity, Tal and Dal were drawn from their lethargy by a noticeable increase in the bickering outside their tent. Listening carefully to the arguments, they realized the bandits were breaking camp. The twins wondered what it meant, but they were unable to overhear any reasons for the change.

Soon Marl entered the tent. He cut the bonds around their legs with a wicked looking knife, then dragged them both to their feet and shoved them roughly through the entrance.

After three days inside the dark tent, even the filtered sunlight of the woods was too bright for Tal and Dal's eyes. Unable to block the light with their hands tied behind their backs, they were forced to stumble blindly where Marl pushed them.

When at last their eyes adjusted to the brightness, they found the camp was almost completely dismantled. Already a stream of bandits was moving off to the northeast. Marl pushed his prisoners in the same direction.

"Where are we going, Marl?" Tal asked. Though their jailor had not shown the slightest warmth toward them, Marl was the only one among the ruffians he thought might answer him.

"We go to join our fellows," Marl replied with what for him seemed almost a happy tone. "There'll soon be blood to spill."

The expression on his face made it clear the prospect that pleased him greatly.

They arrived at the sprawling main encampment late in the afternoon. Tents were scattered over such a large area of woods that the camp's boundaries were impossible to discern. How many bandits were gathered here, Tal and Dal could not even begin to guess. From where their captors began carelessly pitching their own tents, the twins could see several hundred of the villains, but the sounds that filtered through the trees indicated there were many more beyond their sight.

They remembered the ragged mercenaries Penderyn had seen in his dream and wondered if their friends in the city had any idea of the presence of this enemy hidden on their southern flank. Somehow, they had to get word to Kfastia, but when Marl shoved them once more into their tent and bound their feet, there was nothing they could do but lie in the darkness and await whatever fate had in store for them. Eventually, they both fell asleep, but their sleep was fitful and provided little in the way of real rest.

Early the next morning, Marl dragged them from the tent. Brok was waiting outside, a leer upon his bearded face that boded ill for the twins.

"Rorgul wants to see my prisoners," he said pleasantly. "Maybe you'll be worth something after all." He turned to Marl. "Bring 'em along."

Brok turned and set off through the jumble of tents. Marl pushed the twins along behind his chief. The stocky villain's beast-like eyes were filled with anticipation at the thought of turning the twins over to Rorgul.

The bandit leader's tent was a large, four-sided pavilion that stood out from the tents of his men like a maiden among cleaning servants. Its smooth green and yellow sides sloped gently inward and enclosed an area at least twenty feet on each side. The clean, well-fitted panels provided a stark contrast to the crudely stitched hides of the smaller tents surrounding it.

Brok halted before a screen of fine netting that protected the entrance from insects. One of the two burly guards who flanked the opening nodded to the bandit and disappeared into the tent. A moment later he reappeared and motioned Brok to enter.

The twins heard several voices inside, but they were unable to make out whatever was being said. Before long, Brok emerged from the tent, followed by two men. Tal and Dal had no trouble guessing the identity of either of them.

The first was a giant of a man, a full head taller even than Brok. His broad, powerful shoulders seemed wide enough for two men, and the thickly muscled arms that protruded through his sleeveless brown cloak looked like the limbs of a stout tree.

Despite the man's size and power, it was his face that drew their attention. A shaggy black beard covered his jaw and a curved scar ran across his left cheek from his ear to his mouth, twisting his thick lips into a permanent sneer. Small, dark eyes, more like those of a beast than a man, flanked a broad, flat nose that looked to have been broken more than a few times. A large gold hoop dangled from his right ear.

The aura of evil emanating from the giant was almost

palpable. Only a man such as this could rule the villainous army gathered here. The twins knew this had to be Rorgul.

The second man was a stark contrast to the fearsome, unkempt bandit. He was small and slender, shorter than the twins by at least a couple of inches, and immaculately groomed, with smooth black hair and a trimmed beard that tapered to a sharp point. He wore a flowing robe of gold silk that belonged in a palace rather than out here in the woods. Tal and Dal had never seen this man, either, but they recognized him from Penderyn's description. He was Halibur, Lord of Colgoth, meeting here with his secret ally.

Rorgul stared down at the twins with contempt. "These are the prisoners you're so interested in?" he said to Halibur. The giant's voice was deep and gruff. "They look like boys run away from their mother. If they be warriors from the city, this war will be over much too quickly."

Rorgul glowered at Brok. "Untie their hands. Rorgul needs no protection from such as these."

Brok drew a long dagger from his waistband and quickly slashed the twins' bonds. For the first time in four days Tal and Dal were able to move their hands and arms. They tried to show as little discomfort as possible as they gently worked their stiff shoulders and backs.

"By their remarkable likeness, these can only be the twins who came to Kfastia with the boy everyone is calling the Last Born," Halibur said to Rorgul. "It's a shame he wasn't included in the capture, but Arista keeps him safe within her walls."

Tal and Dal smiled at each other. At least Penderyn was still well.

"I would not be too happy, if I were you," Halibur advised them. "Already my army surrounds Kfastia. Your friend will not be safe for long." He smiled. "But I am not a hard man to get along with. A little cooperation from you two might persuade me to be merciful to your young friend. I'm told you and he and some comrades were gone from Kfastia for several months. Perhaps you'd like to share the details of your journey?"

Tal and Dal exchanged glances.

"We went to visit some cousins," Tal said. "No big deal."

Halibur's smile disappeared and his voice grew hard. "Accompanied by the sons of two Majhari and a lore master? I think not."

"If you think you know so much, why bother with us?" Dal asked disdainfully.

"Because I do not like surprises. If you refuse to tell me what I wish to know, the death of your friend will be on your hands."

The twins remained silent.

"I have ways to loosen stubborn tongues," Rorgul growled impatiently.

Halibur thought for a moment. "We're in no hurry," he said finally. "Let's give them a bit of time to think about it. I hope you don't mind keeping them alive a few days more."

Rorgul shrugged. "Their lives are nothing to me. If you wish them alive, then they shall live a bit longer."

As he spoke, the bandit leader unfastened the front of his cloak against the growing heat of the morning. When his cloak fell open, the twins saw a familiar symbol on the breast of his tunic—a black circle, pierced by a jagged line.

The image of his father's mutilated body and severed head flashed before Tal's eyes. This was the man who had burned Ishtor!

Tal exploded in rage, throwing himself upon Rorgul. So sudden was his move that his hands were grasping at the giant's throat before anyone could react. His hand caught upon the earring which dangled from Rorgul's ear, ripping it through the tender flesh. The bandit howled in pain and rage. His huge fists pounded at Tal, but the Tal clung like a leech to Rorgul's neck.

Dal was a half second behind his brother, giving Brok time to tackle him as he lunged to Tal's aid. Dal struggled to break free, but Marl grabbed him as well. He was helpless.

Tal clung tenaciously to Rorgul's throat, squeezing with a strength multiplied by his rage. But even such strength was not enough against the awesome power in Rorgul's giant frame. Tal's hold weakened as Rorgul's fist continued to batter him, until at last the brute threw him to the ground. Two burly guards immediately pinned him there.

Rorgul glowered down at his attacker. His right hand rubbed at his torn ear. When he brought it before his eyes, his fingers were covered with blood.

"You shall not die yet," he said. "Not until you have suffered long and horribly. Only when you can beg no more shall I kill you." He turned to his guards. "Hold out the hand that injured me," he ordered.

Dal looked on in horror as the bandits dragged Tal to his feet and held his left arm extended in front of him. Dal struggled desperately to go to his brother's aid, but Brok and Marl held him too tightly. He watched helplessly as Rorgul withdrew his sword from the jeweled scabbard at his belt.

"Thus do I deal with those who dare attack me," Rorgul said as he held the huge sword poised above his head. The blade flashed downward. Tal let out a single scream as Rorgul's sword severed his hand at the wrist.

CHAPTER 23

Penderyn awoke screaming, his left wrist engulfed in agonizing pain. He thrashed wildly under his blanket, frantically grabbing at his throbbing arm.

As suddenly as it had come, the pain vanished. His wrist felt normal, unharmed. But the agony had been all too real.

Orith rushed into the room. His flickering torch illuminated Penderyn sitting on the bed, his hand gripping his wrist, a puzzled expression on his face.

"What is it, Penderyn?" Orith asked as he quickly scanned the room for any sign of danger. "What happened?"

Penderyn shook his head. "I'm not sure. Bring the torch closer."

He held his wrist close to the flame and examined it carefully. There were no marks of any kind, no sign of injury. He looked up at Orith, who was watching him with concern.

"My wrist felt like it was on fire," he said. "The pain was almost unbearable, but now there's nothing."

Jarrowon hurried into the chamber. The lore master was surprised to find Penderyn and Orith sitting on the bed. He looked at them questioningly.

"I heard you scream. What happened?"

Penderyn explained about his wrist, holding it up for Jarrowon to see. The lore master examined it closely. His wrinkled brow knitted in surprise.

"I sense a faint trace of magic," he said. "But whatever it was is gone now."

"Perhaps it had something to do with a dream," Orith suggested. "Do you recall dreaming about anything?"

Penderyn tried to remember, but his mind was blank.

"No, nothing," he said finally, looking down at his wrist once more.

"Try using the *iffirium* to help you remember," Orith suggested.

Penderyn closed his eyes and began the slow, deep breathing. The familiar sensation of peaceful emptiness filled his mind as he drifted off into the *iffirium*. Slowly, the images from a forgotten dream arose, startling in their clarity.

Tal and Dal stood in front of a large tent. Their hands were tied behind their backs. Two familiar figures emerged from the tent—Halibur and the black-bearded giant.

A third man cut the bonds around the twins' wrists. The giant's cloak fell open, revealing the hated insignia upon his breast. Tal leaped upon the ruffian. They struggled briefly, but Tal was overmatched. The giant flung him to the ground. He drew his sword. Two men held Tal's arm extended out in front of him. The sword descended.

Pain engulfed Penderyn's wrist and blackness filled his mind, but still he did not awaken.

The darkness lightened. Once again he saw Tal and Dal. The twins were tied to two large wooden wagon wheels, arms and legs spread-eagled against the spokes. Their clothes had been torn off. Bleeding cuts covered their bodies.

The vision faded and Penderyn awakened. Pain and sadness filled his eyes. For a moment he sat silently, gathering himself.

"I saw Tal and Dal," he explained when he trusted himself to speak. "Halibur and the bearded giant from my earlier dream are holding them captive." He sucked in a deep breath and rubbed his wrist. "They cut off Tal's hand. That was the pain I felt."

"Our dreams see the future," Orith reminded him. "What you saw has not yet come to pass. Could you tell where they were?"

Penderyn pictured the terrain from his dream in his mind. "I recognized the general area," he said. "It was the wooded land to the south, not more than two or three leagues from here." He stood up. "I've got to go help them."

Jarrowon looked out the window. "It's nearly dawn. There's no way we can leave the city undetected now."

"I have to try," Penderyn insisted. "I can't just leave them."

"Tonight," Jarrowon said. "Under cover of darkness we might be able to cross the plain unseen."

Penderyn hated to delay, but he knew Jarrowon was right. He nodded in acceptance. Though he could not know it, the delay did not matter. In just one hour Marl would awaken Tal and Dal to bring them before Rorgul. Even if the rescuers had left Kfastia immediately, they could not have arrived in time.

Jarrowon had good reason not to try to talk Penderyn out of going on such a dangerous mission. He knew the unswerving loyalty between the Last Born and the twins would make it almost impossible to stop Penderyn in any event, but he had another reason as well, one unknown to Penderyn.

The previous morning, Orith had come secretly to Jarrowon's chamber. It was still dark when the Eirydian entered the lore master's room, but even by the flickering glow of the torch Jarrowon could see the look of deep concern etched upon his features. Orith had just awakened from a dream, a dream he knew he must report to Jarrowon immediately.

"I have seen the Last Born fall," Orith had said ominously.

He recounted his dream to Jarrowon. In his vision, Orith had seen a battle upon the plain before Kfastia. Penderyn rode with the city's cavalry and had engaged the unknown giant in combat. The struggle lasted several minutes, but the outcome had been clear—the giant's sword had pierced Penderyn's breast.

Jarrowon now had little doubt such a battle must eventually come to be—both Penderyn and Orith had dreamed it. Both had also seen the bearded giant. Somehow, Penderyn must be prevented from meeting him in the coming battle. Keeping the Last Born within the city was the obvious choice, but Jarrowon doubted Penderyn could be dissuaded from joining in any major fray. He had asked Orith whether he had seen Tal and Dal in his dream, but he had not.

The lore master had been wrestling with the problem ever since. When Penderyn announced his intention to go to Tal and Dal's aid, Jarrowon had not dissented. Though such a mission was fraught with danger, it would at least keep the Last Born away from any impending battle. And if Tal and Dal were rescued, he knew they would ride with Penderyn in combat, a future that would be different than the one Orith had foreseen.

Penderyn and his comrades had just finished breakfast when a messenger from General Kriselor arrived at Valdor's door.

"Halibur's men are burning farmhouses," the messenger reported.

"What do they seek to gain by that?" Penderyn wondered aloud.

"Halibur must have decided he could not afford to merely sit and wait," Valdor said. "He seeks to provoke us." He turned to the messenger. "I presume Kriselor has sent word to the palace?"

The messenger nodded. "And to the other Majhari as well."

"Do you think Arista will respond to the challenge?" Jarrowon asked Valdor.

"She won't want to," the nobleman replied, "but she may have no choice."

"We should go to the palace," Penderyn said. "Arista will need us."

Valdor shook his head. "Arista will want to see this with her own eyes. She'll go to the wall."

A second messenger, this one from the palace, arrived even as Valdor spoke.

"The Sumara wishes you to meet her above the north gate," the man reported.

Servants were sent to ready four horses. A few moments later, Penderyn, Jarrowon, Orith and Valdor were riding rapidly through the city.

They reached the gate just as Arista and her royal bodyguards were mounting the stairs. They followed the Sumara to the top of the battlement, where General Kriselor awaited them. The general pointed to the north.

Five columns of dark smoke rose like miniature thunderclouds into the blue noontime sky. Soon the rising smoke would be visible from almost any part of the city. From atop the wall, the watchers could even see the yellow tongues of flame that consumed the abandoned farmhouses.

"Such destruction is pointless," Arista said angrily. "What does Halibur think to gain by burning empty cabins?"

"He seeks to provoke us," General Kriselor said. "A battle would do much to reinforce the loyalties of his warriors. Once we attack, we become the enemy."

"Well, I will not be provoked," Arista said. "Cabins can be rebuilt. Dead soldiers cannot be brought back to life."

"It may not be quite so easy," Valdor said. "Halibur's army is not the only place with divided loyalties. There are divided loyalties within our walls as well."

"What are you suggesting?" Arista asked sharply.

"Only that allowing Halibur to destroy our farms unchallenged may be taken by some as further proof of your inability to protect Kfastia. This faction could cause trouble inside the city. With the enemy already camped on our doorstep, we can ill afford such distractions."

"Have I no choice then but to play into Halibur's hands?" Arista asked in frustration. She looked anxiously at each of her advisors.

"Not exactly," General Kriselor replied. "I have an idea."

He pointed toward the burning farms, where a sixth column of black smoke was now climbing into the sky.

"They are burning the outermost of the farms," he explained. "It's the work of several small patrols, less than a hundred warriors total. Right now, they're too close to Halibur's main force for us to interfere, but if they continue their pattern, they'll be moving farther from the protection of the army and closer to us. We can send a small force of cavalry to intercept them."

"What if Halibur sends reinforcements?" Arista asked.

"Then our men break off the skirmish and return to the city before the help arrives."

"What about the army Penderyn saw that may be hidden out there somewhere?" Arista asked, still not comfortable with sending her warriors outside the walls.

"If they were close enough to be a concern, we'd know where they were," General Kriselor replied.

Arista stood in silent thought for a moment. While she waited, another cabin went up in flames. As General Kriselor had predicted, the enemy was moving farther from the main camp. She decided she had seen enough.

"They must be stopped," she said. "How many warriors will you need?"

"Two companies should be sufficient."

"Use your two best then," Arista ordered. "Which are they?"

"The ones commanded by Cornon and by Phrak," General Kriselor replied instantly. "Both are ready."

Arista looked toward Valdor. He nodded his agreement.

"Dispatch them as soon as you think it safe," Arista commanded.

Penderyn stepped forward. "If Cornon's company is to go, then I must go with them," he said.

Arista looked at him in surprise. She had forgotten Penderyn's assignment to Cornon's unit. It would be foolish to risk the Last Born in so unimportant a venture. Before she could tell General Kriselor to send a different company, Jarrowon turned to Penderyn.

"Your duty lies elsewhere this day, Last Born," he reminded him.

In his eagerness to join the fight, Penderyn had momentarily forgotten Tal and Dal. Jarrowon was right. He had a more important mission to think of.

The sound of horses in the courtyard below drew everyone's attention. The two companies of cavalry were already gathering behind the gate. Cornon's warriors were in the lead, their young captain at their head. At his signal the wooden doors swung open and the horsemen thundered forth from the city.

Ten abreast they raced, urging their mounts to all possible speed. Two hundred yards from the city the companies divided. Cornon's column struck directly for the enemy riders, while Phrak's warriors veered to the right, to intercept the raiders should they try to flee back toward their camp. Phrak's position would also allow him to protect Cornon's flank.

So sudden and swift was their attack that the enemy had no chance to flee before Cornon's warriors were upon them. The outnumbered enemy was no match for the Kfastians. The battle was over in minutes. Only a few of the raiders escaped, riding to the north where their foes refused to pursue them.

Halibur's army was slow to react. By the time their cavalry charged from the camp, the attackers were already racing back toward the city.

Cheers rang from the battlements as the horses crossed through the gateway. The last rider through was Cornon. The first battle of the war was ended, and though the victory was but a small one, it belonged to Kfastia.

CHAPTER 24

The sun slowly settled toward the distant horizon, a molten sphere seemingly growing larger and more liquid in appearance as its yellow brightness dimmed first to orange and then deepened to a fiery red. The scattered clouds dotting the evening sky gradually darkened, and the sky took on a purple and orange hue.

Penderyn glanced repeatedly at the setting sun as he paced the southern battlement, as if by force of will he could make it sink more quickly. He took no notice of its beauty. Only the approaching darkness interested him. Unconsciously, he rubbed his left wrist. Night was coming far too slowly.

While Penderyn paced, Jarrowon and Orith studied the movements of the enemy riders patrolling the plain. Watching with them was Soldrok, a grizzled old hunter chosen by Arista to be their guide. Halibur's patrols were small and scattered, but their crisscrossing pattern was enough to cover the wide expanse of open ground by day.

At last the sun disappeared. As the twilight deepened, the watchers atop the wall looked carefully for any sign of increased activity by the enemy, but saw no change in the size or number of patrols. Clearly Halibur did not expect anyone to try to leave the protection of the city, and so was not increasing his patrols. By the time darkness settled over the plain, the comrades atop the wall were confident their small party would be able to reach the forest without detection.

Still, they waited, allowing the darkness to deepen before

finally descending from the wall on a pair of knotted ropes. The gates would be watched, but they would not be seen descending the wall. Invisible in the blackness, they set out quickly across the plain, using the hoof beats of the enemy horses to help them avoid the enemy patrols.

Penderyn had almost forgotten how dark the nights had grown. Only a few dim stars were able to pierce the veil of blackness that was steadily enveloping their world. So thick was the darkness, he had difficulty seeing his comrades from only a few feet away. Until he felt the brush of an unseen branch across his chest, he did not even realize they had reached the forest.

Once within the cover of the trees, the rescue party stopped to wait for Primus to rise. Without some light from the moon, it would be foolish to stumble blindly through the woods. One twisted ankle or poke in the eye could spell the end of their mission.

Finally, a faint glow appeared low in the eastern sky. The light from the rising moon was not much, but it was enough for Soldrok. With a nod to his companions, the veteran woodsman started off into the trees, following well-known paths.

For almost an hour they trekked southward along narrow, twisting trails they could barely see. When their latest path began to gradually veer to the west, Soldrok turned off the trail and led them down into a deep ravine.

They moved even more slowly now, stepping carefully over slippery, moss-covered rocks and invisible roots that seemed to grasp at their feet. The ravine became increasingly damp and the air grew thick and moist with the musky smell of rotting vegetation. Tiny, unseen insects buzzed annoyingly about their heads as they trudged silently along in single file.

As their pace slowed, Penderyn's impatience grew. His boots became heavy with mud, and each step seemed to take longer than the one before. The swarming bugs did not help his mood. He wondered if they would ever find Tal and Dal.

Finally, Soldrok led them up out of the ravine. Even in the dimness, Penderyn recognized the wooded landscape from his dream. Soldrok had guided them flawlessly. The Last Born looked to the hunter and nodded.

"The area you described is just ahead," Soldrok whispered. "If the enemy camp is there, we're almost upon it."

"The camp is there," Penderyn said with a bit more confidence than he felt. "I'm sure of it."

He wished he was really as confident as he tried to sound, but he could not show any doubt to his companions.

The small party moved forward with redoubled caution, testing every step before transferring their weight, probing the darkness ahead for any unnatural shape or outline. At any moment, they might reach the first of the tents. Silence was imperative.

Suddenly, a dark shape loomed up out of the darkness, directly in their path. Despite their caution, they had stumbled upon a sentry whose outline had been hidden by the thick trunk of a tree behind him. There was no chance to hide.

The bandit faltered back in surprise, as startled as they were.

Penderyn reached quickly for his knife, knowing even as he yanked it from its leather sheath that he was too late. Already the man's mouth was opening to shout an alarm.

But somehow, no sound issued from the bandit's throat. His jaw hung open, frozen in a silent shout. Slowly his mouth eased shut and a vacant look glazed his eyes. Penderyn was mystified. What was going on here? What magic had saved them? He turned and glanced behind him.

Jarrowon was moving slowly forward, his brow creased in concentration. His right hand—thumb and fingers pressed tightly into a point—was aimed directly toward the bandit's face. The lore master paid no attention to the Last Born; his gaze was focused on the paralyzed sentry.

Penderyn could almost feel the invisible lines of force connecting the two men. He watched in wonder as Jarrowon closed ever so slowly toward his victim, as if the slightest mistake would sever the fragile thread binding their minds together. When at last the lore master was within reach, he gently touched his fingertips to the guard's forehead.

The bandit collapsed soundlessly into Jarrowon's arms. The lore master lowered the inert form silently to the ground and then motioned for his comrades to follow him.

A moment later, they reached the edge of the camp. The tents were grouped among the trees in scattered bunches, with no apparent pattern to their placement. This was no well-organized army camp, but Penderyn still knew they would find Tal and Dal somewhere near the center of the encampment.

Like soundless wraiths they moved among the tents, keeping to the trees as much as possible as they slowly penetrated toward the heart of the enemy stronghold.

Most of the bandits were sound asleep. What few sentries patrolled the camp took little interest in their task, and Penderyn and his comrades avoided them without much difficulty. Even so, long anxious minutes dragged by before they at last reached their goal.

Penderyn recognized the huge tent from his dream instantly. Pitched in the center of a large clearing, it was bathed in dim moonlight. It's green and yellow panels looked black and light gray in the darkness. Two guards, far more alert than any of their comrades had been, stood watch outside the entrance.

The Last Born hesitated to look further, afraid of what he might find. With a determined swallow he imagined could be heard by the pair of sentries, he forced himself to continue his survey of the clearing. His eyes came to rest on two large round objects near its north edge. His heart sank. Even in the shadows he knew what they were—the wooden torture wheels he had seen in his dream. Once again he was too late. His vision had already come to pass.

He closed his eyes and fought back tears. First his mother and now Tal and Dal—he had failed everyone he loved. The mental anguish was too much for him to bear. Frustration, anger, hate and blame surged through him, churning into an irresistible vortex that tore at his soul. Was this his doom—to see the future but never be able to change it? Would his power always torture him, but never aid him? Would he always be too late?

A series of horrible grimaces twisted Penderyn's features. Orith reached for his young friend, but Jarrowon pushed his arms aside and stepped between them. The lore master watched in dismay, knowing the Last Born teetered on the brink of madness.

Jarrowon knew he had but one chance to aid Penderyn, though such a course was fraught with danger for both of them. He had no choice—he had to try. Hesitantly, he reached for Penderyn's forehead.

When the lore master's fingertips touched Penderyn' skin, he was stunned by the surge of raw power that buffeted him as his mind entered the Last Born's. Pinwheels of blinding colors flashed in his brain. Yawning black gulfs threatened to swallow him. Soundless explosions battered his senses. He had not expected anything so fierce, so powerful.

Desperately he hung on, channeling his magic in search of the core of Penderyn's power. Deeper and deeper he probed, until his mind could stand no more. He must stop, he knew, must pull himself back before he was lost forever. He was about to give up, when suddenly he was no longer alone. Another magic joined with his, strengthening him, guiding him. The *Luminari* had somehow appeared, come to aid him just in time.

He felt the magical spirits' despair as their power began to fade, but perhaps it had been enough. With a final effort, Jarrowon delivered a surge of magic into Penderyn's core before the darkness engulfed him. The lore master collapsed into Orith's arms.

In the small part of his consciousness that still escaped his inner turmoil, Penderyn felt Jarrowon's magic flow into him. Dimly he sensed the battering the lore master was taking from the uncontrolled powers raging inside him, but he could do nothing to stop it.

Suddenly, a white light seemed to explode in his brain. His confusion vanished as his innate magic was unleashed, triggered by Jarrowon's desperate gamble.

The world became filled with shimmering lines of light swirling around him in an infinite array of patterns and colors. Pulsating fields of energy surrounded everything he looked at. He felt the weakness in Jarrowon's flickering blue-green aura and shared Tal and Dal's slumbering pain. Trees, plants, and even rocks gave off their own unique glow.

Guided by some inner instinct, Penderyn placed his hands at the edges of the lore master's weakening aura and let his own energy flow into it. The flickering stopped and the colors grew brighter as Jarrowon's strength was replenished. When Penderyn sensed the lore master was out of danger, he turned his attention to the unsuspecting sentries across the clearing. With a single thought, he caused them to fall soundly asleep.

Sensing that his power was waning and knowing he could do nothing to stop its disappearance, Penderyn hurried across the clearing toward Tal and Dal, feeding what strength he could into their tortured bodies. Orith and Soldrok ran with him. Quickly they cut the leather thongs that bound the twins to the wheels. They gently lowered Tal and Dal to the ground and wrapped them in soft brown cloaks.

As the colors around him slowly disappeared, Penderyn had a fleeting sense that some dark, malevolent power had sensed his magic and was trying desperately to find him. He shuddered as he remembered the evil creatures that had twice haunted his dreams. He was glad his power was fading. He hoped it had faded in time.

There was no time to worry about that now, though. Soon the *mocrah* would begin. If they were not out of the enemy camp before the night brightened, escape would be impossible.

They retraced their steps through the maze of tents, their speed reduced by Tal and Dal, who could walk only with support from Soldrok and Orith. Through a break in the foliage, they saw the tell-tale lightening of the black sky that presaged the appearance of Ferus. Only minutes remained.

A series of shouts split the night behind them. The disappearance of the twins had been discovered.

There was no time to lose. Silence was no longer important. All that mattered was getting past the last few clusters of tents before the bandits were fully alert.

Penderyn knew he had no magic left to save them. He grabbed Tal's free arm to help Soldrok, while Jarrowon moved alongside Dal to aid Orith. Supporting the twins on both sides, the rescuers hurried ahead, heedless of the noise they made as they crashed through the underbrush.

All around them men scrambled from their tents, shouting and rushing about as they tried to discover what was happening. The noise and confusion worked to the company's advantage. Before the bandit leaders could bring any order to their men, the fugitives had vanished into the woods.

Ferus brightened the night just as the last of the tents disappeared behind them. They turned immediately to the west, hoping their pursuers would assume they had fled northward toward Kfastia.

For once, Penderyn was thankful for the slowly spreading veil of darkness. The diminished *mocrah* was still bright enough for them to choose the quickest route through the trees, but too dark for their foes to easily track them in the woods.

Soon the sounds of pursuit were lost behind them. Satisfied they were safe for the time being, they stopped to allow Tal and Dal a few minutes rest. Propped against the trunks of a pair of thick trees, the twins had their first chance to thank their rescuers.

"This is the second time you've saved our lives, Penderyn," Dal said gratefully. "How did you find us?"

Penderyn pointed to Tal's crudely bandaged wrist. "I had a dream about that last night," he replied grimly. "I'd hoped to find you before it happened. I'm sorry."

"We're alive, that's what matters," Tal said. He smiled weakly and held up the stump of his wrist. "Don't worry about this. Now people will be able to tell Dal and me apart."

Penderyn managed a thin smile, but Dal was having none of his brother's humor.

"The villain who did it is the same one who burned our village," he said angrily.

"I know," Penderyn said, his voice growing hard. "I saw the lightning symbol in my dream."

"His name is Rorgul," Tal said. He brought his crippled arm close to his face. "It's worth this to have found him at last. I'm only sorry I failed to kill him."

"He'll pay for his crimes soon enough," Penderyn vowed.

Jarrowon frowned as he watched the grim set of Penderyn's face. There was no doubt now that the Last Born would seek out Rorgul. Somehow, the outcome foreseen by Orith must be prevented.

Hoping they had traveled far enough to the west to avoid pursuit, the company turned north. There was still one more race to be won—they had to reach the city before dawn or risk being trapped outside its walls. Once more Soldrok took the lead, this time choosing wide, level paths on which the weakened twins could maintain the most speed.

They crossed the plain even as the first gray light began to etch the eastern sky. Tal and Dal were too weak to climb, so Soldrok and Orith scrambled up the waiting ropes to gather help. Jarrowon and Penderyn carefully fastened the ropes around Tal and Dal's waists, and then stood back while the warriors above gently hoisted the twins up the wall.

Two more ropes were thrown down, and Penderyn and Jarrowon climbed to safety. Already, white-robed healers were tending to Tal and Dal's wounds. Cornon detached himself from the group around the twins and greeted his comrades warmly.

"Well done, my friends. You made it back just in time." He looked to Penderyn and smiled. "That seems to be a habit with you, Last Born."

Penderyn smiled in return. "I don't plan it this way, I promise you."

"It's been a long night," Cornon said. "I think we all could use some sleep. Our healers will take good care of Tal and Dal."

Penderyn turned toward the twins. The healers had placed them upon stretchers and were preparing to carry them from the battlements. There was nothing more he could do. He suddenly felt very tired.

CHAPTER 25

Penderyn, Jarrowon and Orith stopped just outside the door to Penderyn's bedchamber.

"Before you go to sleep," Jarrowon said to Penderyn, "tell me what happened in Rorgul's camp. Right after I passed out."

Penderyn's brow furrowed in confusion. As hard as he tried to recall the events, he couldn't remember. The time between entering the bandit camp and helping Tal and Dal down from the torture wheels was a blank. He closed his eyes to try to picture the scene. He saw a hazy image of lights and colors, but couldn't make sense of them.

"I can't remember," he said at last. "I sort of remember a bunch of colored lights or something, but that's all." He looked questioningly at the lore master. "Can you help me remember? Did you see any of it?"

Jarrowon shook his head. "You had some kind of seizure. I probed with my magic, trying to help you, but your defenses were too strong. I blacked out. The next thing I knew, Orith and Soldrok were cutting Tal and Dal from the wheels."

Penderyn looked at Orith. "What about you? You saw it all. What happened?"

"I can tell you what I saw, but I don't know how much it will help. When Jarrowon passed out, you seemed to regain control of yourself. You held your hands over him for a few seconds and his breathing got better. Then you turned toward the two guards outside the main tent. A moment later they both collapsed—how, I don't know—and you rushed toward Tal and Dal. You held your hands out toward them while Soldrok and I cut their bonds. I don't know what was going on, but you seemed to know exactly what you were doing."

Penderyn sighed. "I may have known then," he said, "but I have no idea now. What about the colored lights? Did you see them?"

Orith shook his head. "No, I didn't. I'm sorry."

Jarrowon stroked his chin in thought. "Somehow, I must have triggered your magic before I blacked out. For a few moments, your powers were alive, controlled by your subconscious. When your magic faded, your memory went with it."

Penderyn sighed a second time. "So my power remains a mystery, even after I've used it." He shrugged and smiled wryly. "At least it came in handy."

"That it did," Jarrowon said. "Even if none of us knows exactly how."

Penderyn yawned. "I'm exhausted. I need to sleep for a few hours, at least."

"I think we could all use some rest," Jarrowon said. "Even I find myself very tired, and I don't usually require much sleep."

"Whatever happened out there in the camp must have drained you as well," Orith said.

"I think you're right," Jarrowon said. "I wish I could remember exactly what happened. Maybe it will come back to me after I sleep."

"Perhaps I'll remember more as well," Penderyn said. "Maybe I'll even dream about it."

He stepped into his room and then turned back to his companions. "If I'm not up by noon, wake me. I'll want to check in on Tal and Dal."

He yawned again and closed the door. He barely had the energy to get out of his dirty clothes before he was fast asleep atop his bed.

Later that day, refreshed by a hearty meal and several hours of much needed sleep, Penderyn, Jarrowon and Orith headed for the House of Healers. While they walked, they were struck by the change in the mood of the city. The solemn quiet of the past weeks had been replaced by a happy, almost festive air, a direct result of Cornon's victory the previous day. Everywhere they looked, they saw people smiling and talking about the skirmish.

As they passed by the happy clusters of people, Penderyn hoped Arista had been out and about the city today. He knew the cheerful mood of her subjects would do her good after so many months of gloom.

They found the House of Healers without trouble. Set apart from the surrounding structures by a wide plaza, the small round building with its white marble dome glistened like a giant pearl under the afternoon sun. Two colorful gardens filled with the herbs and flowers used by the healers flanked the building.

The three friends entered the House of Healing through a wide archway. Inside, the air carried the faint, tangy scent of freshly crushed herbs.

A young maiden clad in a long yellow robe led them to Tal and Dal's chamber. The twins lay in adjacent beds, heads raised slightly by soft pillows. Clean white bandages covered much of their faces and arms. Despite their wounds, they were in good spirits.

"Ahhh, our rescuers," Dal said, smiling. "I hope you've come to save us from this horrible place as well." He smiled up at Gullinno, the chief healer, who was preparing some kind of medicine for the twins in a large copper bowl. Penderyn could smell its pungent odor. For the twins' sake, he hoped the mixture was an ointment and not a tonic.

Gullinno was said to be the oldest man in Kfastia, though no one knew his true age. He was certainly the oldest person Penderyn had ever seen. His wrinkled head was completely hairless, except for a few small tufts of white that passed for eyebrows, and his cheeks were so sunken his eyes seemed to bulge from his head. He was incredibly thin, and when he moved, which he did in a surprisingly sprightly manner, his bones seemed ready to burst through the pale, mottled skin that covered them.

"Some of our remedies may taste a bit unpleasant," Gullinno said cheerfully, "but they all have their purpose, I assure you."

"For someone who endured Rorgul's tortures with barely a sound, my brother has been making a lot of noise," Tal informed them with a laugh.

Dal's features twisted in feigned indignation. "That's it," he said. "You'll hear no more from me. Do your worst, old man."

"I hope that's a promise you'll keep," Gullinno said as he handed Dal a small cup of steaming yellow liquid. He poured a second cup for Tal. "Drink this."

The healer's lined face broke into a wide smile as Tal and Dal gulped their first swallows of the viscous mixture, their grimaces ample evidence of the drink's foul taste. Dal was about to speak, but remembered his promise and clamped his mouth shut.

Gullinno chucked. "That's much better," he said. "I wish all my patients were so brave." He turned to the visitors. "The drug will soon make them sleepy, but you may stay until then. Rest assured they're both doing fine."

"I like him," Penderyn said as the old man walked away.

"I'll tell him so," Dal said. "Perhaps next time he'll fix a cup of his delicious broth for you, too."

"What's going on with the war?" Tal asked. "We've heard nothing since we got back."

"Not much is happening," Penderyn said. "Halibur shows no sign of attacking, and Arista is content to wait inside the city. There was a minor skirmish yesterday. Cornon's company destroyed a raiding party that was burning farms. They made it back to the city before Halibur's army could react."

"I expect Halibur will bring Rorgul out of hiding now that his ally is no longer a secret," Dal said.

"I would think so," Jarrowon agreed, "if for no other reason than as a show of force to keep Legas or Dewellyn from joining Arista."

"I'll say one good thing about the waiting game Arista and Halibur are playing," Tal said. "It gives us a chance to recover without missing any of the fighting."

Penderyn looked down at his friend. The thought of Tal taking his place in battle with only one hand was not a pleasant one, but he said nothing, for he knew Tal's thirst for vengeance against the raiders who had murdered their parents matched his own. Gullinno's brew was beginning to make the twins drowsy, so the visitors took their leave with promises to return the following morning.

Several quiet days passed with no change in the stalemate around Kfastia. As expected, Rorgul's army of mercenaries had emerged from the forest and joined Halibur's forces in view of the city, perhaps hoping to intimidate the city's defenders.

Early on the fourth day, the quiet was broken by a sudden frenzy of activity in the mercenary encampment. Lookouts atop Kfastia's watchtowers sounded the alarm. The forces along the wall watched in stunned surprise as a column of scarlet-cloaked cavalry broke from the banit camp and galloped toward the city. The battlements erupted into a loud cheer as the defenders recognized the onrushing horsemen. They were the five hundred warriors who had been dispatched to Legas more than a week before.

Their commander had not expected to find his city encircled by an enemy when he returned, but he was an experienced soldier and had maintained his advance scouting parties even as he drew near to Kfastia. When his scouts reported the enemy's presence, he had taken advantage of the situation and struck at the most inviting target—the poorly prepared mercenary camp.

In just a few minutes his warriors had inflicted scores of casualties before breaking off the attack and racing for home. So unexpected was this assault from the rear that the Kfastian losses were almost nil.

Several companies of Halibur's cavalry made a half-hearted attempt to pursue the Kfastians, but they were far too late. The returning horsemen thundered through the gateway amid the cheers of their fellows long before their foes could overtake them.

News of the action reached the palace even before the commander could make his report. When he arrived in the throne room, a smiling Arista awaited him.

"Welcome, Takrill. Your Sumara congratulates you on the success of your return."

"I merely made the best of what I found," Takrill replied. "I hope I acted as Your Majesty wished."

"Exactly as I would have wished," Arista assured him. "Especially in choosing the mercenaries as your target, rather than our cousins from Colgoth. What word do you bring from Lord Mylar?"

Takrill shook his head. "The Lord of Legas bids me bring his Sumara his greetings and his regrets. His concern for his people will not allow him to take sides in this conflict, but he will heed your advice and prepare for war. He prays that you understand his position."

Arista nodded resignedly. "It is the reply I expected, though not the one for which I'd hoped. At least Mylar makes ready; that's something. Go enjoy a well deserved rest, Takrill. I'll inform the Council of the news you've brought."

"Nothing has really changed," Valdor said when Arista had repeated Mylar's message to her gathered advisors. "We did not expect help from outside, so we're no worse off than before."

"But should we continue to wait and do nothing, now that we know help is not forthcoming?" Jaspar asked.

"It seems the safest course," Aurelus said. "We have stores of food enough for some time yet."

"And when they run out?" Jaspar countered.

"Much can happen between then and now," Aurelus replied.

"I agree," General Kriselor said, surprising everyone. It was not like the commander to want to sit and wait. "I've wanted to do something to stir things up for some time now, but Arista has restrained me. Thanks to Takrill, that's now been taken care of. His attack is sure to cause more than enough trouble among our enemies. Rorgul lost many men; he'll not take that lightly. The man is a killer, not a soldier. Halibur will not easily dissuade him from wanting to avenge his humiliation. I think we can afford to wait and see what develops."

"I agree," Valdor said. "Rorgul may force Halibur's hand, making him do something he doesn't really want to."

"It's seems we are in agreement, then," Arista said. "We'll continue to do as we have done. We will wait."

CHAPTER 26

Late that night, something pulled Penderyn from his restless sleep. Whether it was some slight noise or perhaps only instinct that awakened him he didn't know, but he opened his eyes just in time to see a dark shape momentarily outlined against the slightly lesser darkness of the hallway before it slipped stealthily through the doorway. Whoever—or whatever—it was had not moved since.

Penderyn lay motionless in the dark, only his eyes moving as he strained to pierce the blackness of his bedchamber. His mind raced. He was defenseless, his only advantage surprise. The intruder probably did not know Penderyn was awake. Struggling to keep his breathing as rhythmic as possible, he inched his hand toward the sword hanging beside his bed. At last his fingers closed upon the cool leather hilt.

Reassured by the familiar feel of his weapon, he waited. His eyes slowly grew accustomed to the blackness, but still all he could see was a dark shadow beside the door.

His unknown visitor took a slow step forward. Penderyn tightened his grip on his sword and prepared to fling himself from the bed.

Perhaps sensing that the Last Born was awake, the intruder halted. He spoke in a low whisper.

"Penderyn, if you're awake, make no noise."

The voice was familiar, but Penderyn couldn't place it.

"I'll make no sound yet," he replied softly as he swung his legs over the side of the bed, his sword held before him. "But come no closer. Who are you?"

He tensed as the man struck a flint, the sound unnaturally loud in the stillness. A small candle illuminated his visitor's face. Penderyn at him in stared in surprise. The soft yellow glow was enough for Penderyn to recognize Zolar, a warrior from Arista's personal guard. Zolar's sword was sheathed at his side.

"What is it, Zolar?" Penderyn asked, lowering his own weapon. "Why do you come to my room like a thief in the night?"

"I bear an urgent summons from the Sumara," Zolar said quietly. "She wishes to see you at once."

"At this hour? Why?" Penderyn's surprise made his voice louder than he intended. He saw Zolar wince at the sound.

"The Sumara does not explain her commands to me," Zolar said, his voice barely above a whisper. "My orders are to fetch you immediately, and to be certain no one knows of your coming."

Penderyn was puzzled. He could not believe Arista meant to exclude even Jarrowon and Cornon. He would trust either with his life. But it was not his place to question the motives of his Sumara. Her orders to Zolar had been clear. Had Tal and Dal been here, he might have disobeyed even Arista, but the twins were still at the House of Healers. He would do as his Sumara wished.

He dressed quickly by the dim light of Zolar's candle, finishing by strapping his sword snugly about his waist.

"We must be silent," Zolar cautioned. "Are you ready?"

Penderyn nodded. Zolar blew out the candle and then stepped cautiously into the hallway, making certain no one was about before motioning Penderyn to follow. They turned right, avoiding Jarrowon's and Orith's chambers. Silently they crept through the slumbering household, making their way toward the servants' quarters. Zolar signaled Penderyn to stop midway down the corridor that connected the servants' wing to the rest of the house.

"We'll go out here," he whispered, indicating the narrow window in front of them.

The window was at least twenty feet above the flagstone courtyard below, but in the faint moonlight Penderyn saw a small, three-pronged grappling hook fastened over the thick masonry. A knotted rope trailed down to the ground. He knew now how Zolar had reached his room undetected. But why the need for such secrecy from the rest of the household?

"Go first, Last Born," Zolar instructed. "I shall follow."

Penderyn felt strange, leaving the house like a thief, but he pushed his misgivings aside and climbed quietly onto the window ledge. Hand over hand he descended the rope until he stood upon the ground of the deserted courtyard.

Zolar followed a moment later. With a firm shake of the rope, he detached the hook from the windowsill, deftly catching the metal prongs before they could strike against the flagstones.

Penderyn saw it was late enough that the *mocrah* had already ended. Only the dim glow of Ferus illuminated their way as they stealthily crossed the wide courtyard. Using the rope and the hook, they scaled the wall that circled the house. Once over the wall, Zolar signaled Penderyn to draw his hood about his face. The warrior did likewise, and then led Penderyn hurriedly away into the darkness.

The streets were mostly deserted, but Zolar stayed away from the main avenues, keeping instead to the darker and narrower side streets. The young warrior's head was in constant motion, his eyes probing the shadows for any witnesses to their passing. As far as Penderyn could tell, no one had seen them.

Just before they reached the palace, Zolar turned into a narrow alley leading away from the main gate.

"Must we enter even the palace in secret?" Penderyn asked in surprise.

"Those are my instructions," Zolar said. "No one is to know of your arrival, not even the palace guard. The Sumara is unsure who she can trust. She herself will let us in through her gardens."

Penderyn followed Zolar down the alley, wondering what new troubles beset Arista, that she should feel the need for such caution. Whatever it was, he was determined to help.

A muffled cough behind them drew him from his thoughts. He whirled around just as three men emerged from the shadows of a dark doorway. The pale moonlight glinted dully on their bared swords.

"Zolar!" he cried, whipping his sword from its scabbard.

Penderyn waited, but the men made no move to attack. Perhaps they were only thieves, he thought, with no stomach for facing two armed warriors. He felt Zolar's presence behind him. Something was wrong. The warrior was much too close. Should the thieves decide to attack, he and Zolar would only be in each other's way

Suddenly, he knew. He turned in time to see the club descending toward his head, but had no chance to defend himself against Zolar's treacherous blow. Lights exploded inside his head, and then there was only darkness.

Jarrowon was hunched over a collection of faded scrolls when Orith rushed into his chamber, his face flushed with excitement.

"Penderyn is gone!" the Eirydian shouted breathlessly. "He's disappeared!"

The lore master was on his feet in an instant. "Gone? What do you mean gone?" He rushed toward Penderyn's room.

"There's no sign of a struggle," Orith said as he followed Jarrowon into the Last Born's empty chamber.

Jarrowon quickly examined Penderyn's bed and chest.

"His sword is missing and he had time to dress," he said thoughtfully. "I sense no trace of magic. Wherever he's gone, it appears he left of his own free will. Did no one see him leave?"

"Cornon and Valdor are questioning the servants now, but so far, no one knows anything."

Cornon hurried into the room a moment later.

"Nothing," he reported, his head moving back and forth across Penderyn's room, hoping to spy some clue the others had missed. "No one saw or heard anything unusual all night."

Jarrowon scratched at his head, thinking. "I don't believe the Last Born would go anywhere without telling us," he said after a moment, "unless someone ordered him not to. There are few he would trust enough to obey such a summons. Tal and Dal, of course, and probably Arista. Someone should go to the House of Healing right away."

"I'll see to it," Cornon said. He motioned one of the house servants into the room and gave him his orders.

"Why would the twins or Arista wish to see Penderyn without our knowing it?" Orith asked. "It doesn't make sense."

"I'm afraid we'll find that they didn't," Jarrowon said grimly, "but we must check in any case."

"If you're right," Cornon said, "then Penderyn must have been lured away by some clever falsehood."

Jarrowon nodded. "I believe so, probably by a message delivered by someone he had no reason to doubt. By whom or for what purpose I do not know, though I can guess that Halibur may somehow be behind it." He shook his head. "The Last Born's true importance is known only to a few—if anything ill befalls him all Perator shall suffer."

An hour later, Jarrowon, Orith and Cornon arrived in the Council chamber. Arista and the Majhari were already gathered there, along with General Kriselor and a dozen of his captains. The three comrades settled into empty seats at the table. The crowded room quickly grew silent.

Arista spoke first. "Everyone knows why we're here," she said, her voice tight with anger. "Let's not waste any time. Jarrowon, have you learned anything further?"

"Not much. We found scratches on a window ledge and on the wall below that indicate Penderyn probably climbed from the house. It appears he left willingly, so we can only guess he must have been summoned by someone he knew and had reason to trust. Who that might be, or where they went, we don't know."

"I've spoken personally to each of the garrisons on duty last night," General Kriselor said. "They all report no one was seen trying to leave Kfastia."

"Then we know Penderyn is still within the city," Arista said hopefully. "The walls are well guarded. If no one saw him leave, he is still here somewhere."

"Guarding against an attack from outside is not always the same as watching for an escape from within," Jarrowon said. "Still, I think we should act on the assumption that the Last Born remains hidden somewhere in Kfastia."

"Your point about guarding against an escape is well taken, though," General Kriselor said. "I'll issue immediate orders for all sections to be watchful for anyone trying to leave the city."

"I want you to order an immediate block by block search of every building in the city as well, general," Arista commanded.

General Kriselor nodded. "Such a search will take time."

"Use as many men as you can spare. Leave only enough upon the battlements to defend against a sudden attack."

"I suggest we begin our search in the temple," Valdor said. "This kind of treachery smells of Chirops."

Arista nodded. "I agree. I want you to lead the search of the temple personally, Valdor. I know you will not be intimidated by our High Priest, as others might be."

Valdor and Cornon departed immediately to collect a dozen warriors from Cornon's troop, while General Kriselor remained behind with his captains to plan the search of the city. Jarrowon and Orith went with Valdor, for the lore master was eager to observe Chirops when they questioned him.

CHAPTER 27

Penderyn's head throbbed unmercifully, like someone was banging an iron gong inside his skull. For the hundredth time since he had regained consciousness, he cursed Zolar's treachery. Arista had suspected there was a spy within the palace, and she had been right. The traitor was a member of her own personal guard. Even now, Zolar was probably back at his post, awaiting his next opportunity to strike a treacherous blow against Kfastia. And Penderyn was the only one who knew it!

Frustrated, he strained against his bonds. The effort sent a searing pain shooting through his skull. He wished he could at least touch what he was certain must be an egg-sized lump on the back of his head, but his hands were tied firmly behind him to the back of a crude wooden chair. He had no idea where he was, or how long he'd been unconscious. Two candles provided a meager light in the small, windowless room, but the bare stone walls gave no clue to his whereabouts. The only sounds that penetrated his prison were an occasional set of muffled footsteps somewhere in the distance.

That Halibur was behind his misfortune Penderyn had little doubt, but why the Lord of Colgoth had risked kidnapping him was unclear—unless Halibur had somehow learned of his true importance as the Last Born.

Penderyn shuddered at the thought. If Halibur used him as a bargaining tool, Arista would have no choice but to yield. His importance to the future of Perator far outweighed who would be the ruler of Calistan. Somehow, he had to escape before that happened.

The sound of approaching footsteps pulled him from his thoughts. A key rattled in the lock, and the wooden door swung open. Chirops stood in the doorway. Penderyn was only mildly surprised to see the High Priest.

"I knew you were a traitor," Penderyn said, his voice a mixture of anger and disgust.

Chirops smiled. "Traitors are only found among the losers, my young friend. I do not intend to be one of them."

He walked slowly around behind Penderyn and lightly touched his head. The Last Born winced.

"I hope Zolar was not too rough," Chirops said. "I did not want you hurt—not badly, anyhow."

"What are you going to do with me?" Penderyn asked. "Hand me over to your master, Halibur?"

"I serve no master, Last Born, as Halibur will ultimately discover." The priest's voice was cruel and sinister, without the veneer of piousness he maintained in public. "I'll not take you anywhere just yet. You probably won't be surprised to learn that your disappearance has created quite a stir. It will be impossible to get you out of the city until things settle down."

"They'll not spare your temple from their search," Penderyn said, guessing that Chirops was holding him somewhere inside the temple.

"As a matter of fact, I expect them to come calling quite soon," the High Priest said unconcernedly. "But they won't find you. This temple originally served as Kfastia's first palace, used by Sumar himself while the present palace was being constructed. Underneath us are hidden catacombs unknown to anyone save myself. Even I stumbled upon them by only the merest accident. You'll be safe from discovery there, I assure you, until I decide I have need of you."

He cut the bonds holding Penderyn to the chair but left the Last Born's hands tied behind him. "Get up. It's time to move to your new home."

Chirops kept the point of his dagger against Penderyn's back as he ushered him through the doorway. The High Priest removed a torch from a holder on the wall and then directed Penderyn down a series of dim, narrow corridors and steep stairways. They saw no one as they descended ever deeper into the bowels of the temple.

At last they stopped. Before them was an ancient wooden door whose massive hinges were rusted with age and disuse. The huge door screamed in protest as Chirops pushed it open.

Damp, musty air assailed Penderyn's nostrils. The room was filled with piles of tattered old sacks and broken pieces of furniture dumped here and forgotten ages ago. Chirops shoved him inside, directing him along a narrow, twisting pathway between the heaps of junk.

Penderyn grew hopeful. The search for him would be thorough—even this deep beneath the temple, the searchers would find him. Surely Chirops knew that, though.

At the very back of the old storeroom, the High Priest carefully moved a pile of rotting rags. He tripped a hidden catch, opening a stone trapdoor so cleverly concealed Penderyn had not even seen it until it swung open. The flickering torch revealed a crude wooden stairway descending into a black pit below.

"This is your new home, Last Born. There's food and water for at least two weeks, should I be too busy to visit you before then. I'm sorry I can't leave you a light, but you'll get used to eating in the dark. Don't bother trying this trapdoor; it opens only from above."

Penderyn had a brief glimpse of a large stone dungeon as Chirops followed him slowly down the stairs. Suddenly, the priest cut his bonds and pushed him roughly down the last few steps. Taken by surprise, Penderyn tumbled to the hard stone floor.

Before he could recover, the door slammed shut above him, leaving him in utter blackness.

The searchers entered the temple unannounced. Valdor led the way, bursting through the open doorway and ignoring a pair of blue-robed priests who sought to remind them of the ban against bringing weapons into the holy place. The warriors quickly split into groups of three to begin painstakingly checking every inch of the huge structure for any sign of Penderyn.

Almost before they could begin, Chirops appeared from somewhere within the temple. Jarrowon watched him closely. The High Priest appeared calm and unworried.

"I presume you come seeking young Penderyn," he said.

"How did you know Penderyn was missing?" Cornon asked, not bothering to hide his suspicions.

"The whole city knows about it," Chirops responded smoothly. "I am the High Priest. Should I not know what my flock knows?" He turned to Valdor. "I'm not surprised to see you here. Ever are you willing to blaspheme our gods. I shall pray they are not offended as you ransack their temple."

"I need no intercession from you with the gods, priest," Valdor replied. "And do not waste your time trying to intimidate my warriors. They do not fear you any more than I." He signaled his men to continue with their search and then turned back to Chirops. "I want you with me at all times," he said. "As distasteful as your presence is, I prefer to have you where I can keep a watchful eye on you, even as I would a venomous serpent."

The High Priest's lips curled into a sneer. "Do what you will," he said confidently. "You'll find nothing here." Whether that was a boast or an expression of innocence the searchers could not tell.

The temple was huge, and the search took hours. Every storeroom and closet was checked closely, altars were tapped for sounds of hollowness, and every floor and wall examined for any signs of recent construction that might indicate a hiding place. Locked doors for which no key was forthcoming were promptly battered down, and any chest or cupboard deemed sufficiently large was pried open. They found nothing.

"Are you satisfied now, blasphemer," Chirops taunted when at last the searchers were finished.

"Our failure has not changed my thoughts one bit, priest," Valdor said evenly. "I'm as certain as ever you are behind this thing." He waved his warriors to take their leave. "We'll be watching you closely," he promised Chirops. "Have no doubt of that. Whenever you leave this temple, someone will be watching."

He turned his back to Chirops and strode from the temple.

"Should you have warned him that he'll be watched?" Orith asked as they descended the temple steps. "Won't that make him even more cautious?"

"He'll have expected no less," Valdor replied. "What he may not expect is that he'll be watched inside the temple as well."

Jarrowon raised an eyebrow in surprise.

"Not all his priests are happy with Chirops," Valdor said, allowing himself a trace of a smile. "I'll see that they keep a watchful eye on him. Perhaps his arrogance will betray him."

"He bears watching even if he knows nothing about Penderyn," Jarrowon said. "There's treachery in his heart, of that I'm certain."

CHAPTER 28

For two full days, General Kriselor's troops searched the city with painstaking thoroughness, but with no luck. As the areas still to be searched grew smaller, hopes of finding Penderyn dwindled. Finally, they had to admit defeat. If the Last Born was indeed still within Kfastia's walls, he was too well hidden to be found.

Arista was determined to repeat the entire search, including the temple. But before she could issue her new orders, she was confronted by a more immediate problem—a report that Danustiri had added his army to the forces arrayed outside the city.

Danustiri's unexpected commitment to Halibur's side was a demoralizing blow. The Sumara had thought the Lord of Dewellyn would remain ostensibly neutral, at least until the tide of the war was much more certain. Indeed, that had been Danustiri's intention, until Halibur forced his hand with an ultimatum to join forces or risk being considered an enemy. The ultimatum had been precipitated by the very factor General Kriselor had predicted—Rorgul's desire for swift revenge.

The bandit leader had demanded an attack upon the city, refusing to heed Halibur's arguments against such a move. Halibur was left with little choice. Not wanting to risk a frontal assault without a stronger force, he had compelled Danustiri to act. Unknown to anyone but the two leaders, Halibur had promised to give Danustiri rule over Legas once Kfastia was defeated.

The defenders of Kfastia knew that Danustiri's appearance signaled an attack was imminent. General Kriselor immediately doubled the garrison atop the walls and put the entire army at full alert, leaving few warriors for a search for Penderyn. Still, those who could be spared continued to search the city.

The assault against Kfastia began early the next morning.

Halibur aimed his main thrust at the east wall. With the glare of the spring sun at their backs, wave after wave of gold caped warriors surged slowly across the plain. The rhythmic pounding of marching drums boomed ahead of them.

Just beyond the range of the archers atop the wall, the well-drilled attackers halted. Their own bowmen moved quickly to the front, ready to provide covering fire for the infantry when they stormed the city. Even Rorgul's unkempt mercenaries showed surprising discipline as they massed upon the right flank of Halibur's army.

A strange quiet settled over the battlefield. For a brief moment the armies faced each other, until a trumpet blast shattered the silence.

Lines of archers surged forward behind the protective shields of rows of infantry. Arrows rained down upon them from the battlements, but most bounced harmlessly off the wall of shields. When the attackers were fifty yards from the wall, a second trumpet call echoed across the field. Halibur's archers rose from behind the shields and launched their missiles. Momentarily protected by the hail of arrows, the infantry charged forward.

A thousand warriors raced across the narrow stretch of open ground, carrying scores of tall wooden ladders. The defending archers concentrated their aim on the men who carried the ladders, but still the ladders surged forward. Whenever one carrier fell, another warrior replaced him, until finally one ladder, and then another and another were thrust up against the wall.

The Kfastians spilled cauldrons of flaming oil down upon the warriors who scurried up the ladders. Terrible screams of agony rang above the din, and the acrid smells of charred flesh and burning oil filled the air. Still the attackers came on, pushed forward by the crush of their comrades behind. Every foot of progress was paid for with dozens of lives as a withering storm of arrows and stones rained down from the battlements.

Wave after wave of Halibur's troops broke upon the wall, until finally one warrior gained the top. He fell almost immediately, pierced by two spears. Behind him came a second, and then a third. Together they held back the defenders for one brief moment, long enough for more of their comrades to scramble atop the battlements, before they too fell. The enemy had gained a toehold atop the wall.

General Kriselor quickly spotted the breach and rushed reinforcements to the beleaguered section in time to stem the growing tide, but they were unable to push the invaders from their position on the wall.

The attack was costing Halibur's army dearly, but by sheer weight of numbers they forced a second and then a third foothold upon the battlements. Each time the defenders rushed fresh warriors to the danger spot, but Kriselor could sense that the tide of the battle was beginning to go badly. The veteran commander knew he had to gamble, to do something to break the momentum of the attack. He dispatched a messenger to his cavalry.

Minutes later, the main gate was thrust open. Hundreds of horsemen poured through the gateway, led by Cornon's battletested company. The mounted warriors swept into the enemy foot soldiers massed at the base of the wall, cutting through the crowded attackers with gruesome efficiency.

Rorgul's bandits were the first to break and flee under the assault. Their giant leader tried to rally his men, but he was unable to force his way through the mass of humanity to confront the Kfastians. He bellowed and screamed as he bulled his way forward, but he was too late. The damage was done. With the source of reinforcements below disrupted, the invaders atop the wall were quickly decimated. Kfastia's battlements were swept free of the enemy.

Too late, Halibur ordered his own cavalry into the fray.

Cornon pulled his men back toward the gate. The outnumbered defenders formed a box before the entrance, allowing the gates to be swung open while they engaged the enemy horsemen. Slowly the Kfastians gave ground, pulling their box ever tighter around the gateway.

Now came the most dangerous part of the whole plan. The Kfastians had to retreat through the gates without allowing the enemy to pour into the city behind them. The cavalry and the gate garrison had practiced for this moment countless times, and now the safety of city depended on it.

At a signal from Cornon, his warriors suddenly spun their mounts around and charged back toward the city, gaining a split second advantage over their surprised foes. At the same time, the guards above the gate ignited their waiting cauldrons of oil. As the rear of the retreating column neared the gateway, the gatekeepers spilled their fuel. For a moment it seemed the flaming shower would fall upon their comrades, but the timing was perfect. The oil splashed just behind the Kfastians into the faces of their pursuers. Shrill screams of burning riders and horses rent the air as the defenders raced into the safety of the city.

The surprise assault had broken the backbone of the attack. Knowing there would be no victory this day, Halibur ordered his trumpeter to signal a retreat. Fuming, the Lord of Colgoth stormed back to his tent.

CHAPTER 29

In the aftermath of the battle, the Council gathered in the palace. General Kriselor arrived last, making his way directly from the battlements. His uniform was soiled and wrinkled, but he gave little thought to his appearance as he circled the table and stood behind his chair, ready to give his report. Several of the Majhari had watched the battle from the safety of the western watchtower, but only General Kriselor had been atop the east wall where the fighting had occurred.

"Sit down, General," Arista said. "You've earned a bit of rest. Let me congratulate you on your victory today."

"Thank you, Your Majesty," the general replied as he settled into his seat. "Our victory was a costly one, I'm afraid. We lost more than a hundred warriors today. In the face of the odds against us, we can ill afford such losses."

"Can we withstand another assault?" Arista asked with some anxiousness.

General Kriselor shrugged his broad shoulders. "Another attack like today, probably, but I doubt Halibur will allow himself to be rushed into a second attack. If he listens to his generals, he'll build siege towers and a battering ram. Whether we can repel that kind of assault, I'm afraid I do not know."

General Kriselor's bluntness startled some of his listeners. They had thought the city safe behind its walls.

"Are you saying we cannot defend our city against Halibur's army?" Jaspar asked.

"Not at all," General Kriselor replied. "I'm just saying that I cannot be certain of the outcome against a well-planned assault."

"What do you suggest then?" Arista asked.

General Kriselor stood up, more comfortable on his feet than sitting.

"First, we need to restore our defenses to readiness as quickly as possible, in case Halibur does make another rash attack. My men are already doing that. I'd also like to send a few men to spy on our foes. It would be a big help to know in more detail what kind of preparations Halibur is making."

"Hasn't the enemy tightened their watch since the rescue of the twins?" Jaspar asked.

"They have," General Kriselor replied. "But outside of the *mocrah*, the nights are very dark. A small group of careful men should be able to make it past the patrols. Their information could be invaluable. I think it's worth the risk."

"Do it, then," Arista decided. "But ask for volunteers."

"I will, Your Majesty."

Arista looked around at her advisors. "Does anyone have anything else to suggest?"

"Only that we include at least one person among the spies whose main job will be to seek information about Penderyn," Valdor said.

"Consider it done," General Kriselor said, without waiting for instruction from Arista.

No one had anything more to add, so Arista dismissed them with the reminder to come to her immediately should anyone come up with any new ideas.

That same afternoon, Gullinno released Tal and Dal from the House of Healers, but only after extracting Jarrowon's promise that he would keep the twins from all but the most gentle activity for the next few days.

"I'll be glad to be rid of them," the old healer said to the lore master as a pair of his assistants helped Tal and Dal from the coach that had carried them from the House of Healers. "They were getting little enough rest with us, with all their worrying about their young friend. At least out here they'll know what's going on."

He handed two small pouches of herbs to Jarrowon and winked. "Have them drink some of this tonight, to make sure they get some sleep."

Tal and Dal still wore several small bandages on their faces, as well as a number of larger ones beneath the loose white gowns given them by the healers. But as soon as they were out of the coach, they waved away the pair of litters Valdor's servants had prepared for them.

"We can walk," Tal said.

The servants looked to Valdor, who nodded his agreement.

The twins immediately converged on Jarrowon. Gullinno shrugged at the lore master in exasperation and signaled his driver to depart.

"Can we at least go inside before you begin to interrogate me?" Jarrowon asked as the healers rode away. "I promised Gullinno you'd rest. You wouldn't make a liar out of me so soon, would you?"

The twins nodded and hobbled slowly up the wide stone stairway. Once inside the entrance hall, they settled into the closest seats they could find, a pair of stiff backed wooden chairs just inside the doorway. They were not going to wait any longer.

"Now," Tal said. "Tell us what you're doing to find Penderyn."

Jarrowon sighed. "The search does not go well, I'm afraid. I've been crisscrossing the city all day, on the slim hope I might be able to sense some trace of the Last Born's magic. Orith has been trying to use his dream power to try to find some clue to

Penderyn's whereabouts. Neither of us has had any luck."

The twins turned to Valdor.

"Patrols are making random searches throughout the city," Valdor explained. "Chirops is being secretly watched twenty-four hours a day. So far, he's done nothing suspicious."

"Is that all anyone is doing?" Tal said angrily, rising from his chair. "A couple of patrols and a few spies?"

"There's nothing more we can do at the moment," Valdor said. "We've already turned the city inside out. Right now, Halibur is our more pressing worry."

"More pressing for Kfastia perhaps, but not for Perator," Jarrowon said solemnly. He turned to Tal and Dal. "No one wants to find the Last Born more than I do. His safety has always been my primary concern. But Valdor is right. There's nothing more we can do right now."

"Perhaps Halibur has already gotten Penderyn out of the city," Dal suggested. "You and Penderyn rescued us from the enemy's camp, can we attempt less?"

"We were able to rescue you because we knew where you were," Jarrowon reminded him. "Penderyn could be anywhere."

"Halibur could have him in his camp, or even back in Colgoth," Valdor said. "But if he does have Penderyn, ask yourself why he abducted him. Halibur knows nothing of the Last Born's power, so it can only be for his value to Arista as a symbol of the gods' favor. Sooner or later, Halibur will use him to bargain with. That will be the time for us to act."

"I suppose you're right," Tal agreed, his reluctance obvious. "But that doesn't mean we have to like it." He looked from Valdor to Jarrowon. "You'll let us know as soon as you learn anything?"

"Of course," Jarrowon promised.

Three days passed with no threatening activity from the enemy. Halibur had been allowed to send a company of unarmed warriors to the base of the wall to collect his dead, but since then his forces had made no move toward the city. General Kriselor had apparently been right. The Lord of Colgoth was making certain his forces were well prepared before striking again.

The general used the time to restore Kfastia's defenses. Warriors swarmed about the east wall, collecting the stones they had hurled down upon the attackers and returning them to their piles atop the battlements. Porters carried fresh oil from the storehouses and replenished the depleted supplies, while others gathered the ladders left behind by the enemy into a huge pile beneath the wall and set them afire.

Inside the walls, random searches for Penderyn continued without success. Arista was frustrated by the failure to find any clue to the whereabouts of her youngest subject. With the war temporarily at rest, she ordered General Kriselor to pull every spare man from his defenses to conduct a second full-scale search. Twenty-five hundred warriors began to comb the city, while Valdor and Jarrowon returned to the temple, this time accompanied by the rapidly recovering Tal and Dal, as well as a dozen Kfastian warriors.

Unwilling to trust any eyes but their own, the twins insisted on searching every room themselves. With Valdor and Jarrowon behind them, they moved determinedly from level to level, shouting Penderyn's name as they went. Ignoring the exhaustion that steadily sapped the strength from their still weakened frames, they carefully probed every corner and every shadow. Their hopes ebbed as the hours dragged slowly by, but they refused to quit.

Not until well into the evening did they reach the final room: the ancient storeroom at the end of the temple's lowest level. The door screamed in protest as they pushed it open and entered the foul-smelling chamber.

The twins watched as the soldiers moved every piece of junk, but they found nothing. The cleverly constructed trapdoor hidden underneath a simple pile of rotting rags eluded the search. The twins' shouts went unanswered, blocked by several feet of earth and stone from penetrating into the secret chamber below. Despondent and exhausted, they were forced to admit defeat.

They returned home only to find more bad news awaiting them. The army had finished its door-to-door search an hour earlier and had come up empty as well.

In his prison deep beneath the temple, Penderyn sat in the stygian gloom, unaware his friends were even now searching the temple and ignorant that Halibur had launched his attack on the city. Penderyn knew his friends would never cease looking for him, but he was equally certain they would never find him in this long forgotten dungeon. Until Chirops returned for him, there was nothing he could do but wait.

But waiting was difficult. Time had no meaning down here in the unrelenting blackness. He ate when he was hungry—mostly dried fruit and cured meat Chirops had obviously stored down here for just this purpose—and slept when he was tired. How many actual days and nights had passed he had no idea, but he knew it was more than a few.

His gravest enemy was the unending boredom. With no sights to stimulate his vision and no sounds to register in his ears, he began to see and hear things he was certain were not really there. He had to constantly remind himself they were not real. Still, he was not sure how much more of this he could stand before madness claimed him.

To fight off the impending madness, he spent his waking hours exercising—stretching, doing pushups and other calisthenics, and walking back and forth across his cell. Activity would keep the madness away—at least for awhile—and keep him fit should the opportunity for escape present itself.

He spent hours exploring his prison with his hands, carefully tracing his fingers along the walls and floor until he could visualize an exact picture of the rough stone. He knew precisely where the bins and crates of supplies were located and how many steps he could take before crashing into one of the walls. Even so, it was some time before he could bring himself to trust his instinct and walk without his hands stretched out in front of him. Now, he moved about his tiny, timeless world like a man who had been blind all his life.

When he was tired or overly bored, he slept. Each time he closed his eyes, he tried to harness the power of his dreams, hoping to somehow create a future in which he escaped his prison, but such magic was still far beyond his control. His dreams remained as dark as his cell.

CHAPTER 30

Kfastia waited, its citizens and soldiers patient and determined, while Halibur prepared for his next attack. The city's defenses had been completely replenished and were as ready as they could be; there was nothing else to be done until they learned more of Halibur's plans. Six volunteers—four soldiers and two hunters, one of whom was Soldrok—had successfully evaded the patrols ringing the city. A brief candle signal from the south woods each of the last four nights confirmed their continued safety. Thirty minutes ago, one of the spies had returned to the city under the cover of darkness.

Lost in thought, General Kriselor stared out at the hundreds of flickering camp fires that covered the plain outside the city like a carpet of yellow and orange jewels. Laughter, shouts and the clatter of cooking implements from the encampment floated across the plain through the still night air, but the sounds washed over him unnoticed.

The report from his spy troubled him greatly. Halibur was building *two* huge battering rams and fully a score of giant siege towers. The general had not expected so many. That many towers and two battering rams could only mean that Halibur planned to strike simultaneously from at least two sides. The spy had said the siege equipment could be finished in three or four days.

To sustain a two-pronged attack, Halibur would have to commit most of his army, gambling that he could end the war with one giant blow. Kfastia's defenses would be stretched thin—General Kriselor wondered if they would hold.

The rest of the report had been little less bleak. The spies had learned nothing about Penderyn, even though one of them had killed an enemy sentry and donned his uniform so he could wander through the camp. He'd spent most of a day moving about the encampment, managing even to gain a brief glimpse into Halibur's pavilion, but had found nothing to indicate the Last Born was anywhere in the enemy camp. Penderyn seemed to have vanished.

General Kriselor turned his thoughts from Penderyn to the impending attack. He began pacing along the battlement, running ideas through his head as he walked. One thing he knew—something bold would have to be done if Kfastia was to survive.

The following morning, General Kriselor joined Arista and the Majhari at the Council table. He informed them of his spy's report, holding nothing back.

"If we don't take action," he concluded, "our chances of victory are small."

For a moment, the room was silent as the members of the Majhari looked at one another.

"I presume you have a suggestion," Arista said finally.

"I have several ideas," General Kriselor replied, "but each is more dangerous than the next."

"There is no danger in discussing them," she said calmly. "Tell us."

General Kriselor folded his hands on the table in front of him.

"The siege equipment is being constructed near the rear of the enemy encampment," he explained. "A small raiding party could circle through the woods the same way our spies did. A surprise strike might succeed in destroying some of the towers or even the battering rams."

"Such an attack would be suicide," Jaspar protested. "Our

warriors would have almost no chance to escape."

"And what would their sacrifice gain us?" Arista asked pointedly. "A few days at most? Surely Halibur would simply improve his security and rebuild his weapons."

"He would," General Kriselor admitted. "That's why I have another idea."

Arista waited expectantly, but the general hesitated.

"Well?" she asked.

"We could make better use of surprise by attacking Halibur in force."

If General Kriselor expected Arista to be shocked, he was wrong. She sat silently for a moment, considering the idea.

"How large a force would you use?" she asked finally.

"To have any chance of victory," General Kriselor said solemnly, "we would need the entire army."

Surprised gasps erupted from around the table.

"What of the city?" Aurelus asked. "You would leave it defenseless?"

"If we fail, there will be no need to defend Kfastia," General Kriselor replied. "Whether victory or defeat, the outcome will be total."

Arista listened in silence, pondering the general's words.

"Can we win?" she asked. "Surely surprise cannot offset the numbers gathered against us."

"There's one chance," General Kriselor said. "If we inflict a severe enough blow to Colgoth's army before they can organize their defense, Danustiri may withdraw his warriors from the field."

"You may be right," Arista agreed. "Danustiri cannot have his heart in this battle. But can we strike such a blow?"

General Kriselor rubbed his temples. "That's the question I wrestled with all night," he admitted. "The odds are not in favor of it. But I think the chances are better than trying to survive a well planned assault."

"Perhaps there's a way to lessen the odds," Valdor said. "What if we attacked from the rear as well as the front?"

General Kriselor looked at him questioningly. So did Arista.

"That would increase our chances, no doubt," the general said. "But I have no army behind them."

"Then let's put one there. Cannot small groups of warriors do what your spies did? They could slip over the wall a half dozen at a time and gather in the woods, well out of sight."

General Kriselor did some quick calculations. "It would take several hundred men, at least, to have much of an effect," he said. "But if we spread it over two nights, perhaps we could get enough warriors into position." He looked to Arista.

"Is it your judgment that such a plan is our best chance for victory?" she asked.

The general replied without hesitation. "It is."

Arista turned to Valdor. "And you, Valdor?"

"I agree," Valdor replied.

"So be it. General Kriselor, make your plans."

CHAPTER 31

The surprise attack was set for just before dawn. Mounted warriors filled the dark courtyard behind the east gate and stretched in long columns down the broad avenues that fed into the plaza. Behind them waited scores of wagons and carts crammed with warriors who would be sped across the plain behind the cavalry. The rest of the infantry was massed in the narrower side streets. They would follow the wagons through the gate and join the battle as swiftly as they could.

In the two nights since Arista made the decision to attack, almost four hundred warriors had filtered over the wall to join forces in the forest and circle behind the foe. Commanding this vital force was the able Takrill.

At the front of the Kfastian army, ready to spearhead the attack, was Cornon's battle-tested company. Reinforced by three additional companies, their mission was to penetrate as deeply and quickly as possible into the enemy encampment in hopes of reaching Halibur himself. The chance was a slim one, Cornon knew, but if it worked, it offered the swiftest route to victory. Should they manage to kill or capture the Lord of Colgoth, the battle would be ended. If they failed to reach Halibur, they were to keep the enemy divided while the remainder of the army struck into the camp on either side.

Only the faintest yellow glow from the as yet invisible sun tinged the eastern sky when General Kriselor raised his arm in signal. Cornon surveyed his waiting warriors and then waved his arm in acknowledgement. General Kriselor lowered his arm, and the huge gates swung open.

Through the gateway the mounted column spewed, a scarlet arrow streaking through the pre-dawn twilight straight toward the heart of their foe. Thundering hoof beats rent the early morning stillness and the ground shuddered with the weight of their charge.

They sped across the plain and swept away the sentries guarding the huge encampment like dust before a gale-force wind. Horses brayed and men screamed as the Kfastians fell upon the enemy, wreaking a fearsome toll upon the bewildered warriors who struggled half-dressed from their tents. Deep into the awakening army they thrust, until finally the camp's very size and confusion combined to spread the column and slow its charge. Recognizing the danger, Cornon consolidated his forces against the stiffening resistance and put aside for the moment any thoughts of reaching Halibur.

By now, the infantry had crossed the plain as well, striking with grim efficiency at both sides of the divided enemy army. Hundreds of Halibur's men and scores of mercenaries fell in those first few minutes.

Near the front of the column that slashed its way into the mercenary encampment were Tal and Dal. Side by side they fought, cutting and rending like men possessed. With each raider they slew they gained a small satisfaction, but the man they really wanted was Rorgul. Their thirst for vengeance could not be quenched until the villain who had killed their parents and destroyed their village had been brought to justice. So far, they had seen no sign of the murderer.

The battle was going as well as anyone dared hope. Just as the enemy resistance began to stiffen, Takrill launched his attack from the rear. Halibur's forces were swept near panic by the unexpected appearance of a second army at their backs. Their will to fight began to crumble.

Atop the battlements, Arista watched the battle together with the Majhari. General Kriselor's bold plan seemed to be working. Victory looked to be within their grasp. With the tide of the battle so clear, Arista thought there was little chance Danustiri would order his army into the fray.

She might have been right, but she could not know Danustiri was not alone in his tent. Halibur had visited his ally late the previous evening and had remained through the night. Worse still, Rorgul was there with him.

Halibur commanded Danustiri to attack, and Danustiri knew he dare not disobey. One menacing scowl from Rorgul told him his fate would be swift and final if he refused.

With no other choice, he ordered his commander to attack.

Several thousand fresh warriors poured into the battle. Halibur's troops regrouped, their spirits restored by the appearance of their allies. Cornon's advance column was quickly cut off from the rest of the Kfastian army, and Takrill's small force was surrounded moments later.

On the left flank, Rorgul thundered into the fighting. The bandit leader bulled his way to the heart of the battle, his sword red with blood as he rallied his army of cutthroats around him.

Outnumbered now almost three to one, the Kfastians had no choice but to fight on, praying for a miracle that might deliver victory against all odds.

In the center of the battle, Cornon knew he had but one slim chance. He led his men in a desperate attack toward Halibur's gold pavilion. Somehow, his valiant warriors managed to fight their way to the huge tent, but when Cornon rushed through the entrance, Halibur was nowhere to be found.

General Kriselor gathered his forces into a defensive formation, hoping to hold out as long as possible, while on the other side of the battle Takrill did the same.

Though their own column was now surrounded by

mercenaries, Tal and Dal fought on determinedly, pushing ever closer to Rorgul with but one thought on their minds—to gain vengeance against the murderer even in defeat.

CHAPTER 32

In the silent limbo of his prison, Penderyn awoke to yet another day of emptiness, blissfully ignorant of the battle raging outside the city. Once again, he had failed in his effort to direct his dreams. He stood up, stretched his arms out to the side, and breathed a deep sigh that turned into a long yawn. As usual in the unrelenting blackness, it took him a few moments before he was fully awake.

He would no longer try to control his dreams, he promised himself. In the past, his power had always been most useful when it rose unbidden; despite all he had learned, it seemed that might still be true. If his power was going to help him escape, it would do so on its own. Until then, he would wait—and hope.

He wondered what was happening in the world outside his prison. How many days had passed since Chirops had thrown him into this dungeon, he had no idea. Nine times he had slept so far, but how long he slept and how much time passed between sleeps he had no way of knowing. Perhaps as few as four or five days had come and gone, or maybe as many as ten or twelve. It seemed like weeks, but he knew it couldn't have been that long. Chirops had said there was food enough for at least two weeks and there was still plenty left. Penderyn yawned again.

When he opened his eyes, he saw a tiny gold dot floating in the blackness. He rubbed his eyes, wondering if the darkness and isolation were playing tricks on his brain, but when he moved his hands away, the golden globe was still there. Ever so slowly, it grew larger and brighter, like a miniature sun drawing steadily nearer. He thought immediately of the *Luminari*. Had Alythym and Elaemir gathered enough strength to come to him again? Could they somehow help free him from his prison?

Suddenly, lines of crackling red lightning burst from the golden sphere, spreading upward and outward into the darkness. Strangely, the red light had no effect on the blackness anywhere else in his cell. It was as if each bolt was self-contained, with no light to shed beyond its own outline.

Penderyn stepped back. He was pretty sure this was not the *Luminari*. But if not, then what was it?

Slowly the lightning began to ease. The jagged red beams thickened, gradually coalescing into a single form. Penderyn watched in startled amazement as the light transformed itself into the glowing image of a man. He found himself staring into a familiar, red-bearded face, a face he had seen only in his dreams. He wondered if he was dreaming now. This did not feel like any of his dreams, but perhaps it was a new and different kind.

"Have faith, my son. I'm here to help you."

Penderyn could not believe his ears. The sound of a voice was startling enough, but what it said was even more surprising. This apparition could only be Mandrar, the father he had never met and knew almost nothing about. He wondered if he was going mad, or if his father had somehow found him after all these years. He prayed it was the latter.

"Come to me, my son."

Penderyn couldn't tell whether the apparition actually spoke, or if the voice sounded only inside his head. Either way, the words were unmistakable. He stepped slowly forward, his right hand stretched out in front of him.

"Quickly," the voice said. "Every moment we delay increases the danger."

Penderyn shook away his doubts and crossed toward his father. The image floated away from him to the far side of the dungeon. He followed it.

"Take my hand," the image commanded.

Penderyn sucked in a deep breath and reached for the glowing hand, but felt only the stone wall of his cell. He heard a faint click and then a sound like the whisper of a breeze. The image of his father winked out.

He rubbed his eyes again, wondering what had just happened. Had his vision merely been some kind of hallucination? If so, then madness could not be far away. He reached out into the blackness in front of him, feeling for the wall, but found nothing. Impossibly, the wall was gone!

Stunned, he quickly probed the darkness with both hands and discovered there was now a narrow opening in front of him where only seconds before had been solid rock. Somehow, he must have tripped the catch to a secret passageway. Whether his hand had been guided by a vision born of his own power or one somehow created by his father, he didn't know and he didn't care. Something had shown him a way out of his cell, and that was all that mattered.

He stepped carefully into the passage, his left hand extended ahead of him, his right hand sliding lightly along the wall. He walked slowly, testing each step before putting his weight down onto the invisible floor. In the utter blackness, it would be all too easy to tumble into some unseen pit. Any injury down here could mean his death.

For what seemed like hours he crept through the darkness, feeling his way along the wall like a blind man. He should have been afraid, he knew, but he had been surrounded by blackness for so long it no longer seemed threatening. The passage made several twists and turns, but so far there had been no branching tunnels to worry about, at least not to his right, where his hand remained in constant contact with the smooth stone wall. Whether he had passed any openings in the other side, he had no way of knowing.

After a time the stone became rough and uneven, and he

guessed the man-made tunnel had given way to a natural cavern. The cool air took on a faint telluric smell, and the floor felt different under his feet. He reached down and discovered the floor now consisted of packed dirt. Several times he heard soft, scurrying footfalls hurrying away from his approach, but thankfully, whatever creatures shared the cavern with him left him alone.

Suddenly, the wall to his right disappeared. He was so accustomed to its solid presence against his hand that he lost his balance. With a startled cry, he stumbled sideways into the blackness. His knee struck painfully against a stone ledge, and then his hands landed abruptly on a higher platform. It took him a moment before he realized what it was. He had fallen against a stairway!

Hope surged through him. Stairs were not made without a reason; they had to lead somewhere. He prayed these would lead to freedom.

Had there been any light at all, he would have raced up the steps, but he was forced to contain his excitement and slowly feel his way up what turned out to be a steep, curving climb. He hugged the wall to his left, for to the right of the stairs there was nothing but empty blackness. How far a drop lurked there, he did not want to find out.

Eighty-six careful steps he counted before at last he reached the top. Expecting another step, Penderyn almost stumbled, but the slowness of his pace saved him from falling on his face. Chest heaving, he paused to catch his breath.

When his breathing returned to normal, he extended his arms to the sides and felt smooth stone with each hand. This was no natural cave. Someone had built this passageway.

His excitement mounted. He strode forward, his left arm again extended in front of him, but he managed only three steps before he found his way blocked. He reached to the left, expecting that the tunnel had turned, but felt only smooth, solid rock. Frantically he slid his hands back and forth across the unexpected barrier, but there was no opening. The passage had abruptly ended.

For a moment he stood in stunned disbelief, hands pressed against the stone, wondering where he had gone wrong.

He began examining the wall that blocked his way, patiently moving his hands in careful, systematic rows from the floor upward until he felt a small iron handle protruding from the rock. He shook his head and smiled to himself. The passage had not really ended. He had simply reached a doorway.

He pulled the heavy stone door open and gasped in surprise.

His world was no longer black. A dim red glow barely illuminated the tiny chamber in front of him, but to Penderyn's light-starved eyes it was like the coming of a long awaited dawn. He stared down at his hands in wonder. For the first time in what seemed like ages, he could actually see them.

He stepped through the doorway and discovered the source of the light. The glow emanated from a large red jewel, a jewel embedded in the hilt of an ancient sword that lay upon a chest-high marble dais. Even in its simple leather scabbard, Penderyn recognized the weapon instantly. He had seen this same sword on a giant mosaic in the palace. Sumar's Flaming Sword, lost for centuries, had been found.

Penderyn approached the legendary blade reverently. Why Sumar had chosen to hide his weapon in this long forgotten vault, Penderyn guessed he would never know.

Fate works in strange ways, he thought as he stared down at the gleaming red gem. Had Chirops not kidnapped him and imprisoned him in the secret dungeon, the Flaming Sword might never have been discovered.

He reached for the sword, hesitating momentarily before closing his grip around the jeweled hilt. Because of the glow, he thought it might feel warm, but it felt like any other sword in his hand. Gently, he lifted sword and scabbard from the dais.

A sound like the rumble of far off thunder echoed through the cavern as the wall behind the dais swung slowly open, revealing still another hidden passage. At the far end of the passage he saw the soft glow of daylight. Penderyn struggled to hold back his tears. At long last, he was free!

He hurried forward toward the light. When he emerged from the tunnel he was surprised to find himself surrounded by trees—his underground journey had not only taken him beyond the city, but under the surrounding plain as well.

Even the shaded light of the forest was too much for his sensitive eyes, forcing him to squeeze them shut while they slowly grew accustomed to the glare. After several minutes of awkward blinking and squinting, he was finally able to see without discomfort.

He looked down at the sword. In the daylight, the jewel seemed scarcely to glow at all, but when he pulled the sword from its scabbard the gem suddenly burst to life, filling his hand with brilliant red light that reflected from the shining blade like darting tongues of flame. He felt a surge of energy shoot up his arm and through his body.

Here was a weapon all Calistan revered, the symbol of their first and greatest ruler. Surely Halibur's warriors would not fight against an army led by such a talisman. He held the answer to Arista's problems right here in his hand.

But how was he to use the sword's power? Halibur's entire army stood between him and the city; he could not just walk up to the enemy forces and tell them to go home. They would probably kill him and take the sword for Halibur. Even if Halibur's men hesitated to attack him because he possessed the Flaming Sword, the blade would have little effect on Rorgul's cutthroats, who knew nothing of its history and importance.

Penderyn thought of sneaking back to Kfastia under the cover of darkness, but there was the chance he might be captured, and he could not risk letting the sword fall into Halibur's hands. With such a symbol in his possession, the Lord of Colgoth's victory would be all but assured. Penderyn was stymied. He held the key to victory in his hands, but he didn't know how to use it.

He needed an army.

CHAPTER 33

Atop Kfastia's wall, the mood of Arista and her advisors steadily darkened as they watched the battle that would decide her fate unfold. When the first grey light of morning had illuminated the battlefield and revealed the extent to which the enemy had been caught off guard, their hearts had been filled with hope. The swift victory sought by General Kriselor had seemed well within reach.

But as the sun climbed higher it, they realized there would be no quick victory. Arista groaned when Danustiri's army joined the fight; she had not thought the Lord of Dewellyn would send his men into a battle that seemed to be going against Halibur. She had no way of knowing it was the unfortunate presence of Halibur and Rorgul in Danustiri's camp that had prompted his action.

The watchers' anguish mounted as the Kfastian attack was splintered and their forces surrounded. Arista recalled Penderyn's dream—the defeat it had foretold seemed about to come true.

Valdor was the first to openly acknowledge the seemingly inevitable outcome.

"I'm afraid our gamble is lost," he said. "Arista, you must leave the city or your life is forfeit."

The Sumara drew herself erect and faced her advisors, her

bearing both regal and serene.

"I shall not desert Kfastia while her warriors fight for her," she said. "What kind of ruler would I be if I did that?"

"Only a miracle can save us now," Jaspar said. "We must think of your safety."

"No one will blame you," Valdor added.

A sudden trumpet blast echoed across the plain and pulled their eyes back outside the walls. They watched in grateful disbelief as the red-clad cavalry of Legas thundered toward the battle from the west. For some unknown reason, Mylar had decided to join the war, though it seemed to the watchers a futile gesture. His mounted warriors did not seem numerous enough to turn the tide of the struggle.

Mylar's reason for joining the fray rode alongside him at the head of the onrushing horsemen, though no one on the wall had yet recognized Penderyn. The Last Born had known nothing of the battle, but he had needed an army to help him reach Kfastia safely and so had hurried to the only place he could think of to find one. Mylar had needed little persuading. The reappearance of the Flaming Sword had been more than enough to convince him.

A second trumpet blast drew the onrushing column to a halt less than a hundred yards from the suddenly quiet battlefield. Friend and foe alike watched questioningly as two riders walked their mounts a short distance forward.

Atop the wall, Jarrowon was the first to realize that one of the riders was Penderyn.

"The Last Born!" he shouted. "I do not believe it. Penderyn rides at Mylar's side."

Arista was shocked. "How? Why?" she asked. "What can he be doing?"

"I have no idea," Jarrowon said. "But I must get out there."

The lore master raced down from the battlements. Orith hurried after him.

Out on the battlefield, warriors on both sides recognized the Mylar, but only the Kfastians recognized Penderyn. They watched as the two riders drew their mounts to a halt.

Mylar's voice was firm and confident. "Men of Colgoth, men of Dewellyn, hear me," he called loudly. "Your leaders have betrayed you. The time has come to end this senseless war. Here is the only thing worth fighting for."

Penderyn pulled the Flaming Sword from its scabbard. His hand seemed filled with fire as the jewel erupted in a brilliant red light.

"The Flaming Sword!" someone shouted. "The Last Born bears the Flaming Sword!"

The cry spread across the battlefield. The sword's effect was immediate. Hosts of Halibur's warriors laid down their arms in the face of the legendary weapon, for this was truly a sign that the gods favored Arista.

Only Rorgul's band of cutthroats failed to yield before the Flaming Sword. Their giant leader knew nothing of Sumar or his fabled weapon. He knew only that his erstwhile allies had suddenly turned into cowards. He cursed Halibur soundly and would have slain him on the spot had the Lord of Colgoth been nearby. But Halibur was nowhere in sight; all the bandit chieftain could see were ranks of enemy warriors closing in on his band. Badly outnumbered, his knew his only chance was to flee.

He rallied as many of his followers around him as he could and led them in a sudden attack toward the forest. With the battle all but over, the warriors in his way were not anxious to suffer further losses. They moved aside to let the mercenaries escape.

But Penderyn had other plans for the bearded giant. He spurred his mount and raced around in front of the fleeing villains. Two companies of Mylar's warriors followed him.

"Halt, murderer!" he cried, reining his steed to a halt directly in Rorgul's path. "You shall not escape. Your fate awaits you here."

With Sumar's sword flaming in his hand, Penderyn leaped from his mount and faced the bandit leader. The warriors behind him moved to join him, but he waved them back. This was a task he would do alone.

Rorgul's face twisted into an evil leer as he faced the foolish youth who dared to challenge him. He cared little for Penderyn's age or size, or for the shining red blade he wielded. The Flaming Sword's long history meant nothing to him. What mattered was his own strength and skill, which never been matched in countless battles.

"Your fancy tricks may impress these cowards, little one," he scowled, "but they mean nothing to me. I'll take great pleasure in killing you and taking that sword for my own."

He sprang toward Penderyn with surprising speed for one so big, seeking to crush the Last Born with one swift attack. Penderyn darted quickly to the side. He felt a whip of air against his cheek as a vicious slash of Rorgul's huge sword whistled only inches from his head. Rorgul grunted and stumbled slightly when his blow failed to strike its target, but he quickly regained his balance.

The bandit approached more slowly the second time. Penderyn circled warily to his left, sword held in front of him the way Cornon had taught him, trying to keep beyond his foe's long reach while he searched for an opening. The watching armies surrounding them might as well have been invisible; the two combatants' eyes were locked upon each other.

Rorgul pressed his attack, calling upon all the strength and skill developed in a lifetime of fighting. Savage blows rained down on Penderyn from all angles. It seemed impossible the Last Born could stand before such an onslaught, but Sumar's shining blade flashed through the air like a bolt of crimson lightning, blocking every thrust.

Unknown to anyone but Penderyn, magic flowed into his arm

from the Flaming Sword, lending him strength and speed. Indeed, it seemed to Penderyn that the sword had a mind of its own, so quickly did it move to parry Rorgul's attacks. Gaining confidence, Penderyn began to press forward with an attack of his own, slowly forcing his bewildered foe back.

For the first time in his life, Rorgul knew fear. Somehow, unbelievably, this slender youth was his master. He had finally met a power that surpassed his own, and he knew with awful certainty that he was about to die.

Penderyn saw the fear in Rorgul's eyes. The fear was almost enough—almost, but not quite. He watched as Rorgul launched one final desperate blow, a powerful slash that would have separated Penderyn's head from his shoulders had it landed. Penderyn ducked nimbly under the murderer's blade and thrust upward with the Flaming Sword, driving it with both hands. The point pierced the center of the hated lightning insignia on the villain's breast and buried itself to the hilt. Rorgul's jaw fell open and he dropped his sword. For a moment he stood there, impaled upon the Flaming Sword. His skin seemed to take on a reddish hue as the sword's power burned into him. Finally, Penderyn pulled the blade free and the giant crashed to the ground.

Aeta, Harren and Ishtor had been avenged.

CHAPTER 34

All Calistan celebrated in the wake of Arista's victory. For the first time since her husband's death, the entire country was united solidly behind their Sumara. The legitimacy of her rule was now beyond question; any doubts had been ended by the reappearance of Sumar's Flaming Sword. Forgotten for the moment were the barrenness of the women and the encroaching darkness. The citizens of Calistan were certain the discovery of their sacred talisman signaled the beginning of a new, more prosperous and peaceful era.

Arista dealt swiftly but mercifully with those who had challenged her, so that no lingering rancor might spoil this new beginning to her reign. Even Halibur's life was spared, though the former Lord of Colgoth was stripped of his title and his wealth and banished forever from Calistan. Of all his followers, only the traitors Chirops and Zolar shared this harsh sentence. Everyone else was given the choice of accompanying their former master or remaining in Calistan and swearing an oath of fealty to Arista. Only a few of Halibur's most faithful retainers chose to go with him.

Danustiri was also stripped of his title and wealth for his part in the insurrection, but he was allowed to remain in Dewellyn. Arista directed that the confiscated treasuries of the two former lords be used to aid families on both sides who had suffered the most in the short-lived but terrible civil war. She put Rorgul's captured mercenaries to work repairing the damages done to Kfastia and the surrounding farms; when they finished they were to be escorted to the border and warned never to return.

But first, Arista declared a day of holiday, so all her people might attend a special parade honoring Kfastia's many heroes. Joyous throngs of men, women and children from all four of Calistan's cities lined Kfastia's main avenue, cheering and waving banners as their favorites rode slowly by.

At the end of the parade, Arista awarded special honors to General Kriselor, Cornon and Mylar for their parts in the victory. The crowds roared their approval with each presentation, but saved their loudest cheers for Penderyn. Amidst a tumultuous ovation, the Sumara bestowed her greatest honor upon the Last Born, presenting him with the Flaming Sword, to serve him whenever and wherever he needed it.

Penderyn bowed to Arista, then pulled the sword from its scabbard and waved it above his head. The cheers reached a deafening crescendo as the brilliant red flames danced from his hand and shot upward into the air. Few among the onlookers knew how much more yet depended on the slender youth who stood before them.

Later, Penderyn and his friends gathered in one of the sitting rooms in Valdor's home, the one Jarrowon used to study his scrolls late at night while the rest of the household was sleeping. The lore master sat behind his huge desk, but this evening, the scrolls were all pushed aside. Orith perched comfortably atop one side of the desk, his legs dangling over the edge. Tal and Dal sat side by side on cushioned chairs they had pulled up next Jarrowon. Cornon stood by the doorway, leaning against the doorframe.

Slow burning torches in bronze sconces illuminated the room. A warm fire popped and crackled in the marble fireplace.

Everyone's eyes were fastened on Penderyn, who stood

across the desk from his comrades. For the first time since the war ended, he had time to tell them the full story of his escape from Chirops' dungeon.

He recounted the events in as much detail as he could recall. Here in this comfortably appointed chamber, filled with light from the torches and fireplace, his story sounded fantastic even to him. He couldn't even imagine what his friends must be thinking about the miraculous happenings he described. He wondered once again whether his father's appearance might have simply been a dream after all.

"Even when it was happening, I wasn't sure whether I was dreaming or if my father had somehow actually come to help me," he said when he finished his story. "To tell the truth, right now it seems as if it must have been a dream."

His comrades were silent for a moment, digesting everything they had just heard, and then Orith spoke.

"It doesn't sound like a dream to me. Certainly not a dream created by the magic of the Eirydi. I've never heard of one anything like what you described." He looked to Jarrowon.

The lore master's gray eyes bore the familiar vacant expression they always did when he was lost in thought. Penderyn watched him expectantly.

"I do not believe it was a dream, either," Jarrowon said at last. He studied the Last Born closely. "I think your father did help you, Penderyn, in some way I do not yet understand. Tell me, what do you know of him?"

Penderyn shook his head. "Almost nothing. He left Ishtor before I was born. My mother never told me why." His eyes began to mist as he talked about his mother. "She didn't really speak of him at all. I'm not sure why."

"I remember him," Tal said. "Dal and I were only boys at the time, but newcomers were always exceedingly rare in the village, so his arrival was a big deal. He stayed in Ishtor but a month."

"He was always friendly," Dal added, "but I remember feeling there was something different about him, as if matters far more important than our simple life weighed upon him." He turned his gaze to Jarrowon. "I sense a little of the same in you, lore master."

Jarrowon raised his bushy eyebrows at Dal's remark. Penderyn could tell the lore master was gathering the various threads together, but what kind of tapestry they would weave Penderyn had no idea.

"Penderyn, tell me again about your vision in the swamp, when you slew the terriwarg," Jarrowon said.

Penderyn repeated the story, unsure what connection it might have to his father. When he finished, it was again Orith who spoke first.

"There's nothing unusual there," he said to Jarrowon. "Many times a dream is unremembered until the actual event triggers the memory. My people call such a dream a *solana*."

"I'm more interested in Penderyn's actions than his vision," Jarrowon said. "Tell me again what you did, Penderyn. Try to remember every detail."

Penderyn closed his eyes, trying to relive the moment. He told Jarrowon how he had climbed along the terriwarg's back with only Harren's broken spear as a weapon and without really knowing what he was going to do. He described how he spotted the monster's one vulnerable spot behind its head.

"Even though I discovered the weak spot, I didn't know how I could hope to slay the beast," he said. "The target was so small, and even if I somehow managed to strike it, I doubted I had the strength to pierce the leathery skin." He took a deep breath. "I'm not really sure what happened next, but I saw what appeared to be lines of colored energy converging on that single vulnerable spot. I saw similar lights right after you pulled me back from my seizure when we rescued Tal and Dal."

He glanced at the twins for a moment before turning back to Jarrowon. "My mind became focused on that spot on the terriwarg's neck to the exclusion of everything else, even the danger to Tal and Dal. The spear seemed to become an extension of my arm." He paused again and shrugged his shoulders. "Then I just did it."

Jarrowon smiled. Apparently, enough of the threads he had been gathering had fallen into place.

"There's only one answer I can think of," the lore master said. "I believe the blood of the Quirsi flows in your veins."

Penderyn's brow furrowed in puzzlement. He had never heard of the Quirsi. He had no idea who or what they were.

"Who?" he asked.

"The Quirsi," Jarrowon repeated. "An ancient race of mystics, possessors of many magical powers. One was the ability to focus their entire beings into but a single thought, as you did atop the terriwarg. It's said the Quirsi draw their strength from the energy of the world around them. I think that's what you were seeing when you saw the colored lights—the hidden energy of the universe. It's also said the Quirsi can send their thoughts to each other across many leagues. It now seems they can send their image as well."

He pushed his chair back from the desk and stood up. "Your father must have been of the Quirsi, Last Born. I believe that's how he was able to aid you beneath the temple. How he knew of your need, I have no idea, but it's the only answer that makes sense." The lore master placed his hand on Penderyn's shoulder. "I think his magic must also lie within you, Penderyn. Beyond your control, maybe, but there nonetheless."

Penderyn was speechless as he tried to digest Jarrowon's words. Had the lore master at last unlocked the secret of his heritage? It seemed incredible, but Jarrowon appeared convinced the blood of the Quirsi flowed in Penderyn's veins. If the powers of the Quirsi were indeed inside him, perhaps they would be the key to fully controlling his dreams. He still had much to think about, but he knew now where his path lay.

"I must find my father," he said.

Here ends Volume One of the Legend of the Last Born.

ABOUT THE AUTHOR

Scott Prussing was born in New Jersey, but was smart enough to move to beautiful San Diego as soon as he received his Master's degree in psychology from Yale University. In addition to writing, Scott enjoys going to the movies (not renting!), hiking, riding his bicycle near the beach, and golf. He remains one of the few people in the United States without a cell phone.

Contact Scott and learn all about his books at www.scottprussing.com.